ALL THAT GLITTERS

A NOVEL OF THE GILDED AGE

LINDA BENNETT PENNELL

Black Rose Writing | Texas

The author grants the final approval for this literary material.

First printing

ISBN: 978-1-68513-577-5
PUBLISHED BY BLACK ROSE WRITING
www.blackrosewriting.com

Printed in the United States of America
Suggested Retail Price (SRP) $20.95

All That Glitters is printed in Minion Pro

*As a planet-friendly publisher, Black Rose Writing does its best to eliminate unnecessary waste to reduce paper usage and energy costs, while never compromising the reading experience. As a result, the final word count vs. page count may not meet common expectations.

PRAISE FOR
ALL THAT GLITTERS

All That Glitters is an excellent read... a great mystery to solve!
–*In D'Tale Magazine*, October 2020

5 Stars ...a wonderfully done atmospheric book, and the characters were so finely drawn...Very well written...
–Bestselling author of historical fiction Hebby Roman via *Goodreads*

5 Stars ...as a history buff, I thoroughly enjoyed this read...highly recommend...
–Grant Leishman via *Readers Favorite*

5 Stars ...will keep you reading long into the night.
–Mary Anne Yard via The Coffee Pot Book Club

Bronze Medal Winner
Coffee Pot book Club Book of the Year Award

ALL THAT GLITTERS

CHAPTER 1

Is she dead? The flesh on her face feels cool to the touch. It would really be too bad if the whore is in fact no longer among the living. Killing is not a taste I have developed thus far. Much more satisfying to think of them permanently marked and remembering. Checking her throat is in order.

Ah, good. My method holds true. A strong pulse thumps beneath her surprisingly alluring flesh. If she were a lady instead of a whore, she might even tempt me into an actual relationship. As it is, she will live, but with considerable bruising around her windpipe and an ugly scar near her hairline.

See how the moonlight brightens the blood trickling over her temple toward her ear. Perhaps I should deepen the rouge on her tawdry cheeks by smearing some of it on them. Yes. That's better. She now looks exactly like what she is – a whore who will remember tonight for a very long time.

If she hadn't resisted, I wouldn't have hurt her. But then, they always force me to hurt them. All they have to do is submit, but the stupid trollops never catch on until it is too late.

CHAPTER 2

Oglethorpe Island, Georgia
1890

The sound of buggy wheels crunching over crushed oyster shells would now forever be associated in Sarah Anne Mercer's mind with loss and unexpected beginnings. This position was not what she had dreamed of, but there was no going back for all other doors had closed. Nervous hands twisted mesh gloves until the fibers dug into the webbing between her fingers, raising red welts between the strings. Glancing down at the mess, she forced her hands to rest primly in her lap and stretched her neck to relieve the tension building at the base of her skull. Dwelling on what might have been was a useless, unedifying occupation. Acceptance was the only course. Instead of wishing for a different life, she must focus on this time, this future, this place.

The buggy bounced over a rut, sending a tingle up Sarah Anne's spine. As she grabbed an armrest for support, dampness rose on her forehead and beads of moisture formed on her upper lip. Drawing her gloves from her hands, she attempted to fan herself, but nothing could decrease the discomfort of air so thick it felt liquid against the skin. South Georgia's heat and humidity had not diminished simply because the calendar declared autumn had commenced. Heat and nerves were not a good combination. She trained her gaze ahead and fixed it upon a clump of palmettos to avoid embarrassment. Fouling the vehicle's leather appointments with the contents of her predawn breakfast would be a disastrous introduction.

The road curved around a stand of pines and her destination came into view situated upon a broad expanse of manicured lawn. A small gasp escaped. So Uncle Zach's prejudice had not influenced his opinion after all. His description, while uncharitable, was quite accurate. Ripon House, all three glowering stories of it, squatted on Oglethorpe Island like a boil on the backside of a beautiful woman. Rumor among the locals had it that the boil was filled with corruption, but Uncle Zach did not place credence in such speculation. As a man of science, he dealt with facts. Of course he did. He wouldn't have sent her here if he suspected anything untoward. All would be suitable and she would be a great success. This house was now her destiny for better or worse. As the vehicle rolled to a stop, Sarah Anne straightened her posture and plastered on what she hoped was a confident expression.

The driver cleared his throat. "Best not keep Miz Bogard waiting, Miss. She gets in a powerful stir when folks wastes her time."

"Oh. Of course. Thank you. I guess I'm a little awestruck by all of this." Babbling was a nervous habit Sarah Anne thought she had rid herself of long ago. To staunch the flow of words, she jumped from the buggy before the driver could get around to her side, but when she made to grab her satchel, he stepped forward.

"We cain't have that, Miss. Wouldn't be right."

Heat rose in Sarah Anne's cheeks. "Thank you . . ." She looked inquiringly at the driver.

"George, Miss."

"Thank you, George. I hadn't thought of that."

A wry smile spread over the driver's features. "Pardon me saying, but I suspect there's lots about this place you ain't thought of just yet. Give it time and you'll settle in fine. I can see you a young lady with grit."

Sarah Anne gave her advisor a weak smile. Oh joy. Grit would be required. It wasn't that she didn't possess a certain amount of the stuff. Orphaned at age ten and sent to live among people who cast sidelong glances at her dark hair, dark eyes, and prominent cheekbones, she learned early on how to deal with snide comments and left-handed compliments. The only issue presently at hand was how much grit would be needed. Sarah Anne peered up at the house and fought back a sigh.

The driver waited patiently for her to precede him up wide stone steps that led onto a deep veranda. Such a fixture of Southern architecture looked very odd tacked onto this particular house, as though someone had been determined to sneak in a feature that actually made sense in their subtropical climate. All he had accomplished was to enhance the granite pile's sinister appearance. A small shiver ran down Sarah Anne's spine.

As Uncle Zach told it, controversy had swirled from the moment of the house's conception. The architect, a graduate of Virginia, surely knew better, but he didn't allow something so pedestrian as training to get in the way of a colossal fee. The builder, a Savannahian by birth and inclination, must have had objections, but according to local gossip, generous compensation had overcome any qualms he may have had. The good people of Mayweather County absolutely had objections, accustomed as they were to unmolested access to the riches of the island's acres and waters. Uncle Zach had often railed against Mr. Jedediah Littlewood's iniquitous defilement of the land in having his monstrosity of a house built. The fact that the Yankee industrialist owned the entirety of the barrier island did nothing to lessen his enmity. Of course in the end, Ripon House had gone up stone by craggy gray stone. Nobody was happy except the man who had the thing built.

Sarah Anne shifted from one foot to the other before mahogany double doors, her hand stranded at her side unable to knock. Hesitation in the face of the unknown had never been her nature, but today it froze her into a state of inaction. This was so unlike the woman she thought herself to be. To complete her humiliation, her midsection once again threatened open rebellion. This would never do. Inhaling slowly, she held her breath for several beats then allowed the air to escape in one measured stream while she distracted herself with an inspection of the house's exterior.

Despite the day's warmth, the windows stood firmly shut and the drapes drawn. If windows were the eyes of a structure, Ripon House chose to be blind to the world around it. An atmosphere of gloom seemed to hang about the place. The house might have been in mourning, but no one had mentioned a death and no black wreath decorated the door. It was as though Thornfield Hall, the haunted Yorkshire manse of Charlotte Bronte's *Jane Eyre*, had been transported to the Georgia coast. It did not suit. Not in the least. There might not be an insane Bertha Mason guarded by Grace Poole hidden away in the attics, but Sarah Anne couldn't quite rid herself of a niggling sensation of unease. The place just didn't feel right.

Sarah Anne bit down on her inner cheek to rein in her rushing thoughts. This was not the time to let her imagination run free. Failing in this position simply was not an option.

With that, she squared her shoulders and yanked the gloves back over her hands until her fingers strained against the mesh. The force of her knock served as a physical reminder of why she stood upon the Ripon House threshold awaiting admittance to its world.

CHAPTER 3

Damn this unseasonable heat. These sidewalks trap it and send it back up in waves. Perhaps Delmonico's will provide a respite. This blasted handkerchief is so damp from mopping my brow that I dare not put it back in my breast pocket. Ah, there is an obliging trash receptacle. Indian Summer is upon us with a vengeance, but this last gasp of warm weather alone does not account for my excessive perspiration. My God. Is that person looking at me with suspicion? I have taken great care that my fellow passersby will not see anything untoward in my manner or appearance. No, he passed by without a second glance.

The events of last evening have made me paranoid. The whore managed to regain consciousness and wrench free before I made my escape. A most alarming occurrance. And to think I initially feared her dead. The bitch should be grateful I didn't kill her. Instead, she ran screaming from the alley into the street. Shouts from tenement windows brought out ruffians calling for blood. I was lucky nothing blocked the other end of the alley. Jumping into a passing hansom saved me.

Did the woman in that cab just point me out to her companion? What could she possibly know? I am being a fool. She could know nothing of me unless we have met at some tiresome social function or other.

God, I need distraction. My need for release will not lay dormant forever. It seems to be taking on a life independent of my own. The invitation to Mrs. Astor's New Port house party might have provided diversion. Too bad this damnable luncheon engagement could not be avoided.

But wait. Perhaps there is another option. After all, she will give herself to me freely and I do not even need to go out into the night to find her. She has indicated her desire through her words and actions. A liaison with her may satisfy sufficiently to enable a reasonable period between encounters with whores.

CHAPTER 4

A uniformed maid opened the door for Sarah Anne, and then left her standing alone in the foyer. Not a breath of air moved through the cavernous space. Flapping a handkerchief near her face, Sarah Anne gazed about a room unlike any she had seen. In place of the light, simple interiors so evident in the coastal region, dark wood paneling covered the walls and thick oriental carpets covered the floors. Paintings in heavy gilt frames rose up the walls in a gathering of portraits and landscapes of near, but not quite, museum quality. High-backed chairs and ornately carved consoles covered edge to edge with bric-a-brac crowded the wall space not covered by artwork. The effect was claustrophobic. She wanted to throw open windows and toss expensive porcelains into a trash pit. But she would get used to the overstuffed atmosphere. She had no choice.

Her gaze swept over the space a second time. This must be what people meant when they called someone *nouveau riche*. While her experience of the wider world extended only as far as Wesleyan Female College in Macon, it was pretty evident Mr. Littlewood had spent vast sums to create an entry intended to impress. Whether he had achieved his goal was open to question.

Sarah Anne locked her fingers at her waist to prevent fidgeting and checked her reflection in the gold-framed Empire mirror on the wall beside the grand staircase. The girl who gazed back appeared younger than her twenty years. Her wide eyes gave her the appearance of a schoolgirl called upon to give a recitation for which she was woefully ill-prepared. That was the last impression she wished to give. She adjusted her features until she was satisfied she looked confident and competent. Glancing at her journey-stained, simple gingham day dress, she ran her hands over the skirt. Examining the fruit of her efforts, she inwardly sighed. Her capabilities would just have to make up for her appearance.

In any event, the Littlewoods had not hired her for the way she looked or the cut of her clothes. She may be inexperienced, but she could do the teaching. Of that she was sure. This was going to work. She would be a resounding success. Of course, it would work. It had to. She had turned down the only other offer she'd received. Uncle Zach had beseeched, and when that failed, had used guilt. Her dreams of being an independent woman helping the children of her native north Georgia mountains had been dashed upon the rocks of obligation, duty, but most of all, of love. A stinging sensation rose in her eyes. She purposely bit the flesh of her inner cheek. Dwelling upon loss and regret would not help her make a good impression. She pushed all thoughts of what might have been from her mind. Her future lay with Aunt Edith, Uncle Zach, and the Littlewood child.

Bustling movements and a swish of skirts in the adjoining room caught Sarah Anne off guard. Surprise curled through her as she gazed beyond the open door that led into the drawing room or maybe a parlor. My lord, at least six people worked there. Nobody in St. Anne had more than a woman who came in sometimes to help with the wash and maybe do a little cleaning and cooking. She watched with interest as menservants unrolled carpets and maids dragged dustsheets from the furniture. The family was apparently not in residence after all but must be expected shortly. Why, then, had she been asked to come out to the island as quickly as possible? The ways of the rich were certainly a mystery. Perhaps the figure approaching from the hallway behind the staircase would provide an answer.

A little woman, remarkably resembling a five-foot square of gray gabardine, planted herself near the bottom of the stairs. Placing a hand on each hip, she gave Sarah Anne an evaluative going-over. "You'll do,

I guess." Her accent had been formed somewhere up north, perhaps in New England. "Wasn't expecting a white girl. You'll stick out among the Coloreds. Nothing to be done about it now. You'll find your uniforms in a wardrobe at the top of the house. Get yourself changed. There's no time to waste. They're due tomorrow before luncheon. And another thing, do not ever again presume to use the front entrance. It is for the family and their guests only." The older woman turned to go, muttering under her breath about the ignorance of these Southern yokels being almost beyond endurance.

Sarah Anne gulped. "Wait. There's been a mistake. I'm here to teach the Littlewoods' daughter. I'm not a maid." Her voice rang from the foyer into the drawing room where all work stopped and inquiring eyes turned toward the source of disruption. Heat seared Sarah Anne's cheeks. Nothing to do but start over. She extended her hand. "I'm sorry. I'm Sarah Anne Mercer, the new teacher."

The other woman's features hardened. "Well, why didn't you say so from the beginning? Furthermore, why are you here? You're a week early."

Sarah Anne made a concentrated effort to control her rising alarm. Withdrawing an envelope from her pocket, she handed it over. "I am supposed to see a Mrs. Bogard. Would you be she?"

"I am." After reading the letter contained therein, comprehension dawned in the housekeeper's eyes. "I see the mistake is mine. Obviously I got two unfamiliar names mixed. That is unlike me, but we have just been so rushed. Now we'll be short one maid for an entire week and with preparations still unfinished. Oh well, we will just have to manage. Your bedroom is in the east wing next to Miss Adelia's. You might as well settle in as long as you're here. One of the maids will show you the way."

Oh, dear. Another misunderstanding. Sarah Anne looked closely at the housekeeper. The poor woman appeared exhausted and now there would be another, perhaps upsetting revelation. Maybe she could do something to ease Mrs. Bogard's distress. Glancing at the tall-case clock ticking in a corner, Sarah Anne made a quick calculation. "While this will not be my duty when I begin teaching Miss Adelia, I will be happy to help out this week until the maid arrives. I've kept my uncle's house since I was ten. My aunt is an invalid and unable to deal with household responsibilities."

The expression on Mrs. Bogard's face made Sarah Anne want to laugh out loud. If ever a person looked shocked, appalled, and grateful all at one time, it was the housekeeper. As quickly as the expression settled over her features, it disappeared. "That will not be necessary. It would be most unseemly. I'm surprised you do not understand to lower yourself to maid's work would cause the other staff members to lose respect for you. Governesses do not do maid's work anymore than maids teach the family's children."

"Oh. In St. Anne, nobody thinks like that. Most of the women do housework in one way or another."

The housekeeper's eyes narrowed. "You are entering a house clearly unlike anything in your experience. I'm wondering if you're up to the task. If that feckless governess had not disappeared on the eve of the family's departure south, I would not have been asked to find an interim replacement."

Interim? No one had said anything about this being a temporary position. Heaviness curled through Sarah Anne. Uncle Zach had much to answer for. She forced her breathing into a smooth rhythm before replying, "I assure you I am well qualified to teach a seven-year-old. And while we are correcting misunderstandings, I must inform you I will not be living here. My uncle needs me at home at night. He's called out on medical emergencies at all hours and my aunt cannot be left alone. She's completely incapacitated. She has no movement below her waist." Her voice sounded priggish to her own ears, but this situation had to be taken in hand.

Mrs. Bogard's nostrils flared, but this was the only indication she was anything other than calm and controlled. "I see. Dr. MacAllister failed to mention that detail when he recommended you for the position. I don't know what Mr. Littlewood will say. Tutors and governesses have always lived in."

Sarah Anne met the other woman's gaze with a directness she prayed masked her inner turmoil. "I'm sorry he did not tell you the entire story, but then I was not told this is a temporary position. If I had known, I would have accepted the other offer made to me. As it is, it seems we must each accept we were not fully apprised of the facts."

Mrs. Bogard's attention lit on the satchel at Sarah Anne's feet. Pointing, the older woman asked, "If you are not to live in, why did you bring that?"

"Teaching supplies and things for the classroom."

The housekeeper rolled her eyes and huffed, "Did you think a family such as the Littlewoods would not provide what you need? The schoolbooks are already on the shelves."

Not to be bested, Sarah Anne allowed her gaze to linger on Mrs. Bogard for a moment longer than necessary before responding, "There is more to teaching than books and slates. Now if someone will show me to the schoolroom, I will prepare for Miss Adelia's arrival before I must meet the afternoon ferry." Her imperious tone sent a chill through the foyer.

Mrs. Bogard snapped her fingers at one of the maids in the drawing room. "Show this person to the schoolroom." To Sarah Anne, she said, "It is not known how long you will be employed here. My guess is your tenure will be short." With that, the older woman whirled away toward the service hall.

Following the maid up to the third floor, Sarah Anne gave herself a mental kick. What had she been thinking in speaking to the housekeeper like that? If she was to succeed here, she needed friends, not enemies. With persons of her own age, she made friends easily. The older generation was another matter. Sarah Anne's butting heads with St. Anne's self-appointed social mavens had been the bane of Aunt Edith's existence. Poor Aunt Edith hadn't been able to provide much mothering, but she did give one piece of advice. Repeatedly. *You will catch more flies with honey than with vinegar, Sarah Anne. People don't like a sharp-tongued woman.*

The path to the schoolroom led through a labyrinth of hallways. At the end of a short passage, the maid stopped before a single door and flung it open. Sarah Anne stepped into the room and peered at her new domain. Her heart sank to the soles of her boots.

CHAPTER 5

5th Avenue is damnably jammed with traffic today. If I'm not careful in crossing to the park, I will be run down. I will have to dodge these carriages and cabs soon because the 59th Street entrance is just ahead. I can see its pillars topped by the equestrian statues. Aw, here's a break between vehicles.

The Mall with its canopy of trees is a welcome relief from this everlasting heat. That elegant couple looks vaguely familiar. No doubt I have met them at some social engagement among the second tier of society. They have nodded, but their expressions communicate they find something amiss in my demeanor. I must shorten my stride and bestow my most charming smile upon them. It appears to have worked, at least with the lady. I must govern my pace henceforth. I must not bring undue notice to myself.

Oh, good. The isolated bench under the elm by The Lake is deserted. Watching the breeze create ripples on the water eases my tension and calms my soul. It has begun to work its magic. This blessed solitude has created a mantle of peace that settles around me like a comforting embrace, soothing my feverish brain, allowing me to think.

Instead of receding to dormancy, my need is growing. In the past, an encounter would assuage my desire for weeks, but it seems I can no longer depend on that. Damn it to hell! Can I risk another encounter so soon? My punishment of whores provides relief through the complete domination of those denizens of the gutter. It soothes my rage, but the recent liaison took an unexpected turn and now my need grows precipitously. Strange how that unplanned feature left me less satisfied than with the previous encounters. Perhaps in breaking the pattern, a new dimension to my work has been revealed.

Regardless of the form the next encounter takes, without release in the near future pressure will build until it may force me to do something foolish. I must take care. I cannot make a mistake that would reveal my identity for my work is righteous and must continue. I alone among the men of the family have the courage to erase a cancerous plague from our world. This dilemma is more than most men could bear. To go out to seek them and risk detection or stay my hand and suffer the torture of knowing the succubi still stalk the night? I must decide soon.

CHAPTER 6

One week after the disastrous interview with Mrs. Bogard, Sarah Anne returned to Ripon House to work in the schoolroom. Placing her fists on her hips, she once again gazed about and shook her head in dismay. While statement pieces and artwork, albeit not to her taste, filled the other areas of the house, an air of sterility pervaded the schoolroom. It was as though no child had ever entered, much less learned there. No curtains covered the windows. No rugs softened one's tread upon the floor. The only chairs were rigid ladder-backs with wooden seats rather than woven rush. Blackish brown paneling and dark floors created a gloom that was difficult to penetrate. Although sunlight blazed through a bay window, the effect was more one of creating glare than illumination. The schoolroom bore greater resemblance to a dungeon than to a space meant to inspire young minds.

Raiding the linen cupboard at home might help improve the atmosphere. Aunt Edith wouldn't miss what they never used. Perhaps Adelia would enjoy helping to make the room their own. Despite the dreary atmosphere, a little thrill of anticipation curled through Sarah Anne. There might just be a bonus in the lack of décor. She would be able to put her own touches on this, her very first schoolroom.

Sarah Anne tilted her head to one side and sucked on her lower lip. To the maid who had guided her through the labyrinth of still unfamiliar hallways she said, "Would there be any discarded pieces of furniture in the house? Perhaps in the attic?"

Surprise filled the girl's dark eyes. "Yes'am. I suppose so. I never go to the attic. It's a fearsome place. If they have leftover furniture, that's where it'll be."

"If you'll show me the way, I'll take my chances." Lifting her hand in a sweeping gesture, Sarah Anne continued, "A little girl needs a learning environment that inspires. This room needs some help."

The maid grinned. "It sure do." A look of consternation flitted across the girl's face. "If you forgive me saying so. I didn't mean no disrespect."

"There is no disrespect in telling the truth. Just the opposite, in my opinion." Truth telling. Another trait Aunt Edith worked to quell. Sarah Anne smiled and extended her hand. "I'm Miss Mercer. What's your name?"

The girl hesitated, her gaze shooting from Sarah Anne's face to the proffered hand and back. Finally, the maid placed her hand in Sarah Anne's. "Pleased to meet you. I'm called Eliza."

"I've always loved that name. What type of work do you do in the house?"

"I clean upstairs and downstairs. I polish the furniture. I tend to the fireplaces and the like." Eliza's eyes flitted nervously toward the direction of the stairwell. "Well, Miss, if you ain't got nothing else, I need to get back downstairs."

"Of course. I apologize for detaining you, Eliza. And the attic?"

"You just follow the hall either way. There's a door to the attic on each end." Eliza looked at Sarah Anne and smiled shyly. "Well, I'm going now. If you need something, you just ask."

"Thank you. I will." Sarah Anne watched Eliza scurry toward the grand staircase. What a sweet girl. Maybe they would become friends, or as much as the family's teacher and a maid could be.

Not for the first time, Sarah Anne contemplated the injustice inflicted on people who had done nothing wrong other than being born with the wrong color skin. She witnessed it every day in ways large and small. Her own heritage had given her some perspective on the issue.

She was reminded she came from a mixed background every time she looked in the mirror.

Her coloring and features, inherited from her mother's side of the family, had been a topic of gossip since she first arrived in St. Anne. The town's old biddies had whispered about her when she passed and her schoolmates had taunted her until she beat the business out of the meanest boy in class. Afterward, only the gossip continued. Rumors had her being everything from part Cherokee to part Oriental to Black Irish to mulatto to Melungeon.

It was said that even Aunt Edith, usually the kindest of women, had been put off when she first met Sarah Anne's mother. Such was the price of looking unlike one's neighbors and family. Sarah Anne had made her peace with her appearance long ago, but the occasional impolite comment or intrusive inquiry still cut. Perhaps they always would.

Arriving at an attic door, Sarah Anne threw it open and peered into an enormous space. Patches of light drifting through dirty dormer windows relieved the semidarkness to varying degrees and served to highlight the thick layer of dust covering everything. The attic had the appearance of a place unloved and long neglected. A sense of sadness and desolation flitted through Sarah Anne. It felt like one could get lost in there and never be found. A shiver lifted goose bumps on her arms. In disgust, she gave herself a mental shake. *Stop it. It's just an attic, no better or worse than any other. Quit letting your imagination take flight.*

Sarah Anne took two steps into the space and stopped. She blinked several times before sneezing. When her eyes adjusted to the gloom, a small smile played over her features. Unhappy place though it was, the attic proved to be the place where yesteryear's furniture went to live. She placed a fist on each hip and surveyed a jumble of wood and upholstered pieces. Surely among these she would find something to soften the schoolroom and make it more comfortable. Considerable pushing and shoving revealed a pair of chintz-covered armchairs, feminine in both color and design. Sarah Ann dropped down onto the nearest one. Yes, this would do nicely. Sturdy and comfortable, but nothing that would cause worry in a space where a child might wield a paintbrush.

Next she found a piecrust occasional table perfect for placing between the chairs. In a corner under an eave, she found a few oil lamps of various shapes and sizes, most with cracks in their glass or missing chimneys. At the very back of the clutter, she came upon exactly what she was looking for. A lovely old lamp with what seemed like a hand-painted base and matching globe, chipped and cracked on one side. It needed a good washing, but under the grime pinks and greens peeked through. The lamp appeared to have been bought to go with the chairs. If she mended Aunt Edith's old lace curtains presently residing at the back of the linen cupboard, she would be able to transform the dungeon schoolroom into a place fit for a young girl to explore the world through books and discussion.

Sarah Anne lifted the corner of one chair. It slipped from her hands and dropped onto the bare floorboards with a thud. It was much too heavy for her to get downstairs on her own. Maybe if she could drag the chairs to the door, the menservants would move them to the schoolroom for her. A few minutes pulling brought the first chair to the attic door amid so much clattering and scraping that Mrs. Bogard was sure to come flying up to the attic to complain. Well, let her. Adelia deserved a nice schoolroom and so did she.

No sooner had the thought floated through her mind than pounding footsteps sounded on the stairs. Sarah Anne squared her shoulders and turned to face her antagonist, but it was not the housekeeper who darkened the attic door. The figure was decidedly too tall and much too masculine.

CHAPTER 7

"What have we here? Why, it isn't a demon after all, just a pretty girl. What on earth are you doing?" Her inquisitor loomed in the doorway, but made no move into the attic or to step back into the hall. His face and figure appeared in hazy relief, shadowed and highlighted in turn by the light from the small windows scattered about the attic.

Sarah Anne's head jerked back a fraction of an inch and she blinked. Clearing her throat, she responded, "I am gathering furniture. I—"

"But why?" the stranger interjected. "Aren't Uncle Jed's rooms already full to overflowing? Or perhaps you prefer wall-to-wall furniture with only narrow pathways."

Sarah Anne's anxiety dissolved into irritation as the man turned to lean against the doorjamb and she saw his teasing smile. He had the effrontery to toy with her, a perfect stranger and a lady at that. "I am Miss Adelia's new teacher and I want to prepare the schoolroom. It needs additional furniture."

It was her interlocutor's turn to appear surprised. "Teacher?" An arched brow and a lopsided grin indicated his quick return to levity. "But you are surely too young for such a lofty position. You are right on one count, however. That wretched dungeon needs some help."

Despite herself, Sarah Anne laughed. "Those were my exact words when I saw it earlier this morning. May I ask your name, sir?"

The man leaned toward her and waggled his brows. "You may ask, but I may choose to make you guess. So, who am I?"

Sarah Anne decided to play along with his little game. Tilting her head in what she hoped was a coquettish manner, she answered, "Other than what you have already stated, that you are Mr. Littlewood's nephew, I have no idea."

A genuinely crestfallen expression settled over his features. "You really don't know, do you?"

"Why would I? I only accepted the position last week and this is my first day in the house. I know no one really."

"That is probably just as well. It gives me an advantage."

"In what way?"

"Why, in making your acquaintance first, of course, before my cousins descend and make themselves a nuisance." Sarah was confused for a moment until she recalled Uncle Zach mentioning the Littlewood's two grown sons.

When the gentleman offered his hand, she extended her own. He bent from the waist and brushed her wrist with his lips, then raised his eyes to meet hers. "John Edgar van Beek at your service. Sometime journalist, son of Mrs. Littlewood's late brother, frequent subject of society pages, object of pursuit by ambitious mamas with unmarried daughters, and general gentleman at large. And you are?"

Dear lord. This man was a member of New York high society. The women he mingled with wore the latest fashions and went to finishing schools. How inadequate I must appear in his eyes.

Flustered by the man's pedigree, Sarah Anne marshaled her thoughts with a deeply drawn breath and withdrew her hand from his grasp. "Sarah Anne Mercer and I'm afraid our society pages do not extend to persons so exalted as yourself. Our local weekly tends more to church bazaars, Garden Club socials, and who was seen in town during the week." Had her attempt at ironic sophistication worked? Who knew? Sarah Anne certainly didn't.

"Perhaps you've noticed my byline? My articles for *The New York World* are usually syndicated to major regional papers."

Feeling out of her depth, her reply jumped from her lips before thought could modulate it. "No. Sorry. So you're a newspaper reporter?" Though she wasn't very worldly, even Sarah Anne knew working as a newspaperman was unusual for the scion of a wealthy, socially prominent family.

"Oh, no. Nothing so formal as that. I enjoy research and writing, so I freelance when there is a topic that catches my interest. My latest work for Pulitzer and Co. featured a series of crimes against women of the lower classes. Something of an American Jack the Ripper without the bloodletting." His voice dwindled almost to a whisper, as though he realized he had ventured into inappropriate conversational territory. "No one killed, only hurt rather badly. The articles made the Atlanta and Savannah papers, I'm sure."

Sarah Anne's discomfort sent heat rising in her cheeks. "We don't subscribe to the Atlanta or Savannah papers." Put off balance by the strange progression of the conversation and Mr. van Beek's rather intense scrutiny, Sarah Anne hesitated, searching for something else to say. She settled on, "Have they caught him?"

Apparently Mr. van Beek was caught off-kilter as well, for confusion flickered in his eyes. "Caught whom?"

"The criminal?"

A self-conscience smile warmed his features. "Oh, him. Sadly not. He's still at large without a clue to his identity. If you ever go to New York, you must be sure to take care."

"I see. How horrible." Did he realize what he had just said? Sarah Anne had no desire to continue conversing with the gentleman. His good looks would have turned the heads of most girls, but she didn't like the way he spoke to her. It felt almost like he was taking liberties. Furthermore, his comments about a trip to New York implied he considered her of the lower classes. He had some nerve. Instead of speaking, she merely stared at him with an unsmiling countenance.

Van Beek frowned and broke eye contact. After a couple of beats, he responded, "Yes. It is horrible." With a shake of his head and a quickly drawn breath, the lopsided grin returned and his focus shifted back to Sarah Anne. "Please forgive me. I should not be discussing such an indelicate subject with a young lady. In fact, I am sounding like an arrogant blowhard, an uncouth, ungentlemanly one at that. Please believe me. I do not usually behave in this manner. I fear I occasionally display an awkwardness when meeting new people, especially when I'm trying to impress."

That he felt the need to impress her was a new experience. Although unsure why he felt such an inclination, it was rather pleasant. Sarah Anne had always felt at a disadvantage and a little awkward in social settings also. Surprisingly, it seemed they had something in common. How touching to find someone of his background shared her insecurities.

If the arrangement of his features revealed the inner man, Mr. van Beek was truly contrite. She had never seen a more hangdog expression and had to choke back a giggle. With a smile, she gave him an answer. "You can be forgiven, but you must earn it."

Mr. Van Beek straightened into a posture of military precision. "Anything, dear lady. Do with me as you will if it will gain me your favor." Nothing about him moved from the rigid pose except his gaze, which dropped sideways to meet hers.

She couldn't prevent herself laughing. "All right. Relax. No need to give yourself muscle spasms. If you'll help me get a few pieces of furniture to the schoolroom, all will be forgiven."

"Gladly. You only need point out your selections." With that, he removed his coat. A moment of guilt trickled through Sarah Anne as she noted the lovely embroidery on his waistcoat and the snowiness of his fine linen shirtsleeves. He must pay a small fortune for his clothes, but then he would have the fortune to spend, so she brushed aside her concern.

Several trips between attic and schoolroom completed the job. Remarkably, Mr. van Beek's clothing appeared no worse for the effort. Her dress, on the other hand, showed signs of needing a good washing. He had lifted and carried chairs with little effort. More impressively, he had not called servants to do the job for them. Strong, handsome, wealthy, considerate, and humble beneath his façade of bravado—no wonder New York mamas thought him good son-in-law material.

Surveying their work, Sarah Anne's spirits rose. The chairs, table, and lamp created a cozy reading nook in the bay window. Aunt Edith's old lace curtains would soften the space even more.

She looked up at Mr. van Beek with a smile. "Thank you so much. The schoolroom looks more inviting already, don't you think?"

"It does indeed." He might have said more, but Eliza's appearance in the doorway silenced him.

"Miz Bogard, she say she don't know you was coming, Mr. van Beek. She say your room ain't gonna be ready 'til this afternoon, so can you come to the morning room and make yourself comfortable there 'til dinner . . . I mean luncheon is served?"

"Hmm. I'm afraid that's my fault. Uncle and Aunt Littlewood did not know to expect me. Please give Mrs. Bogard my apologies. I'll be down shortly." To Sarah Anne, he said, "I'm afraid I've a bad habit of just turning up unannounced on my relatives' doorsteps. They are a very tolerant lot."

"I take it you're giving up your newspaper writing?"

"For the present. Although the perpetrator is still at large, the attacks have stopped. No one knows why. My last piece presented possible explanations. There is nothing more I want to write on the subject and I needed a change of scene. One can only come into contact with violence for a limited time before one begins to feel violated oneself."

A shiver ran down Sarah Anne's spine. She could only imagine. On the other hand, it must be nice to have the leisure time and money to travel and to have an extended family who welcomed unexpected visits. The rich really were a species apart, people beyond anything in Sarah Anne's experience.

Eliza, looking unsure and confused by the turn in conversation, did a quick bend of the knee and left. Mr. van Beek waited until the maid's steps faded. "I'm sure the invitation extends to you, Miss Mercer. Unless you have made provision for luncheon elsewhere, won't you please join me? It would be a pleasant change from dour faced relatives and I hate dining alone."

Sarah Anne was very sure the invitation did not include her, but she appreciated Mr. van Beek's considerate attempt at covering the slight. She glanced down at her dust-covered dress and could not imagine Mrs. Bogard allowing her anywhere near the family areas of the house. "Thank you, but no. I have too much work remaining."

"But surely you must eat."

"I will be fine until supper. My aunt's cook prepares generous meals and there will be plenty for me when I get home this afternoon."

"So, you are going to allow me, your devoted servant, to languish dejected and abandoned in the cavernous dining room? Surely your heart is not so hard."

A rueful smile lifted the corners of Sarah Anne's mouth. "I doubt Mrs. Bogard will approve."

"Leave her to me. She's putty in my hands."

"Are you sure? She seems pretty unyielding to me." Sarah Anne's stomach took that moment to growl loudly. Her cheeks had to be the color of the red clay in her maternal grandmother's North Georgia garden.

"See. You're starving. I cannot be responsible for your perishing for lack of sustenance. I insist you take luncheon with me. I will ensure Mrs. Bogard's cooperation. Until Uncle arrives, my rule is law in this house."

His masterful manner and self-assurance almost made Sarah Anne believe what he said.

CHAPTER 8

Despite disgruntled looks and grumbling from Mrs. Bogard, Sarah Anne enjoyed a delicious meal of griddle oysters with lemon butter, broiled stuffed flounder that Mr. van Beek insisted on calling sole, boiled potatoes, and green peas. Sarah Anne refused the wine offered, but watched with interest as her luncheon companion filled his glass almost to the brim. When his glass was empty, he poured himself another, which he consumed rather quickly. A little shocked, Sarah Anne watched Mr. van Beek's throat move while he swallowed the final sip of his third glass and poured himself a fourth. His hand still around the neck of the bottle, he gestured toward her empty glass. "Here, my dear. I insist. A small taste only. Uncle Littlewood keeps an excellent cellar even here in the wilds of rural Georgia. This one is particularly fine."

She had never had spirits of any kind and didn't particularly want to start then and there, but took a small sip anyway. It seared her throat and sent her into a spasm of coughing. She couldn't help but notice the humor dancing in Mr. van Beek's eyes.

Red-faced and a little angry, she placed her glass firmly on the table. "I would rather not finish the glass, if you don't mind." If he caught the edge in her voice, he gave no indication. Wine in the middle of the day indeed. No one in St. Anne behaved that way. Whether Mr. van Beek approved or not, she would stick with water since iced tea seemed to be something unheard of in Ripon House.

By the end of the meal, her good mood had returned. She dabbed her lips with her napkin and looked across the table. "That was lovely. I can't remember ever having such well-prepared food. If this is Ripon House's usual fare, I suspect I shall come to regret not living in."

Her companion's eyes grew slightly wider for a second or two before his manners returned. "That is unusual. I'm surprised Uncle Jed agreed to such an arrangement. I ought to say I hope he doesn't try bullying you into changing your mind, but then that would not be to my advantage. He is something of an autocrat, you know."

No, she didn't know. In truth, she was in complete ignorance regarding her employer and his family, but she could not bring herself to admit such to Mr. van Beek. Warmth spread upward from Sarah Anne's throat and over her cheeks. Blushing was becoming an all too common experience in this place. She hadn't felt this off-kilter since first coming to live in St. Anne. It didn't help that Mr. van Beek gazed at her with real concern. "I'm afraid Mr. Littlewood may not know, but there was no other way I could take the position. I must care for my aunt at night and I believe my uncle, Dr. MacAllister, may have neglected to mention it when he recommended me." At this point she knew exactly what had transpired, so why did she feel the need to allow Mr. van Beek to believe less than the truth? She had never cared one whit for other's people's opinions, but this man's good opinion suddenly mattered. She must get a grip on herself.

Laying her napkin aside, she said, "And speaking of my aunt and uncle, I really must be getting home. I have things I must attend to there. Please excuse me and thank you, Mr. van Beek, for persuading Mrs. Bogard to allow me in the dining room. The meal was wonderful."

"How unfortunate." When he saw Sarah Anne's dismay, he quickly amended, "That you must leave and that your aunt is so indisposed. Please allow me to see you across the bay in my uncle's motor craft. I'm always in need of fresh air after a few hours in this house."

"How very kind, but I can't impose on your time any longer. I'll just take the ferry."

"But I'm afraid you can't if you are wanting to leave the island now. The ferry doesn't run again until four o'clock and it is now only just gone two."

Heavenly days, she knew when the ferry ran, but a sudden overpowering need to be away from Ripon House had trampled on her ability to think. "Oh, yes, but I don't understand."

"About the ferry?" Incredulity colored his words.

She sounded like an idiot. What he must think of her. "No, I mean what is a motor craft?"

"Ah. I see." A smile warmed his handsome face. "It's my uncle's latest acquisition. He saw one in operation when he was in England last year and had to have one for himself. Just imagine. Lurssen Yachts has put a Daimler engine into the hull of a skiff, sort of an automobile for the water. Uncle Jed doesn't like being dependent on the ferry. Says the local ferryman is unreliable. I've never experienced such, but my uncle has decided opinions and once set, they are not easily dislodged. I, of course, am delighted he is enamored of this particular *idee fixe*. The thing is great fun." Mr. van Beek grinned at her over the rim of his wine glass.

She returned his smile with a wry one of her own. "The products of industry truly are amazing. It is fortunate for you Mr. Littlewood is so *au courant*." Wistfulness settled over Sarah Anne. "A few automobiles were beginning to appear on the streets of Macon while I was at college there. We girls would marvel at them, but we were not permitted to socialize with the general public, so none of us ever rode in one."

Van Beek hit the table top with his palm, rattling the glassware and utensils. "Well, that settles it. I will ferry you across the bay in my uncle's motor craft. I will brook no refusals."

Sarah Anne laughed at the determined expression and excitement that lit his features. "If you insist."

"I do. I will await you in the foyer while you gather your things."

The walk to the boathouse took them down a path beneath a tunnel of live oaks. Their steps crunching in the deep white sand was accompanied only by the sounds of nature. A mutual shyness seemed to have befallen them. As they approached the docking area, a young doe gazed at them from the shelter of a palmetto clump, eyes wide and nose twitching.

Mr. van Beek watched her bound away, hind hoofs aloft and white tail flagging. "I guess she didn't like the smell of us. Too bad she got away. She would have made lovely venison roasts of which I am particularly fond."

Sarah Anne cut her eyes at him from beneath her lashes to see if he was joking. He appeared in earnest. "I don't think we're outfitted for killing and field dressing a deer. It's a messy job."

Mr. van Beek seemed confused. "Field dressing?"

She decided his question was sincere rather than mocking. "You know. Gutting, bleeding out, and skinning the carcass as soon as the animal hits the ground to preserve the meat."

He kicked at a mound of sand surrounding a hole and a little crab scurried away. "So that's how it's done. I had no idea."

Sarah Anne couldn't keep the surprise from her voice. "I take it you don't hunt."

"Foxes from horseback, yes. Stalking through a muddy swamp for hours on end, no. *Surely* that is not something you have done." He drew out the word "surely" to such an extinct the irony could not be missed.

Sarah Anne laughed and replied, "When I was much younger, my uncle indulged me in my wish that I'd been born a boy. I think he felt sorry for me because I was an orphan and was having a hard time adjusting to life in St. Anne. I went hunting with him and his friends until I began to look too much like a female. I shot my first and last deer when I was eleven. Not much later, he said I was too old to be trailing behind a bunch of old men and should learn the female accomplishments. Life has been a little less interesting ever since."

"I, for one, am delighted you were born female. It makes life on this island much more interesting, I assure you." There was something about his tone and the way he looked at her that set Sarah Anne's teeth on edge.

Discomfort settled over her. She couldn't let this go on. She had to say something even if it put her in a bad light. Familiarity between a member of the family and an employee wouldn't improve her chances of success in her position. Even if he didn't comprehend this, she knew it instinctively.

Sarah Anne stopped and turned to face Mr. van Beek. "While I appreciate the compliments, you must not continue to speak to me in this manner. I am your cousin's teacher, and as such, I must maintain an appropriate distance from my pupil's relatives. I hope you understand professionalism demands it."

Van Beek threw up his hands in a defensive gesture. "Forgive me. I meant no disrespect and please, it's John or J.E., whichever you prefer. May I address you as Sarah?"

"My name is Sarah Anne, but I must be Miss Mercer to you."

"My goodness. So formal, but have it as you like, Miss Mercer. Will you tell me one thing?"

"Perhaps."

"Why does every lady I meet down here have a double first name? It makes for quite a mouthful on occasion." The irritation in his voice was unmistakable.

She refused to be baited. She would keep her voice calm and her tone cordial even if it killed her. "It's a Southern tradition and I have no idea how it got started. Now, I believe I see a boathouse just beyond those trees. Shall we get started for St. Anne?"

Sarah Anne was grateful for the noisy chugging of the skiff's engine. It made conversation impossible during the twenty-minute trip to the mainland. When the vessel bumped against the St. Anne dock, Sarah Anne rose to her feet so abruptly the boat started rocking, sending her slightly off balance. It was a state in which she had found herself too often since arriving at Ripon House that morning.

John grabbed her arm to prevent her toppling into the bay. "I hope I was not being too familiar, Miss Mercer. I'd hate to see you fall into this water laden as it is with dead fish and rotting vegetation." Sarcasm colored his words, making Sarah Anne look at him askance. Rudeness did not become him. The man had the good grace to have color rising in his cheeks. "I apologize. That was uncalled for. I am unaccustomed to being corrected or refused. I'm afraid I have been rather spoiled by the ladies of New York."

Sarah Anne's eyes narrowed and she searched his face, but found only sincerity. A trickle of regret coursed through her for what might have been had they met under different circumstances. "And I apologize for putting a distance between us, but it is how it must be. Surely you understand my relationship with Adelia can in no way be compromised."

"I am contrite and stand corrected. To make up for my shortcomings, please allow me to escort you to your home."

"No. You can't." The words flew from her mouth before she could stop them. The tone of alarm and their volume only served to amplify her rudeness. The effect was clearly written on John's face. "I apologize. Please let me explain. People here are inveterate gossips. They have very little to entertainment them, so talking about one another is a chief pastime. I have always been under scrutiny and do not wish to cause additional speculation. The news of a well-dressed stranger at my side would spread before we reached my uncle's front walk."

"Such is the nature of small towns the world over, or so I have heard. With your express permission then, I shall leave you here and pray we have not been observed too closely."

While humor danced in his eyes, other emotions lurked there as well. She had no trouble laughing at herself, but she truly disliked being an object of derision or pity. Both of those qualities seemed mingled with the mirth. But perhaps her overactive imagination was at work again, so she bit back a stinging reply.

Shaking his hand firmly, she marshaled her words, stamping back what she really wanted to say. "Thank you for understanding. I'm sure we will meet again at Ripon House. I will return when the family is settled. Until then, I wish you well." She turned on her heel and marched up the dock toward Water Street before he could do or say more. A soft chuckle followed her from the direction of the skiff sending heat rushing to her cheeks. Charming, handsome, and audacious—a combination that might prove persuasive if she allowed herself to be in a romantic frame of mind.

Romance? Ridiculous and impossible under any circumstances. The thought settled over her like a musty, smothering blanket. She couldn't afford to indulge in such fantasies. John Edgar van Beek was a man of wealth, family, and position, while she was merely a temporary employee in his uncle's house. Temporary. The word made her pulse pound against her eardrums. Interim governess. That was how the housekeeper had described her. As she marched toward home, a spasm of dissatisfaction gripped her. The more she thought about her situation, the faster she walked. An important task lay at hand, one she had initially rejected because she had not wanted to upset Uncle Zach. He worked so hard caring for everyone in his far-ranging practice and had shown her nothing but love and kindness, especially since her parents' deaths. He was the one person with whom she hated to argue. Because she adored him, she had accepted her fate without accusations of having been manipulated. Well, no more. Uncle Zach had some explaining to do.

Sarah Anne continued past the village square until she reached her own front walk. Turning in at the gate of their white picket fence, she made her way around to the side door that served as the entrance to her uncle's office. The door to the consultation room was closed and muffled voices emanated from the other side. She flounced onto a seat in the outer office, her fingers drumming on the wooden armrest. Presently, the inner door opened. Doctor and patient passed through to the reception area. Uncle Zach observed Sarah Anne's expression and ushered his patient on her way.

"Now Sarah Anne, calm down. I know that face."

Anger bubbled up and spilled over. Sarah Anne jumped to her feet and placed a fist on each hip. "How could you? I turned down a perfectly good full-time job for something that may not last for more than a few weeks. I cannot believe you lied to me."

Uncle Zach dropped his gaze before answering. "I did not lie. I simply didn't share all of the facts and you didn't ask. You assumed it was permanent." His eyes rose to meet hers. "And furthermore, I don't understand how you could have considered a job 300 miles away in Clayton. Especially as you know how badly you're needed here. Your aunt and I were surprised and hurt that you even applied for it." Although the words were direct and might have been harsh if spoken by someone else, Uncle Zach had a way of softening any blow with a gentle tone and kind expression. As the only doctor serving a far-flung rural area, he had had plenty of practice delivering bad news.

His admonition worked. Guilt thrust through Sarah Anne like a rapier in the hands of a skilled swordsman, piercing the bubble of her anger until shame took its place. "I'm sorry. I know everything you say is true. I never meant to hurt you and Aunt Edith. I wouldn't have qualified as a teacher if you hadn't sent me to college. I owe y'all everything. From taking me in as a child to paying for my education, you both have been nothing but kindness itself. I love y'all dearly. Can you forgive my selfishness?"

Uncle Zach reached out and gently squeezed her hand. "Now, now. No need to dwell or become maudlin. Time for you to be on your own will come soon enough." Sadness darkened his features for a moment, then disappeared, replaced by a forced smile. "I believe Dorcas is fixing collards, peas, and cornbread for supper. Why don't you see if she needs help?"

That evening, Aunt Edith felt able to rise from her bed only long enough to use the chamber pot. The effort seemed to sap every ounce of strength she had. Heaviness wrapped its fingers around Sarah Anne's heart while she helped her aunt with her final preparations for sleep. A gray pallor had replaced Aunt Edith's normal rosy glow and a coughing fit announced that her asthma had taken hold with a vengeance.

CHAPTER 9

The article in this wretched newspaper reveals more than I thought possible, but perhaps all is not lost. Egad, but the sofa's horsehair upholstery scratches the back of my neck. Although I hate this particular covering, the sensation does not disrupt my train of thought. In fact, I relish the discomfort because it keeps me sharp and focused. I must think clearly as I dissect what I have just read.

The police have released details provided by the whore whom I initially feared I had killed. Fortunately, the only description she gave could fit any man. The ignorant bitch did not even recognize me as a gentleman. All the same, my work in that area of the city must cease for the time being. The public outcry has been heard by the police commissioner and extra patrols sent into the Tenderloin. I will continue elsewhere for my need has become a demanding taskmaster, especially since the other was such a disappointment.

As it turned out, she denied her intentions and desires. She said I was a monster and tried to run from me. She proved false and had to be punished. Because of her, my need is strong now and release will soon be necessary. I must carefully consider my next. . . What? These encounters must have a name worthy of the work. The word event comes to mind. It fairly rolls off the tongue and these encounters are certainly events the whores will never forget. Yes, Event is an excellent term for my encounters with whores. I believe it fits. From now on, the encounters that grow from my mission will be termed Events.

CHAPTER 10

Two weeks after her introduction to Ripon House, Sarah Anne stood at the front window polishing Aunt Edith's best table when she saw the Littlewood driver pass through the front gate. At his knock, she put her lemon oil and dust rag aside.

Opening the door, she smiled warmly. "George, to what do I owe the pleasure? I thought they didn't want me for a couple more days."

George removed his cap and returned her smile, but with a flash of something in his eyes she could not quite put her finger on. "Mr. Littlewood says you should come to the house tomorrow. Miss Adelia is settled enough to meet you now." An unexpected quality in his tone and the way his eyes darted away when he mentioned the child piqued Sarah Anne's interest.

"I hope all is well with Miss Adelia and her family. Has she been ill?"

"Sick? No, ma'am. She just . . ." George paused as though searching for the right words. "She sort of a delicate child, but she ready for you now." His words did not reassure. A moment of apprehension rose and fell in Sarah Anne.

There are all kinds of delicate. The word might connote anything from frequent, minor illnesses to insanity. What if this, her first pupil, was beyond her abilities? What if she had a serious condition?

Oh for goodness' sakes, stop it. You will "what if" yourself into a big ole mess. The girl is seven years old. She has been groomed for New York society since birth. Her manners and deportment should be impeccable.

To George, she said, "I see. Please tell Mr. Littlewood I'll arrive on the morning ferry. Would it be possible for someone to meet me at the dock? If not, it's really only a short walk."

"Mr. Littlewood says I'm to make sure you get to and from the house every day. He don't want time wasted walking from the dock. If you'll excuse me, I got to get back. Good day to you, Miss."

George didn't wait for her reply. He turned on his heel rather abruptly and his long strides carried him from sight in a heartbeat, leaving Sarah Anne with an uneasy feeling all was not as it should be within the Littlewood family. She stared at the empty street and wiped perspiration from her brow. With the temperature in the low seventies and the humidity in the high nineties, the concrete sidewalks actually gathered moisture resembling drops of sweat on an overheated brow. This weather was worse than the intense heat of summer.

The morrow would reveal the nature of Adelia's delicacy. Until then, all she could do was speculate. Sarah Anne's stomach churned with anticipation, then soured with a touch of anxiety. That night, her mind would still not let go of the question. Sleep eluded her until well after midnight.

To her great relief, the morning dawned bright and cool. A front had moved through during the night bringing much-needed rain and freshening the air. As good as his word, George and buggy stood waiting to transport Sarah Anne to Ripon House when the ferry from the mainland drew up to the island dock.

Assisting her into the vehicle, George seemed to have recovered his cheerful, friendly demeanor. "Beautiful day, ain't it? The cool air makes a body feel more like doing things."

Sarah Anne smiled and nodded, but did not speak. The breeze off the Atlantic sent a shiver through her and she pulled her shawl closer about her shoulders. As George slapped the reins on the horse's rump, she considered how she might obtain more information about her pupil without making George uncomfortable. Nothing useful presented itself.

When the silence grew awkward, she finally said, "Thank you for bringing the buggy. I hope this didn't take you away from more important work."

George looked at Sarah Anne with surprise. "No, ma'am. I ain't got no work more important than driving whenever Mr. Littlewood says to."

"Oh, of course. How silly of me." Sarah Anne squeezed her hands together to bolster her confidence and plunged ahead. "I'm afraid I was mystified by something you said yesterday. It's been worrying me. What did you mean about Miss Adelia being a delicate child?"

George jerked back on the reins so sharply the horse's chin snapped down almost against its chest. It strained back against the reins' pressure causing George to let up a little. The animal shook its head and turned to give its handler a sharp glance filled with rebuke.

Looking straight ahead, George said, "Miss, I don't mean no disrespect, but you cain't ask me questions like that. I shouldn't of said what I did. I cain't lose this job."

Guilt stabbed Sarah Anne. "I'm sorry. I shouldn't have asked and I certainly won't mention what you said. It's just if I'm to do well in this position, knowing more about Miss Adelia would help. In a way, you and I are alike. I need this job, too. Will you forgive me? Please?"

George nodded, but did not speak or look at Sarah Anne. He flicked the reins. The horse snorted and began moving again. Sarah Ann kept her torso facing forward, but glanced at him from beneath her lashes. He didn't seem to be angry anymore, but he no longer wore the sunny, kind expression that had impressed her when she first met him. Sarah Anne sighed inwardly. Another bridge that needed mending. First Mrs. Bogard and now George. She always seemed to be saying the wrong thing or ruffling someone's feathers with her outspoken, inquisitive nature. Still, it was he who had led her to think something might be amiss at Ripon House.

George clicked to the animal and it moved out into a trot. Fragrances floated on the air, some earthy, others fresh, but each one something to do with salt—saltwater, salt grass, salt marsh—and all of them clean and pure. Sarah Anne breathed deeply, hoping the salty air would cleanse her of the niggling foreboding that had disturbed her sleep the previous night.

At the edge of the front walk, George assisted Sarah Anne from the buggy, but did not linger. Touching his cap brim in farewell, he silently led the horse away toward the stables. Chastened by the knowledge that she might have created a lasting rift with someone who had been kind to her, she proceeded up the walk to the door where she waited to be admitted. She locked her hands at her waist to prevent fidgeting and breathed in and out slowly to calm her nerves. Presently, a tall man in tailcoat, waistcoat, stiff collar, and black tie answered her knock.

Sarah Anne smiled and extended her hand. "You must be the butler. I'm Miss Mercer, the new teacher."

The gentleman gave her a good once-over, but did not take her hand in return. "Indeed. Please follow me." The man's manner of speech took her by surprise. While she had not traveled and was unworldly by most people's lights, even she recognized the man's cultured English accent and his unaccountable superiority. Well, he could think whatever he liked. She dropped her hand and plastered a neutral expression on her face, tamping down her irritation in the process. She would ignore his slight so as not to burn yet another bridge. Furthermore, this man's behavior could not be allowed to affect her interview with Mr. Littlewood.

The butler led her into the library where someone who could only be her employer sat behind a large mahogany desk. Behind him, open French windows gave out onto a large terrace that overlooked the rolling Atlantic. The breeze off the ocean freshened the room, though it made the space cooler than she liked.

"Miss Mercer, sir."

"Thank you, Benson. That will be all."

The butler withdrew leaving Sarah Anne standing before the great expanse of wood separating her from Mr. Littlewood. He did not rise nor did he look up from his paperwork. If he wanted to establish that he was master and she an employee quaking in his presence, he had accomplished his goal. After what seemed an eternity, he laid aside his pen and cast his gaze in her direction.

"Mrs. Bogard tells me you hold a baccalaureate degree from . . ." He paused and consulted a paper on his desk. Surprise coursed through Sarah Anne once more as she detected yet another English accent, but this one had a coarser quality than that of the butler. "Here it is. Wesleyan Female College. Unusual. Tell me, what did you study? Sewing, drawing, music, and the like?"

"Yes, sir, but far more, as well. Wesleyan provides an education equal to that of any institution men attend. I studied a full curriculum of literature, higher mathematics, the sciences, history, foreign languages, as well as, art, music, and dance."

"I see. Quite commendable for a female. The housekeeper also tells me you will not be living in. Explain yourself." For what felt like the umpteenth time, she shared her circumstances at home in St. Anne. Mr. Littlewood nodded. "Again, you are to be commended for your devotion, but one point is upper most. Your employment depends upon your success with my daughter. I couldn't care less about your domestic arrangements. As the only medical man for miles around, your uncle's services are mandatory. Yours, however, are merely a contingency. Have I made myself clear?"

Equal measures of anger and anxiety flooded Sarah Anne. Her employer seemed to consider her not much above the station of servant rather than as the professional she thought herself to be.

Digging her nails into her palms, she forced evenness into her reply. "Of course, sir. I am confident Miss Adelia and I will do well together."

Mr. Littlewood harrumphed once then said, "That remains to be seen. The rope is beside the door. Go pull it."

Somewhere in the depths of the house a bell tinkled and the door opened within moments. Mrs. Bogard swished through, came to rest at the edge of the oriental carpet, and dropped a small curtsey.

Mr. Littlewood gestured toward the second floor. "Fetch Miss Adelia. If she resists, tell her I will come myself." Sarah Anne did not miss the subtle threat in his words or tone. George's hint replayed in her mind. Perhaps the child had reason to be delicate.

With the housekeeper's exit, he picked up his paperwork again. He neither made conversation nor invited Sarah Anne to sit, leaving her shifting from one foot to the other while they awaited the child's appearance. Two or three minutes passed before a loud thump overhead drew her gaze upward. Several more booms that could have been stamping feet filtered through the floorboards, then a door banged against a wall, a sound she recognized only too well from her own turbulent arrival in St. Anne as a newly orphaned ten-year-old. Angry voices rolled down the grand staircase and into the library followed by a deadly quiet.

Finally, muffled stomping on the staircase announced that Miss Adelia was on her way to the library. Within seconds, a red-faced Mrs. Bogard and a sullen-faced girl strode into the room. Only then did Mr. Littlewood look up from his papers. With a crook of his hand, he beckoned his daughter forward. She came to rest in front of the desk but as far away from her new teacher as possible. Sarah Anne would have loved to give a disgusted sigh, but knew it would do more harm than good.

Father addressed daughter. "Thank you for joining us, Adelia." Sarah Anne glanced sidewise to check the girl's reaction to her father's ironic tone. She resisted his baiting by remaining sulkily silent. Mr. Littlewood gestured toward Sarah Anne. "Say hello to Miss Mercer. She will be conducting your education for the time being. You will do as she says. Do you understand me?"

Adelia turned, but did not meet Sarah Anne's eye. "Pleased to meet you." Frost clung to the girl's words. Maybe if Sarah Anne smiled and tried to seem friendly rather than authoritative, the child might soften a little.

"I'm so glad to meet you, Adelia. You are my very first pupil, so we will be learning together. I suspect I shall make some mistakes, which I hope you will forgive, but I promise we will have fun as well. What is your favorite subject?" The girl stayed stonily silent. "Perhaps science?

There're many wonderful things we can explore on this beautiful island."

The girl glanced at her father who had returned his attention to his papers then she looked at Sarah Anne with narrowed, glaring eyes. "I like to read because it is an activity I can do alone." A slight emphasis highlighted the final word.

Sarah Anne swallowed and sighed inwardly. This child was going be more of a challenge than she had anticipated. Perhaps a more neutral setting would ease the situation. To Mr. Littlewood, she said, "Sir, perhaps I might show Adelia what I've done with the schoolroom. I hope she will like the changes."

The father barely glanced up. With a distracted wave of his hand, he replied, "Do as you like. She is your responsibility now."

"No. I won't go with you! I want Miss Ballard. I want Margret!" The sudden wail split the quiet atmosphere of the library. Sarah Anne watched in dismay as the child fled the room. Pounding footsteps echoed from the foyer and seemed to be heading toward the hallway behind the grand staircase. Sarah Anne didn't wait to request dismissal. She followed the sounds of those flying feet down the hall, through the kitchen where the staff watched her progress with interest, and out the backdoor. Adelia was nowhere in sight. Sarah Anne's heart pounded with exertion and the rising fear that she might actually fail at her first teaching job. The child had simply disappeared. Sarah Anne forced herself to stand very still so that the only sounds she heard were the wind in the trees and her own pulse thumping against her eardrums. Within a moment, faint voices floated from the direction of the carriage house.

Sarah Anne's boots crunched on crushed oyster shells as she marched across the back drive. Her fear had begun to devolve into anger. It appeared the child had been allowed to develop the habit of displaying rudeness when faced with what she considered adversity. This was no way to start a pupil-teacher relationship. Sarah Ann increased her pace, but when she reached the open carriage house door, she pulled up short. Adelia was inside all right. She had her arms flung around the midsection of George's tall, lanky frame.

He patted the child's back awkwardly while making soothing sounds. "There, there, sweet girl. It's gonna be all right. I was the one what brung your new teacher to the house and she's a nice young lady. It ain't her fault Miss Ballard took off."

"Margaret didn't take off! She wouldn't do that. Why won't anyone believe me?"

"I can't answer that 'cause I don't know." While he spoke, George met Sarah Anne's eyes and shook his head. She stayed still and quiet while he continued, "I tell you what. If you'll try to do your schoolwork today, I'll have Merrybelle all saddled and ready for you this afternoon. That little pony's gotten too fat waitin' for you to come back to Georgia. We both missed you something awful."

"I missed you, too, George. You're my only friend now that I don't have Margaret. No one cares about me but you."

"Now, Miss Adelia, you know that ain't true."

Adelia leaned back so she could see George's face. "Yes, it is! Promise you won't leave me. Promise!"

A sad expression full of empathy and pain filled George's eyes. "I'll stay as long as your daddy'll let me."

A shudder passed through Adelia's small body. She sniffed and ran her sleeve under her nose. "Will you ride with me and Merrybelle this afternoon?"

"We'll have to see what work I got to do." George looked at Sarah Anne. "Maybe your teacher could go with you." He then nodded at Sarah Anne encouragingly.

She moved a few steps into the carriage house. Keeping her voice quiet and mustering as much confidence as she could, she responded, "That is an excellent idea, George. Riding is one of my favorite pastimes, but one I don't often get to enjoy."

The girl flung herself around, glaring. "I don't want to ride with you." The petulant whine in Adelia's voice was more suited to a four-year-old than a girl of seven.

That was enough. At this point, Sarah Anne pretty much had the child's measure. Rudeness and obstinacy must be addressed, but perhaps challenging the girl at this particular moment was not the best plan. Behavior correction could come later. Instead of chastising Adelia, Sarah Anne took a different approach. "I know how it feels to lose everyone you love. It hurts beyond anything you ever thought possible. Maybe we can spend this morning just getting to know each other better. We don't need to start lessons right now." Looking beseechingly at George, she continued, "I don't think I remember my way around the island. I haven't been here since I was a child. A ride would be wonderful on this beautiful morning. George, won't you please come with us?" Thank goodness for the equestrian requirement at Wesleyan. If it had not been for the riding instructor there, she would have no idea how to stay mounted sidesaddle. She fought back the feeling that she was in way over her head with little Miss Adelia Littlewood.

The driver glanced at the child whose head bobbed up and down. "I guess I can spare y'all a hour."

Horses saddled and mounted, shawls fetched from the house, the trio started out past the south wing of the house with Adelia between the adults. Sarah Anne craned to catch a better view of this side of the house, which she had not seen before. Movement at a second-floor window caught her attention. When she looked more closely, she saw John Edgar van Beek smiling and nodding. The triple warmth of success, approval, and relief wrapped Sarah Anne in a lovely cocoon.

CHAPTER 11

Sarah Anne remained wrapped in the warmth of Mr. Van Beek's approval until they entered a trail shielded from the house by a forest of pines and live oaks. Without warning, Adelia kicked Merrybelle's sides and the little pony dashed away. Sarah Anne leaned forward in the saddle preparing to gallop after the girl, but George caught her reins in time to stop her.

"Let the child go. She knows these woods better than most folks. She won't come to no harm."

Sarah Anne's heart raced after rider and mount, but when she looked angrily at George, she saw that he remained calm and determined. He seemed confident in Adelia's ability to find her way and stay in the saddle. Perhaps she should heed his advice.

"If you are *sure* she'll be safe."

He nodded, dropped Sarah Anne's reins, and nudged his horse forward. They rode on at a leisurely walk. Neither of them spoke for several minutes. Finally, Sarah Anne mustered the courage to ask the question that hung silently between them.

"Adelia seems to be such an emotional child." She watched for George's reaction with a sidewise glance. His shoulders tensed, but he did not look at her, so she forged ahead. "Is this what you meant when you described her as delicate?"

His expression hardened. "Miss, you wasn't going to ask me no more questions."

Sarah Anne rolled her dry lips between her teeth and moistened them with her tongue. If this job was going to pull her under, it would not be without a valiant effort to keep herself from drowning. "You're right and I'm sorry to break my promise, but please believe I only want to help Adelia. At this point, I have no idea where to begin. You seem to know her well. She trusts you. I need for her to trust me." She didn't have the courage to look at him, so she simply plunged in heart first. "What has happened to cause someone so young to be so angry?"

George yanked back on his reins so hard his mount stumbled over its own feet. Sarah Anne had no choice but to pull up also. It was his turn to look angrily into her eyes. She prayed what he discerned there was a sincere desire to do well by the child, that he saw she meant him no harm, and that she could be trusted. After a few moments, he gave his mount a pat on the neck, then stretched forward and rubbed the horse's poll, the itchy place between the ears that could never get enough attention.

Finally, he sighed heavily. "It ain't what's been done *to* her. It's what ain't been done *for* her. A child's got to know it's loved."

Sarah Anne suspected she knew the answer before she asked the question, but she needed to keep him talking and divulging what he knew from years of association with the Littlewoods. "And Adelia doesn't feel loved?"

George's features became a study in neutrality. He looked at Sarah Anne, then away. His chest rose and fell as though controlled breathing might help him maintain a grip on his emotions. Perhaps she had pushed too hard or too fast and had made him angry. Just when it seemed he would never answer, he straightened up in the saddle and replied, "Adelia's got everything a little girl could want—dolls, toys, pretty dresses"—his volume dropped so low she leaned toward him in order to catch his final words—"but they just things." He then looked away, far off into the distance and urged his mount ahead into a faster walk.

Sarah Anne fell in behind him without another word. As great as her desire for additional information, the need for discretion outweighed the urge to assault him with a stream of questions. Patience had never been her particular virtue, but she couldn't risk offending him into permanent silence. He needed more prompting, but he wouldn't be pushed. That much was now very clear. They rode on in silence until they reached an opening in the trees where Sarah Anne found herself gazing out at the Atlantic. Packed sand showed a route through the dunes, which they followed. The sound of rolling waves, rhythmic and constant, soothed her turmoil, promoting clearer thinking.

As they rode on down the beach path, she considered the situation. It didn't matter whether George liked her or not. His good opinion, when weighed against the child's welfare, could not be paramount. She had to find out what he knew. She moved up beside him and glanced his way. No tension marred his face nor stiffened his body. Perhaps the ocean had the same effect on him that it had on her. Judging the timing might be right, she asked her next question.

"Was Miss Ballard able to give Adelia what she is missing?"

He froze for a moment, pulled his mount to a stop, and looked at Sarah Anne with suspicion. This was the moment of truth. He would either trust her now or never. He sucked on his lower lip for a few beats then nodded. "She saw how things was. Pretty soon Adelia was stuck to Miss Ballard like a barnacle on a old boat."

That was promising. Maybe a nudge more would bear even sweeter fruit. "It sounds as though Miss Ballard was devoted to Adelia."

George nodded in emphatic agreement. "She was for sure."

A question arose now that seemed more important than any she had previously asked. "Why do you think Miss Ballard left the Littlewoods so abruptly?"

Instead of replying, he bent down and toyed with the buckle on his nearside stirrup. He glanced up at Sarah Anne with a neutral expression. "They saying she run off with a man." His voice was almost a whisper. Discomfort radiated from him like heat from an over-stoked fire.

It was apparent that one key to working successfully with Adelia lay in understanding her relationship with her former governess. At the risk of upsetting George further, Sarah Anne plunged on. “Would it be in her nature?”

George straightened up in the saddle. He turned glittering eyes on her. “She was pretty enough. If she left on her own, I guess she had her reasons.”

Sarah Anne’s attention pounced on one phrase. *If she left on her own.* A shock of surprise mixed with trepidation coursed through Sarah Anne. “Are you saying she didn’t leave of her own volition?”

“I done said enough,” George answered and clicked to his mount. The horse’s ears pricked up and it moved out in a rapid walk.

When she caught up with him, she forced herself to speak calmly. “Thank you for telling me. I only asked to understand how best to work with Adelia. I promise to do what I can to help her as long as I’m here.”

George jerked around to face her. His eyes narrowed. “What you mean?”

Sarah Anne plastered an apologetic smile on her face. “I’m afraid I may only be temporary. It isn’t my choice, but it’s how I was hired. I didn’t even know until I had already accepted the position.”

George made a guttural sound of disgust deep in his throat. “That child’s going to be hurt all over again.”

The trust that had been in his eyes moments earlier disappeared behind the veil of reserve usually displayed by a servant of low status when dealing with someone higher up the social ladder. Whatever bond they briefly shared had been shattered by the revelation of a situation over which she had little control. Sarah Anne’s spirits popped like a soap bubble. The child chose that moment to reappear on the path ahead of them. George kicked his mount into a trot and rode off to join her.

The ride back to Ripon House took place in complete silence with George and Adelia in the lead. A need for haste had become evident when the day began to warm, bringing fog rolling in from the much colder Atlantic waters. The girl pointedly kept her back to Sarah Anne save for one or two baleful glances over her shoulder. If disapproval could be expressed simply in one's posture, little Miss Adelia Littlewood had mastered the attitude to perfection. So what should they do for the remainder of the day now that the ride Sarah Anne had such high hopes for was ending in disaster? The schoolroom was all that remained. Enticing the girl up to the third-floor room presented a challenge Sarah Anne anticipated with an emotion not even remotely akin to joy.

CHAPTER 12

The need is growing. Every day it increases and every night, oh yes, especially at night the torture becomes more exquisite with each passing hour. The pain I feel before each release is almost as satisfying as the images I carry with me after an Event. Mere mortals could never conceive the exaltation of the double-edged sword of pain and pleasure. Pain, inflicting pain, release, pleasure. It is a simple formula. One I have applied to each Event.

Event. A simple term for something that takes days, sometimes weeks, of planning. Yes, they are certainly events the whores will remember for the rest of their lives. The euphemism is all the droller for the irony. It often leaves me chuckling at my own cleverness. Events are what dreams and nightmares are made of. Certainly the bitches will never forget choosing the gift of experiencing an Event with me.

But wait. I must be honest. I would never stoop to the level of being disingenuous. I am not insane. Dishonesty is a form of insanity reserved only for weak-minded, ordinary men. In truth, all save one accepted my gift by their own choosing, but not she. That one exception mars my otherwise perfect record. She will never know how I have suffered for what I did to her, but it could not be avoided. She called me a monster and would have raised the hue and cry. She would have ruined me, sent me to prison or worse. It was her fault, after all. Indeed, she tempted me into an Event by her feigned interest and now the pressure is building beyond any I have known.

An Event will be called for in the very near future. I need the release to ensure I can maintain the façade of my dreary everyday existence. But when? Where? Who?

CHAPTER 13

When Sarah Anne's mount trotted onto the patch of lawn in front of the stables, she saw that the ride would end as it had begun. Adelia glared at her then promptly turned on her heel and ran away from the hated new teacher with her little legs churning as fast as they would go. Fortunately, she only made it to the edge of the paddock next to the stalls before George called out to her.

"Miss Adelia, come back here."

Sarah Anne watched in surprise and with gratitude as the child skidded to a stop and turned to follow his directions, albeit with a dragging, shuffling gate and a face that would have seared the flesh from anyone too close by. Bless the man. He may not trust her, but he at least seemed to understand what was important where Adelia was concerned. Running off into the rapidly gathering fog could spell disaster. Even those completely at ease with a particular geography could become disoriented and lost in dense fog. The girl came to rest beside George and placed her hand in his. He kneeled down on one knee so he was eye level with her.

"You know you got to go with your teacher. Your daddy say so."

Adelia's mouth twisted and tears rose in her eyes. "I know." Her voice was barely above a whisper.

George dropped her hand. "You go on now. If you don't, Merrybelle'll get sold. He done told you. Any more trouble and the pony's gone."

The child began to cry in earnest. "Please don't tell Papa I ran away from her today." Adelia jerked her head in Sarah Anne's general direction.

Despite the child's behavior and attitude, a twinge of pity tugged at Sarah Anne. With tears streaming down her upturned cheeks, Adelia looked very small and very unhappy. More than defiance showed in those tear-brightened eyes. Beneath the willfulness and bravado lurked something else. Fear perhaps? The child would fear her pony being sold, but this was something more, something Sarah Anne could not put her finger on. Could it be that in addition to being neglected, at least from George's perspective, Adelia was being ill-used in some way? Sarah Anne pushed the thought away as soon as it popped into her mind. Parents had a right and a duty to discipline their children.

George stood up with a hand pressed to his back. His gaze met and held Sarah Anne's. "If you go with your teacher and don't argue, I think we can forget about it." Adelia's head swiveled toward Sarah Anne. Her eyes held pleading edged with defiance.

Sarah Anne nodded. "I love horses and ponies. I would never want to see sweet Merrybelle sold." She unconsciously held out her hand to the child. Adelia ignored it but stepped beside her. Silently, they made their way to the house.

Sarah Anne glanced up at its windows and an unexplained shiver ran down her spine. Wrapped as it was in semi-opaque moisture, the house appeared soulless and sinister. Gray encased in gray like some enormous corpse in a dirty shroud. Its blind eyes gazed at them without any hint of welcome. It was as though the house exhaled the breath of evil. She shook her head.

Goodness gracious! Stop it! You're letting your imagination play havoc with your common sense. It's just a house, for pity's sake. Enough.

After giving it a final upward glance, she cast her gaze firmly ahead toward the service entry. The place may look and feel like a mausoleum, but it sheltered the living. And providing shelter was about all the good in it she saw. Granted, she had not grown up with such architecture, but surely Ripon House could never feel like a home.

They passed no one on their journey to the schoolroom. It was as though they were alone in the house. Other than the occasional sound of domestic occupation coming from the service area and that of their own carpet deadened footsteps, all was silent. Mr. Littlewood must have still been behind the closed library door, but he made no effort to see how his child and the new teacher were getting on. There was no sign of Mr. van Beek. Presumably he was pursuing his own interests, whatever they might be. Mrs. Littlewood remained a specter in Sarah Anne's imagination as there was simply no indication of when or where they might meet. For a mother, she seemed to take precious little interest in her young daughter. Of course, she could be ill or otherwise indisposed, but really. One expected a mother to at least want to meet the person charged with the welfare of her child. How ungracious and lacking in charity. Sarah Anne chided herself for the judgmental attitude while she kept an eye on the back of her pupil who picked up speed when she reached the staircase.

Sarah Anne was winded by the time she stepped into the third-floor hallway. Adelia had already disappeared, hopefully headed toward the schoolroom. A game of hide and seek held no appeal after the morning's antics and acts of defiance. Making her way to the back of the house, Sarah Anne glanced down hallways and into alcoves. Adelia was not in any of them. She broke into a run.

A fear overtook her that had no basis in reality. No one had mentioned or even implied that Adelia was in danger or might be a danger to herself, but Sarah Anne had an awful vision of a lost child and only herself to blame.

She came to a skidding halt at an arched hallway entry. At the door to the schoolroom, Adelia stood with her arms crossed over her chest and a smirk on her face. The brat clearly intended to make things as hard as she could without bringing any condemnation down upon herself. She would skirt the edges of manners and push the boundaries of obedience, but remain just on the right side of correct behavior. Smart and tricky. A lethal combination in one so young.

Sarah Anne stood at the end of the hall long enough to regain control of her breathing. Once at the schoolroom door, she opened it and stepped aside. Adelia stood on the threshold and peered in at the room. A little gasp escaped her rounded lips. She started to step forward, then stopped and glanced over her shoulder at Sarah Anne. "Did you do this?"

"I did. The room seemed a little uninviting when I first saw it. Do you like it?"

Adelia started a nod then stopped herself. "It's okay, I guess. Miss Ballard made our room in New York a lot prettier."

Sarah Anne watched as Adelia took a tentative step into the room. Her gaze swept the space until it came to rest upon the reading nook in the bay of the window. She hesitated then went across the room and fingered Aunt Edith's lace curtains. Delight with the redecorated surroundings and devotion to Miss Ballard clearly warred within the little girl. Her loyalty to her former governess was touching, but somewhat misplaced if the rumor was true about Miss Ballard running off with a man. Adelia must see Sarah Anne as an interloper, an intruder on a very special relationship. Only time, patience, and understanding would create the bond teacher and student needed to accomplish anything meaningful.

Sarah Anne slipped up cautiously beside Adelia. Together, they gazed through the window at the salt marsh edging the property. Fog creeping among the reeds, cattails, and salt grasses could make one believe in ghosts.

Shaking off the supernatural turn of mind, she cautiously said, "I'm sure Miss Ballard would have made this a lovely place to learn. She must be a wonderful teacher to inspire such loyalty in her pupil." Sarah knelt down until her knees touched the floor. Adelia turned ever so slightly toward her. Sarah Anne drew a silent breath in and let it out slowly. "I know you miss her terribly. I'll do my best, but I know I will not take her place. I don't want to. I want us to make our own place for each other."

The child tilted her head and studied Sarah Anne. Reaching some unspoken decision, she replied, "No, I don't suppose you will ever take Miss Ballard's place." Ice clung to Adelia's words. Such a grown-up remark from one so young. Just then, the girl sounded a lot like her father.

Sarah Anne stood and lifted her arm to indicate the books stacked on the table between the chairs. "Be that as it may, we should begin work. Let's sit here in the window. I would like to hear you read."

"Why?"

"So that I will have an idea of where we need to start instruction."

"I know how to read. I don't need instruction. Can't you teach anything I don't already know?"

"Oh, I suspect I can, so why don't you show me what you know? After that, we can think about what you don't know."

Suspicion flashed from Adelia's eyes, but she did as Sarah Anne asked. No doubt George's words echoed in the child's mind. For the remainder of the day, the duo explored the depths and shallows of Miss Adelia Littlewood's previous acquisition of knowledge and skills. Sarah Anne discovered in Adelia a pupil with a quick mind and surprisingly mature understandings of literature, mathematics, and rudimentary sciences.

If she could convince the child to trust her, the task of teaching would be quite easy. It might even be a lot of fun for both of them. The difficulty, of course, lay in the trusting.

• • • • •

Over the course of the next month a pattern developed. Sarah Anne would set out lessons and Adelia would reject them at first, but would ultimately comply. Sarah Anne made it clear they would not leave the room until compliance and learning had been demonstrated and in that order. During the month, Sarah Anne saw little of the other members of the family. Mr. Littlewood was always locked away in his library when she arrived and Mr. van Beek had been invited to a lengthy house party and hunting trip near Savannah.

It was on the first day that could actually be called cool, a day with a blue, cloudless sky and a sharp breeze, a day in mid-November, when Sarah Anne was finally to learn more of the Family Littlewood. She and Adelia were seated in the window bay reading from a history of colonial America when Eliza appeared in the open door.

The little maid dropped a brief curtsey. "Begging your pardon, Miss. Miz Littlewood says can you and Miss Adelia come to her sitting room?"

An immediate squeal of joy came from the chair opposite Sarah Anne. "Momma wants to see me." The little girl jumped up, tossed the book aside, and was at the door before Sarah Anne had even risen from her chair. There was something startling and very sad in the way the child danced around in anticipation of an interview with her mother.

"Come on, Miss Mercer. Hurry up. Momma shouldn't be kept waiting. Come on before she changes her mind." Adelia grabbed Eliza by the hand and started pulling.

The light of understanding dawned for Sarah Anne. While the day outside was gloriously bright and sunny, the one inside the house grew suddenly gray and cold. At ten, Sarah Anne had lost her parents when their buggy tumbled down the side of a mountain, but even so, she remembered how they made her feel. She never once had to wait to see her mother or to talk to her. Her father had taken his little girl with him whenever he could because he knew she enjoyed outings even if it was only to the feed store. Her parents had made her feel cherished, an important member of the family. They did not give her material things beyond what she needed, but they gave her something far more important—a parent's deep, abiding, unconditional love.

Sarah Anne watched Adelia race ahead, her little legs churning, but instead of disappearing as she was want to do, the child would slow and glance back to ensure her teacher followed as instructed. The child practically dragged the maid by the hand. Heaviness wrapped itself around Sarah Anne's heart and a lump rose in her throat. So there really were such things as poor little rich girls.

They traveled areas of the house Sarah Anne had not seen thus far. When they reached a set of double doors, Eliza knocked then opened the door a crack.

"Miss Adelia and Miss Mercer, ma'am."

"Thank you, Eliza. Tell them to enter and then you may go back to your duties." The voice that spoke held a musical quality, melodic and high pitched.

Adelia burst through the door and ran across a great expanse of thick carpet colored in greens, pinks, and creams. Sarah Anne's art history professor would have called it Aubusson. Mrs. Littlewood's parlor was a breath of springtime and femininity in Ripon House's otherwise cloyingly dark ambiance. The room in decoration, furnishings, and wallpaper was a throwback to an earlier time. Instead of dark, heavy furniture, delicate gold and white painted Louis XVI settees and chairs graced the space around the carved marble fireplace. Fine embroidery covered their seats, backs, and cushions. Sarah Anne had never seen the real thing in person nor did she have any education in the decorative arts, still, the room looked like a piece of feminine heaven to her untrained eye. These furnishings might be reproductions, but somehow she didn't think so. The juxtaposition of this room against the others in the house fairly took one's breath so striking was the contrast.

"Miss Mercer, won't you join us?" The voice came from a window bay much like the one in the schoolroom only this one had a view of the Atlantic. Adelia stood beside a chaise upon which reclined an elegantly dressed woman whose dark-blonde coloring, clear blue eyes, and over generous mouth were an older version of the child.

Sarah Anne blinked as heat filled her face. She realized she stood frozen in place so transfixed had she been by the unexpected nature of the room. "Yes, ma'am. And you must be Adelia's mother."

"Please draw up a chair so we may chat."

Having done as instructed, Sarah Anne sat waiting for her employer to begin the conversation. The woman said nothing more. After several uncomfortable beats, Adelia began to pick at a loose thread on the chaise's braiding. Finally, she said to her mother, "I am so glad you are able to get up today." She leaned in and put her arm across her mother's shoulders. To Sarah Anne she said, "Momma suffers from spells. It is a terrible burden, but one which she endures with dignity and forbearance." Again, very mature words for a child of seven. Sarah Anne began to suspect the source from whom the child learned such phrases.

"Yes, it is true. Adelia is very solicitous." Mrs. Littlewood ran her fingers across Adelia's cheek then said to Sarah Anne, "I understand you are local."

"I am. I believe you may know my uncle, Dr. MacAllister?"

"Indeed, I do. A most capable physician. Now tell me about yourself."

For the next quarter hour, Sarah Anne shared the details of her college experience, and when pressed, the facts of her life prior to her attending Wesleyan.

Sarah Anne had just mentioned her parents' deaths when Mrs. Littlewood interrupted her. "How did it happen?"

Sarah Anne choked back a gasp. Even after ten years, the pain of loss lay raw and burning just below the surface of her well-developed defensive shell. Mrs. Littlewood's question, while not unexpected, had been delivered in a manner so direct and its tone was so lacking in actual sympathy as to be what some people might consider rude. Sarah Anne drew a deep breath and exhaled slowly.

"My parents and I lived in Rabun County on a farm near the North Carolina state line. Mrs. MacAllister is my father's sister. She and my uncle were visiting us. It was a Sunday and I should have gone to church with the family, but I was running a high fever. My uncle, being a doctor, was the logical choice to stay behind with me. When my parents and aunt were returning home after church, their buggy overturned and tumbled down the side of a steep cliff. It was a long drop. My parents were killed and my aunt was left paralyzed."

"I see. Why did they overturn?" Once again the words were not out of place, but their tone was devoid of any appropriate emotion. It was as though Mrs. Littlewood was only going through the motions of normal conversation.

"My aunt says that a gunshot in the woods above the road spooked the horse and it bolted. When the horse was found, my uncle took his pistol and shot it."

"Do you still have family there?"

"No, my grandparents have all passed away, as well."

"So, you are an orphan. You must count yourself lucky to have been sick on that fateful Sunday." Mrs. Littlewood's eyes were beginning to glaze over as though she was either bored with Sarah Anne's details or her attention was wandering.

"I suppose one might view it that way." Sarah Anne had reached her limit with this line of questioning. She mustered her most professional smile. "Perhaps you would like to discuss Adelia's academic progress?"

Mrs. Littlewood dismissed the suggestion with a wave of her hand. "Another time. I wished to inform both of you that the week of Thanksgiving Mr. Littlewood and I are hosting a large house party. Miss Mercer, it is imperative you live here at Ripon House during that time and for at least two weeks prior to the house party. My daughter enjoys neither the preparations nor these events themselves and will need constant supervision. Why my husband agreed to your not living in is another matter. It is most irregular."

A tenderness tinged with sadness and colored by anger settled over Sarah Anne as she watched the light fade from Adelia's eyes. The child wasn't stupid. She understood what her mother had just communicated, however unwittingly, but the message came through loudly and clearly all the same. Ignored. Neglected. Perhaps unwanted.

Easily discarded in favor of more stimulating, more entertaining company. No wonder the child was angry and lashed out where she thought she safely could.

"Mrs. Littlewood, I am afraid it is quite impossible." Sarah Anne explained her home situation now for what seemed like the thousandth time. She watched in some amusement as the light of comprehension dawned in her employer's eyes. It was highly likely the woman could count on one hand the number of times an employee had rejected her demands. "So you see, I must be home in St. Anne every night. My aunt's welfare depends on it."

At that point, Adelia's lower lip began to quiver. "Will Jacob be here?"

"Of course not," Mrs. Littlewood snapped. "Oliver and Jacob must stay in New York. Oliver is very busy learning the workings of your father's businesses. Jacob will use the long weekend to study. Columbia Law is a demanding institution. Neither of your brothers will come south until the Christmas season. How many times must I tell you?"

Adelia straightened up and removed her arm from around her mother. The child appeared to marshal her emotions. The effort clearly cost her a lot. "I'm sorry, Momma. Who is coming to your party? Will there be any children?"

"Children? Whatever gave you such an idea? Children are never invited as you well know."

It dawned on Sarah Anne as she watched the exchange between mother and daughter that Adelia was a lonely little girl, one who would find no solace or understanding in the person who should most have provided those supports. An idea suddenly popped into her head. It would probably be rejected, but it was worth a try—anything to extricate herself and Adelia from the awful interview and the prospect of a miserable little girl hidden away in her room for the duration of what should have been a happy family holiday.

"Mrs. Littlewood, I can see what a disruption to your plans my inability to stay overnight is. Would it be possible for Adelia to spend the duration of the house party with me at my home?"

Emotions played strongly across the faces opposite Sarah Anne—relief in the mother and astonishment in the child.

Adelia's face turned bright red and she burst into tears. "I won't go. I will not!"

CHAPTER 14

Sarah Anne stood alone in the schoolroom packing up books and the other teaching tools she would transport to St. Anne so lessons could continue during the Thanksgiving week. Adelia was in her room watching Eliza pack her valise. In less than an hour, Sarah Anne and her pupil would be crossing the bay and Adelia would be entering a world she most likely had never experienced or even knew existed. Sarah Anne dreaded the responsibility of two entire weeks with the child, but the more she had seen of family interactions, or rather the lack of them, the more convinced she was that taking Adelia with her was the right course. It had occurred to her that the child might not know how a loving family actually behaved. The experience would be good for Adelia and would also be good for Aunt Edith, who sometimes focused too closely on her own situation. Those two might even be good for each other if Sarah Anne handled the situation well.

Movement at the door caught Sarah Anne off guard, making her jump. She jerked around to find a grinning John Edgar van Beek leaning against the doorjamb.

Gathering her wits, Sarah Anne placed a fist on each hip to fight any outward sign of the little thrill coursing through her. "I see you have returned from your hunting trip. You startled me. Is there something I can do for you, Mr. van Beek?"

He didn't answer for a moment then chuckled. "I do apologize. I shouldn't have lurked in the doorway, but watching you unbeknownst was too tempting. Has anyone told you what a winsome vision you are when intent upon a task?"

Heat flooded Sarah Anne's face. This man created an effect she had not heretofore experienced or expected. "I don't believe they have, but it is not really my or your concern. Adelia and I are bound for St. Anne on the afternoon ferry." It may be the norm for gentlemen of his class and northern upbringing to pay compliments that felt a little too intimate and yet could not be faulted as inappropriate in their wording. Sarah Anne had no idea how to react to such.

He must have sensed her confusion for a sardonic smile lifted one corner of his mouth. "So I have heard. Your courage in taking the child with you is to be commended."

"I'm sure her parents will find entertaining easier without us under foot. Are you looking forward to the festivities, Mr. van Beek?"

"Oh, I will not be here to enjoy them. I'm called back to New York to spend time with another uncle and aunt from among my large assortment of relations, so I will be taking the ferry with you. I have to make my way up to Brunswick to catch the morning train north."

"Then I wish you a safe journey. If you will excuse me, I still have some packing to do."

"Until the ferry then." His eyebrow rose ever so slightly. Something in the simple movement seemed suggestive, but Sarah Anne couldn't say exactly what. He lingered just long enough to bring the heat to her cheeks for a second time, so she turned away to signal dismissal. She could hear gentle laughter and light footsteps floating back to her from the hallway.

Nothing he had said was untoward, but something in his tone had left her feeling off balance, at a disadvantage. She didn't know whether to be flattered or offended by the attention he was paying her. His behavior flew in the face of what she had been brought up to believe appropriate in a gentleman's deportment. If he were to show up on Uncle Zach's doorstep, what kind of reception would he receive and why was she even thinking about it? She shook her head in disgust. John Edgar van Beek was no more interested in her than he was in last month's newspaper. He probably enjoyed many minor flirtations that were quickly forgotten when something or someone more interesting came along. She would put him out of her mind.

In reality, she might not see him again after today since her employment was only temporary. Adelia's parents could be searching for a permanent replacement at that very moment, one who could live in and travel with the family. What a depressing thought. She was pouring her heart and soul into reaching the child, but she could be cast off at any moment. Might as well find her charge and make their way down to the dock.

During the ride across the bay, Adelia sat pouting in a corner as far away from Sarah Anne as she could get. Mr. van Beek seemed lost in his own thoughts and did not even glance in Sarah Anne's direction despite sitting beside her. For her part, Sarah Anne made a mental list of things to do in St. Anne that might interest a seven-year-old born and bred in New York. The list was short indeed.

When the ferry reached St. Anne, Mr. van Beek offered Sarah Anne his hand and assisted her step onto the dock. She couldn't remember when the train to Brunswick left, but he had been so kind to her that offering hospitality felt in order.

"My uncle's home is only a short walk. Perhaps you would rather wait for your train in our parlor. It would be much more comfortable than the wooden benches at the depot."

Surprise flashed in his eyes. "That is very kind, but my train leaves shortly." No doubt he remembered her refusal to allow him to see her home upon the last occasion when they crossed the bay together. "I have just enough time to purchase my ticket. If you will forgive my refusal of your invitation, I must be off in search of the ticket office."

"Oh. Of course." A flush rose in Sarah Anne's cheeks. Mr. van Beek's simplest conversation now had an unsettling effect on her. She had never before reacted to anyone in such a flighty manner. In his presence, she often felt callow and naïve. She must regain her grip on composure. To cover her embarrassment, Sarah Anne launched into a detailed description of the five-minute trip to the train depot. "So, as you can see, St. Anne is very small. You can't miss the depot." Her words ground to an awkward halt.

Amusement danced in Mr. van Beek's eyes. "Thank you. I'm sure I shall find it without difficulty. Now I must bid you adieu." He bent slightly at the waist. "Miss Mercer. Cousin Adelia."

Confused and a little irritated by his manner, Sarah Anne watched him walk away and disappear around a corner. A true gentleman would not have the effrontery to find an offer of hospitality amusing. Then, the explanation dawned on her. He had arrived in St. Anne by train and probably had done so many times in the past. He knew where the depot was without her rambling directions. He must think her an utter fool, or at the very least, an unworldly, socially awkward yokel. So much for making a good impression. But then, why did she care what he thought of her? He was of no importance in her life or she in his. They were from different worlds. He was of her employer's family and she was merely hired help. It was how things lay and they could never change.

Sarah Anne looked down at Adelia who had a knowing grin spread across her face. The child was quick. She had to give her that. "Home is this way. You can carry your own things, Adelia."

A spark of shame flickered in Sarah Anne as she watched the child lugging her valise. Reprisal against a seven-year-old did her no credit. Adelia was on the small side and rather skinny. Even though the walk was no more than five minutes, she struggled to keep her bag from dragging the ground. Halfway to the house, Sarah Anne's conscience got the better of her. "Here. Give your valise to me."

Adelia gave Sarah Anne a red-faced scowl. "Don't touch my things. I'll do it."

"Okay. Suit yourself." Sarah Anne's patience with rudeness and petulance was near an end. Feeling disgruntled with the child and herself, she picked up the pace of their march. The faster they got home to Dorcas's good, simple food and the comfort of people who loved her, the better.

The sight of Aunt Edith sitting on the front porch signaled a good day, one during which she had been able to leave her bed. Good days were less frequent with each passing month. Sometimes when Aunt Edith was having a particularly rough time, Sarah Anne could hear Uncle Zach late at night pacing in his office. Because of the ten-year age difference between them, his most desperate fear was that he would die before she did, leaving her alone and defenseless against the world.

Though by all accounts Uncle Zach was an excellent physician, he was a country doctor whose patient list was comprised of smallholding farmers, sharecroppers, and fishermen. He worked to cure their ills, not to get rich and so took as payment whatever they could give. Last week, the proud father of Mayweather County's newest citizen paid the doctor's midwifery fee with a peck of corn. Sarah Anne assured her uncle that Aunt Edith would always have a home with her if the worst happened. After one of her declarations, he would give her a weak smile and call her a good girl, but she could see in his eyes that her assurances did nothing to lessen his fear.

Sarah Anne, with Adelia in tow, turned in at the gate in their picket fence and rushed to give Aunt Edith a big hug and kiss on the cheek. "It's a lovely day. I'm so glad you are able to enjoy it. Have you been out here long?"

"Not too long. I wanted be here to greet the little girl. It will be so nice to have a child in the house again." Aunt Edith loved children, but sadly, had not been blessed with any of her own. She had always doted on her only brother's child, even more so after the buggy accident left her a cripple and Sarah Anne an orphan.

Sarah Anne glanced back to the middle of the front walk where Adelia stood holding her big valise looking not unlike a little girl lost. Her big blue eyes were brighter than usual and her lower lip quivered. Her gaze shifted from Aunt Edith's sweet face to her wheelchair several times. Perhaps the child had never encountered a disabled person and feared what she saw.

Using her gentlest voice, Sarah Anne said, "Come meet my Aunt Edith. She is like my mother and loves little girls. She is excited to meet you." She kept one arm around her aunt and held out the other to the child.

Adelia hesitated. Fear, confusion, yearning, and surprise all played across her features in a jumble of conflicting emotions telling a sad tale. She appeared desperate to be included in the affectionate exchange on the porch, but also afraid, of what it was hard to say. Sarah Anne gestured with her free arm, beckoning the child forward.

Adelia dropped her bag and went onto the porch. She refused Sarah Anne's offered embrace, but looked at Edith with interest. After several moments of observation by both the child and the adult, the fear seeped out of the child, but the confusion remained.

Adelia tilted her head to one side. A crease formed between her brows. "You are excited to meet me?"

Edith smiled and leaned forward until she was as close to Adelia's eye level as possible. "I am. This house has been too long without the laughter of a child. I had Dorcas get Sarah Anne's toys out of the attic and clean them up just because you are coming to visit."

Adelia considered this for a moment, and then asked, "Who's Sarah Anne?"

Edith's hug tightened around Sarah Anne's waist. "Perhaps you know her as Miss Mercer?"

Adelia looked up at Sarah Anne with wide eyes. "Oh." Her disappointment could not be missed. Perhaps she hoped for another little girl as the week's playmate. "Who's Dorcas?"

"Our cook and my nurse."

"Will she like me?" The wistful note in Adelia's voice touched Sarah Anne's heart almost to breaking. The girl was a bundle of contradictions. On the one hand, she could parrot adult phrasing and opinions with an authority far beyond her seven years. On the other, she could devolve into an attitude and mannerisms more suited to a younger child.

Edith smiled gently. "Oh, I am quite sure she will love having you here as much as I will. She made teacakes just because you were coming."

"What are teacakes?"

"Cookies. Do you like cookies?"

Adelia nodded. Edith glanced up at Sarah Anne then held out an arm to Adelia. To Sarah Anne's surprise, the child moved into the offered embrace. She looked stiff and unsure, but the tears had disappeared and her lower lip no longer telegraphed her distress. Progress was being made thanks to a gentle, loving woman in a wheelchair. Sarah Anne prayed Aunt Edith's magic would last for the duration of their stay. Adelia gave all evidence of desperately needing what their simple home life had to offer.

CHAPTER 15

"Sarah Anne, why don't you pull up two more chairs then go to the kitchen and bring the teacakes out here." Aunt Edith grinned at Adelia. "You won't let a cookie or two spoil your supper, will you?"

A big grin lit the child's face. "No. I promise to eat my dinner."

"Sweet Girl, we have dinner in the middle of the day here in St. Anne. Supper is what we eat in the evening. You won't let a teacake spoil your supper, will you?"

"No. I promise."

"No what?"

Adelia looked completely perplexed. "No, I won't let a teacake spoil my supper."

"That's not what I'm looking for."

Adelia looked to Sarah Anne in complete confusion. Sarah Anne explained, "Here in the South, children answer adults' questions with yes ma'am or no sir. It doesn't matter who the adult is, southern children always show respect to their elders."

Adelia looked back at Edith. "No, ma'am."

"That's much better. You're going to fit in just fine here in St. Anne. I've sent word to my friend Mrs. Butler that we would appreciate a visit while you're here. She has two little granddaughters about your age."

"Would they play with me?"

Edith chuckled lightly. "Of course. The children have no interest in us adults."

"I do."

"Do what, Sugar?"

"I'm interested in you." Adelia's tone and face held an earnestness that could not be doubted. "I want to know all about you. You're the nicest person I've ever met."

It was Edith's turn to have tears well up. This time when she drew the girl to her, Adelia melted into the embrace. "That's just about the sweetest thing anyone has ever said to me. I am so glad you are here with us."

Well, would wonders never cease? As Sarah Anne stood glued in place marveling at the magic she observed, memories came flooding back of Aunt Edith's spells working upon her own disoriented, grief-stricken ten-year-old self. Despite Aunt Edith suffering her own grief and terrible injuries, she had let Sarah Anne know she was wanted and loved.

The late afternoon sun painted a golden glow over her aunt's face, a face that should be lined and weary with age and infirmity, but somehow managed to appear more youthful and rested than it had in many months. Perhaps Adelia had worked some magic of her own. Edith caught Sarah Anne's eye over the top of Adelia's head and flicked her gaze toward the front door.

On the way back from the kitchen with a tray containing a plate of teacakes and lemonade, Sarah Anne met Uncle Zach in the central hall.

"Is the little girl with you?"

"Yes, and she's having quite an effect on Aunt Edith. I think this may be one of my best ideas yet. Come take a peek."

"I'll do better than that. I'll get some coffee and join y'all."

Back on the porch, Sarah Anne watched Adelia with interest as Zach dragged up a chair next to Edith. He was something of a big ole soft bear of a man—tall, paunchy, gentle, and kind. He put out his hand to the child. "I'm Sarah Anne's Uncle Zach and you must be the little girl we are so looking forward to having with us for a visit."

Adelia appeared shy at first, then a little smile lifted the corners of her mouth and she took his hand. "My name is Adelia. It's nice to meet you."

"What nice manners you have. You must be very well behaved." Adelia practically glowed in the warmth of such praise. Zach pointed at the tray containing the refreshments. "Aren't you hungry? I am. Would you pass around that plate of cookies, please?"

"Yes, sir, but they're called teacakes."

Uncle Zach and Sarah Anne exchanged brief smiles before he replied, "Of course. Teacakes. I forgot. I leave the cooking to Dorcas and Sarah Anne."

As Adelia offered the plate to the adults, she asked, "Are you the doctor who came to see my mother?"

"I am. She was in a delicate way then, but she's much better now. You don't need to worry about her."

"She thinks you're a good doctor. Are you?"

"I certainly hope so. If not, I'm drinking a lot of water to get a little coffee." Seeing Adelia's confusion, he added, "What I mean is I try to take very good care of my patients, which takes hard work, long hours, and traveling many miles."

Adelia stopped beside his chair. A pensive expression darkened her small features. "If I am sick, will you take care of me so I won't die?" There was something in the way she asked the question that implied the topic was not new to her.

Zach looked surprised perhaps that one so young should dwell upon so tragic a subject. His expression softened as he slipped an arm around her. "Of course. I would come right away with good medicine to make you better. I would take care of you like you were my own granddaughter." The shadow that had fallen over Adelia only a moment before lifted at once. In fact, a lightness Sarah Anne had never before seen in the child appeared in her face and her step.

Watching Adelia bloom under the positive attention filled Sarah Anne's heart. Clearly, her description of the little girl's plight had touched her aunt and uncle and helped them understand what she needed. They were compassionate people who should have been blessed with children of their own. Sarah Anne smiled as she watched their three heads bent toward one another in deep conversation about Zach's medical practice. Adelia seemed mesmerized.

Was it possible the child had never, or at least had infrequently, been the center of her parents' attention? While Sarah Anne could not change the Littlewood's home life, she made a silent vow to see that Adelia felt cared for and protected as long as it was permitted and most especially during the two weeks the child was with her in St. Anne.

After their successful first day, time passed much as it had started. Sarah Anne conducted lessons in the morning in Edith's bedroom. Edith enjoyed helping Adelia with her spelling and listening to her read. In the afternoon when Edith needed to rest, they took their studies to the parlor where Adelia's aptitude for math and interest in science made for great success.

Walks about the village and along the bay in late afternoons when the weather permitted proved far more interesting to Adelia than Sarah Anne had first imagined. Mrs. Butler's granddaughters came to play several afternoons and lessons were canceled. As a child, Sarah Anne had taken care of her toys. They provided a new generation of little girls with several hours of fun.

By Thanksgiving Day, Sarah Anne hardly recognized the difficult, petulant girl who had arrived in St. Anne. Adelia had become affectionate with Edith and Zach who did indeed treat her as though she was a grandchild. Moreover, she had begun to cling to Sarah Anne, wanting to hold her hand wherever they went and insisting on being kissed and tucked in with one more story at bedtime. Most surprising, she had become Dorcas's kitchen helper, setting the table, taking food to the dining room, clearing up, and drying the dishes while Dorcas washed.

The cook grew up in an isolated island community where Gullah was spoken. It caused Sarah Anne some concern that the child was picking up so many of the Creole words and expressions. She considered the possible repercussions as she stood in the kitchen doorway listening to the two of them chattering away like lifelong friends.

Dorcas handed Adelia a pan of dressing. "Chile, tek dis tuh de table."

"Yes'm." The heavy pan wobbled a little in Adelia's spindly arms then righted itself.

Sarah Anne moved out of the way and held the door open. "Do you need help with that?"

Adelia smiled up at her and passed by with a swish of skirts. "Thank you, but no ma'am. I can do this. Dorcas said I need to build up strength in my arms if I'm going to be a cook." Oh, Lord, what would Mr. and Mrs. Littlewood say about their daughter's ambition to become a Low Country cook? Have some grits and redeye gravy, y'all? A shudder ran through Sarah Anne at the thought.

The Butlers, who could not afford a cook, and their granddaughters, were invited to Thanksgiving dinner. When Sarah Anne asked why the girls' parents weren't with them, Aunt Edith had given a vague answer having to do with far-flung business interests. In other words, it was a taboo topic, one not to be mentioned again.

At precisely 2:00, the MacAllisters and their guests sat down to a table groaning with good country food. Mrs. Butler cast a scandalized glance when Dorcas pulled out a chair for herself, but as Aunt Edith brooked no reproaches on the subject, the good lady said nothing. As was sometimes the case in the South, servants of long standing became quasi members of the family. The MacAllisters went a step further with Dorcas, who had no family of her own and upon whom Aunt Edith depended completely during the days when the doctor made house calls and Sarah Anne was on the island.

Uncle Zach's dearest friend provided the turkey. The gentleman owned a farm where the wild birds were fed and given shelter until one was needed for the table. Sweet potato soufflé, collards, black-eyed peas, and yeast rolls completed the meal. Sarah Anne breathed in the fragrances of food prepared by experienced hands and said a silent prayer of thanks for having been born to a family that valued a simple life well-lived among neighbors who cared for one another.

The next three days passed uneventfully. The only change was church on Sunday. Sarah Anne watched Adelia watching her as they sang, prayed, stood, sat, and knelt in Christ Episcopal. She added failure to provide religious training to the list of the Littlewoods' deficiencies as parents.

Monday morning arrived bright, cool, and with return to Ripon House looming over them. Adelia stood watching Sarah Anne packing the school things into her bag. "Do I have to go back? Why can't we stay here with Uncle Zach and Aunt Edith? They like me. They said so. You like me, too. I know you do." Without warning, she threw her arms around Sarah Anne's middle and buried her face in long skirts. "I wish you were my mother and Aunt Edith was my grandmother. I could live here in St Anne and play with Mrs. Butler's granddaughters and go to school like they do." The child's shoulders heaved while a lump rose in Sarah Anne's throat. It caught so hard she was unable to speak for fear she would match Adelia's tears now dampening the skirt of her shirtwaist. "Oh, please, please. I don't want to go back to Ripon House."

Sarah Anne placed her hands on Adelia's arms and gently pulled them away from her waist so she could bend down to the child's level. "I do like you very much. If I ever have a little girl of my own, I hope she is just like you—smart, kind, a good reader, interested in all sorts of things—but I can't keep you. It wouldn't be right because you belong to your mother and father. If I don't take you home, they will be very angry and I might never see you again. We don't want that, do we?" Adelia shook her head and wiped her running nose on her sleeve. "Then let's get ourselves down to the dock."

The scene was repeated thrice more, first with Zach in his office, next with Dorcas in the kitchen, and finally with Edith in her bedroom. Dorcas was stoic, but Sarah Anne saw her wiping a tear away when she thought no one was looking. Zach held his emotions in check, but tears streamed over Edith's cheeks like a creek at spring flood. Edith patted the child's back and between sniffles said, "Oh, Sweet Girl, I would keep you if I could. You've got to go home, now, so Sarah Anne won't get in trouble, but you can come back here whenever your momma will let you. Now give me a kiss and be on your way. Like time and tide, the ferry waits for no man."

The trip to Oglethorpe Island was as quiet as the previous one to St. Anne had been, but with a major difference. Instead of sitting as far away from Sarah Anne as she could get, Adelia huddled against her and clung tightly to her hand. As they neared the dock, Adelia's head dropped against Sarah Anne's shoulder. Her little body shuddered with an immense sigh. Although she knew better, Sarah Anne could not stop herself. She instinctively kissed the top of Adelia's head.

When the ferry pulled up to the island dock, Sarah Anne saw George standing next to the buggy with one foot propped on a piling and a hand looped through the horse's headstall. She started to wave, but the look on the ferryman's face froze her hand at half-mast. If the consequences of violating the social norms had affected only her, she would have given the old bigot a hard look and waved until her arm fell off, but George didn't deserve trouble. A display of friendship from a white woman would fall hard on him or any Colored man. It had confused her as a child that the admonition to "love thy neighbor as thyself" only extended to those deemed socially acceptable by so many of the people she knew. Now, she understood it for what it was.

One day, maybe things would be different, but not today or anytime soon. Such was life in deep South Georgia, or in reality, any place below the Mason Dixon Line. So much for the War Between the States abolishing slavery for all the good it did the Coloreds. Indignation flooded through her tightening the fibers of her muscles like new woven cotton cloth thrown into boiling water. She drew in a long breath in an effort at self-control and stepped onto the dock.

George doffed his hat at their approach and came forward to retrieve their bags from the ferry. With the innocent abandon of childhood, Adelia ran to him and flung her arms around his waist. "I've missed you, George. How is Merrybelle? Has she missed me?"

George looked over Sarah Anne's head at the ferryman whose schedule dictated he must wait at the dock for thirty minutes before returning to St. Anne. The welcoming smile faded from his face, replaced by an expression so neutral that he resembled the automaton brought to town by a traveling carnival a couple of years back. He eased the child's arms back to her sides. "Good to have you home, Miss Adelia, Miss Mercer. Mr. Littlewood said to see him as soon as you get to the house."

Sarah Anne glanced over her shoulder. The old bigot stared at them with an expression so cold it chilled the marrow in her bones. "I guess we'd better be going, then." To Adelia she said, "We shouldn't keep your papa waiting."

"Father."

"I beg your pardon?"

"You know he is called Father or Sir. He says daddy and papa are too familiar."

Too familiar indeed. What kind of father told his child not to be familiar with him? This job was becoming difficult, but not in any way Sarah Anne had ever anticipated. How long she would be able to hold her tongue depended on how many other signs of distancing from and neglect of their child the Littlewoods displayed. Pray God they had already shown their worst. She really needed this job and would need a good reference when it ended. Despite her uncle and aunt's kindness, they would not live forever and she didn't want to be a burden to them. An orphan had to be able to make her own way in the world.

"Of course. I forgot." Taking Adelia by the hand, she led the way to the buggy. Stopping at the footrest, she knelt down to the child's eye level. "When we see your father and mother, it might be best not to mention certain things that happened in St. Anne, things like you helping Dorcas in the kitchen or wanting to be a cook. I don't think your parents would understand."

Adelia rolled her ocean blue eyes and flipped her dark blond sausage curls. "Never. I'm not stupid, you know."

Sarah Anne couldn't keep from chuckling. "You're so grown up sometimes it fairly takes my breath away." Pointing to the buggy, she continued, "Shall we?"

They did not speak again until they stood before Mr. Littlewood's massive mahogany desk in the library. He made a bridge of his fingers and pinned Adelia and then Sarah Anne with a gaze that communicated nothing at all and yet everything one needed to know, if one only had eyes to perceive the message.

"I assume your time on the mainland was productive?" No warmth at his child's return. No words of welcome. No loving embrace. The blasted man barely masked his boredom with what he must see as his paternal duty. Sarah Anne glanced down to see if Adelia noticed her father's indifference, but the little girl's eyes glowed as she basked in the warmth of her father's presumed attention.

"Yes, sir." Mr. Littlewood's brow rose slightly at the use of the word sir. "I have learned twenty-five difficult new words since we last met. Miss Mercer's aunt helped me practice my reading every morning."

"Really." His gaze drifted to Sarah Anne. "And how was Miss Mercer occupied while her aunt did the teaching?"

"Mrs. McAllister didn't teach me. She just listened to me read. She's an invalid and doesn't get out too often. She likes it when people read to her. She says it is an act of Christian charity. Miss Mercer corrected my essays while I read. She made sure I used my new words correctly in my writing."

"I see. So what words did you learn?"

Adelia tilted her head and tapped her jawline with an index finger. "Hmmm. Let me see. There is alacrity, expeditious, and precipitous, all having to do with speed but in slightly different ways. The differences are nu . . . nuan . . . nuanced. Is that right?" She smiled up at Sarah Anne proud in her accomplishments and showing she had not forgotten the word nuanced at all, but simply wanted to include her teacher in the conversation.

Smart little thing. Sarah Anne returned the conspiratorial smile. "It is indeed. You learned your vocabulary well." Adelia giggled with pleasure. The child really was a contradiction. One minute she spoke in a manner advanced far beyond her years, the next she was still just a little girl.

The interview continued with a recitation of learning in the other academic areas. After about ten minutes, Mr. Littlewood leaned back in his chair with an air of impending dismissal. "I see your time in St. Anne was well spent. You and Miss Mercer are to be congratulated on your acquisition of knowledge and the remarkable improvement in your manners." Without further comment, he began shuffling papers on his desk. When they made no move to leave, he looked up again in some impatience. "That will be all."

The crestfallen expression on Adelia's face sent a tangle of emotions coursing through Sarah Anne. Anger, frustration, pity all swirled together in a dark, sucking sinkhole, but none of that could be allowed to show in her face, voice, or demeanor. She didn't give a flip about Mr. Littlewood's feelings, but the child must be protected. She would be damned if she would let him off the hook with a wave of his hand in his daughter's direction.

"Thank you, sir. I know you are as proud of Adelia as I am. She really is quite accomplished, especially for one so young." She remained rooted in place silently demanding the man give her a reply.

After several beats, he looked up and met her gaze. "Yes. Of Course. Well done."

Even an infant could surely hear the distracted tone and see the disinterest in his face. Sarah Anne didn't dare look at Adelia. Instead, she took her hand and led her away to the schoolroom.

Once the door closed on what Sarah Anne had come to think of as their private sanctuary, Adelia dissolved in tears. "Why doesn't he love me? He loves my brothers. I know he does because he says so and acts like he does. Why not me? Am I such a bad girl that Father can't love me?"

Sarah Anne went to the bay and sat down in one of the chairs beneath the window. When she patted the arm of the chair, Adelia flew across the room and crawled onto Sarah Anne's lap like a child of two.

With her arms around Sarah Anne's neck, Adelia's tears subsided. "Promise you won't ever leave me. Margaret promised, but she didn't keep it."

It tore her heart, but Sarah Anne gave the only answer possible. "I won't make a promise I can't keep. It wouldn't be fair to you. Your father has hired me as a temporary teacher. You know that. We have talked about it several times. Perhaps Miss Ballard didn't have time to tell anyone she needed to go away. That happens sometimes with train and ship schedules. Maybe her mother was taken gravely ill and that's why she had to leave without saying goodbye."

Adelia sat up, wiped her face, and cocked her head to one side. "Momma says she ran off with a man, but that can't be right. I would have known if she had a gentleman admirer. Do you really think her mother might have been ill? She never talked about a mother. Of course, she must have had one. Everyone does."

"I'm not sure why she left, but I am very sure that whatever her reason, it was a very good one. Otherwise, she would never have left you. You are too precious to just up and leave behind."

"Do you really think so?"

"I know so. Now, we really must get to work, young lady. Go choose a book and we'll read for a half hour, then you must practice your penmanship. You may have noticed I did not mention the lack of quality in your script." Adelia giggled and jumped from Sarah Anne's lap.

The child began placidly pulling out books, but when the chair creaked under Sarah Anne's shifting weight, Adelia jerked around. Distress filled her eyes. Did she fear this teacher might evaporate into thin air before her eyes? Sarah Anne smiled and nodded encouragingly at a selection, but her mind churned with Adelia's mystery.

No one really seemed to know what had happened to the former governess, which was strange considering how close she and Adelia appeared to have been. By all accounts, Miss Ballard had been liked by the family and popular with members of staff. She was reported to have been reliable and responsible, yet she chose to leave without warning and without saying goodbye to the charge who adored her. If there had been trouble in the governess's life, surely she would have mentioned it to her employer and requested a leave of absence. Perhaps the woman did have a lover. It would explain a lot.

CHAPTER 16

The pressure is becoming unbearable and all because the stupid bitch threatened to tell who I am and what I have done. How she had figured it out is beyond me. But wait. Had she actually accused me? I can't remember. God, why can't I remember? Did I strangle her with my bare hands for nothing? No, it had been for the very good reason that she knew me. Of course she didn't know my true self until the very end.

Now I remember. Only at the end did she accuse me and threaten me. Why, oh, why did I not ignore her? She had not even come willingly to me as anticipated. I was forced to use a ruse to trick her to the isolated spot by the river. With any luck, her body will not float to the surface. As long as the rope tying her to the weight holds, she will simply have disappeared, a woman who turned out to be feckless, careless, and undeserving of the faith placed in her. As long as the rope holds. That fucking rope haunts my dreams.

Stupid, stupid, stupid. I can never make that mistake again. Stick to the unknown whores who gladly approach hawking their dubious wares. No more waltzing around with the hired help.

CHAPTER 17

Lessons during the first day back at Ripon House went more smoothly after Sarah Anne managed to distract Adelia from the heartbreaking realization that her father was an indifferent parent at best. Unfortunately, other aspects of the day degenerated to depths not yet plumbed. The child, who could at times demonstrate an exaggerated maturity, regressed to baby talk, thumb sucking, and clinging. Adelia had never before sucked her thumb in Sarah Anne's presence. She wanted to sit on Sarah Anne's lap or under her arm, seeming to need physical contact in order to function. While Sarah Anne's heart ached for Adelia, her common sense told her this behavior was not normal for a girl of seven going on eight. Adelia was truly complicated and in need of much more than mere academics.

As time drew nearer for Sarah Anne to depart for the ferry, Adelia's agitation returned. She followed Sarah Anne from bookcase to table to chairs all the while twisting her hands around her crossed forearms. "Please don't go back to St. Anne without me. They don't really care if I'm here or not. Aunt Edith and Uncle Zach said I could come anytime I wanted. Please take me with you."

Sarah Anne turned from her tidying and knelt to Adelia's eye level. "That's not true. Your parents may not be as demonstrative as my aunt and uncle, but they love you and want you here with them." She was not convinced what she said was true, but a child needed to believe it was wanted and loved by its parents.

"No they don't and you know it. I'm going with you."

"We will do what your parents tell us to do. That is simply the way it must be. Do you want to say goodbye here or in the foyer?"

Without answering, Adelia turned on her heal and marched toward the door, muttering under her breath as she went. It sounded very much like the child said, "We'll see about that."

Sarah Anne finished tidying the schoolroom and closed the door behind her. At the head of the stairs, she paused and pondered the wisdom of going in search of the child. When Adelia still had not appeared after a minute or so, Sarah Anne started down. Halfway to the foyer, she caught sight of her student. Adelia waited by the front door, a determined expression creasing her brow and turning her mouth down at the corners. By her feet stood her little valise. Next to the valise stood Mr. and Mrs. Littlewood. When they heard Sarah Anne's tread upon the stairs, all three looked up. Adelia's expression communicated silent pleading as clearly as if a telegraph line ran between them. Both parents looked as though they would take great pleasure in tearing someone, presumably Sarah Anne, limb from limb. She drew a long breath, exhaled slowly, and continued her descent.

When she drew near the trio, Mr. Littlewood took Adelia's arm none too gently. "For the last time, you are not going to St. Anne tonight or any other night." He shot a steely glance at his wife. "You should never have agreed to such unseemly foolishness in the first place." Pushing the child forward, he continued, "Now say goodbye to Miss Mercer."

One second Adelia stood beside her father. The next Sarah Anne had to grab a newel post in order to keep her balance. The force of Adelia flinging her arms around Sarah Anne's waist nearly took them both down. Wailing bounced off the foyer walls and echoed down the service hall. Frozen in astonishment, Sarah Anne looked from the child to the parents, aghast at their reactions. The color ebbed from Mrs. Littlewood's face until it matched flour paste. Crimson flooded Mr. Littlewood's features until they could have blended in with sweet gum leaves in the fall. Sarah Anne gently pulled at Adelia's arms to free herself. Impossibly, the wailing and accompanying agitation grew until gasps alternated with screeches. Without warning, Adelia went limp and slid to the floor. Horror stabbed Sarah Anne. She knelt and put her ear to the girl's chest. The heartbeat was steady and strong, the breathing even. Was she faking or had she really fainted? It was hard to say.

"Get up immediately, you silly girl." At first, it seemed Mrs. Littlewood spoke to Sarah Anne, but then the mother bent down and yanked on Adelia's arm. "Oh do get up!" Her hiss rolled through the foyer. Adelia moaned, opened one eye then shut it. Her mother apparently did not notice the affirmation of defiance.

Sarah Anne leaned close and whispered, "Stop this right now."

Magically, Adelia groaned once and sat straight up. She looked at her mother. "I am going with Miss Mercer."

Mr. Littlewood loomed over the trio of females. "The hell thee ayre. When I wast a lad in Yorkshire, my pap woulda beat me within a inch of me life." So it was Yorkshire that set his accent apart from that of the butler, Benson's cultured tones. Mr. Littlewood must have worked hard to lose it, but strong emotion brought the sounds of his childhood into instant bloom. His roar continued. "Hey up, me gel. Miss Mercer's aleavin' and thee ayre goin' to tha room 'til thee've learnt to do as thee're tolt." He stuck his finger in his wife's face. "I tolt thee afore. The gel is tetched in the head. I will not abide her much longer." Turning his attention back to Adelia, he continued, "Test me again and it will be the asylum for you." The Yorkshire twang had disappeared. Perhaps he wanted to ensure his daughter clearly understood his message.

For once, Mrs. Littlewood's attention focused on someone other than herself. Her arms flew around her daughter. "Jedediah, you don't mean it. Please! I must have my baby with me."

His face turned to stone. "Take this as fair warning. Any more of this . . . this outrageous behavior and she'll be put away." The library door slammed after him, then a stunned silence settled over the foyer.

Mrs. Littlewood slumped beside her child. "You must do as your father says. He means it this time."

Tears brightened Adelia's eyes. "How do you know? He's never meant it before." Her voice trembled and broke on the final word.

"I've been married to the man for thirty years. I know his moods better than anyone."

Adelia melted into her mother's arms and sobbed with what sounded like authentic anguish. "Oh, please don't let him send me away. I'll be good. I'm just so scared."

"What on earth do you have to be afraid of?"

"I told you but no one believes me."

"Oh, do not dare go on about that feckless governess again. It is that, among other things, which has your father in such an uproar. If he sends you away, it will be your own doing."

"Please let me go with Miss Mercer." Adelia buried herself in her mother's skirts and shook with silent weeping.

A red glow crept over Mrs. Littlewood's face. Anxiety mixed with anger shone in her eyes when she looked at Sarah Anne. "This is what comes of not living in. Surely you can now understand you must come here."

Late afternoon sunlight pouring through sidelights at the front door created a dazzling pool on a section of bare hardwood floor. Sarah Anne stared into its glow, mesmerized by the blinding reflection and the impasse in which she now found herself. Caught between duty to her family and that to her pupil, she bit down on the inside of her lower lip to prevent herself screaming in frustration.

She was on the verge of telling Mrs. Littlewood she must regretfully resign her position when the older woman made a dismissive gesture with her hand. "Yes, I remember your inconvenient domestic situation. I am not the imbecile everyone takes me for." A calculating expression flitted across her face. "I have a small income of my own from a grandmother. Mr. Littlewood can neither touch it nor control how it is spent. Is there someone you can rely upon to stay with your aunt and uncle at night?"

Within the week Sarah Anne found herself ensconced in a bedroom on the other side of a connecting door that opened into Adelia's room. Dorcas had been very happy to move into the extra bedroom in the St. Anne house. The additional income from Mrs. Littlewood made the move all the easier. Aunt Edith found the change advantageous, as well. Having Dorcas at her beck and call twenty-four hours a day made her feel very secure. Uncle Zach seemed to take the change in stride with a nod and comment that it was probably for the best. Adelia shrieked with joy when Sarah Anne arrived with her belongings. The only person with reservations about the move was Sarah Anne herself.

Adelia's dependence and clinging had changed her life. Whether it was for better or worse was yet to be determined, but had changed it in a decidedly unexpected manner nonetheless. With the move into Ripon House, an old, unwelcome feeling crawled through Sarah Anne.

Females had little control over their own lives, children even less so, and orphans least of all. While gratitude to her aunt and uncle for taking her in would always supersede all other emotions, in small secret pools within her heart and mind, subtle resentment at not being given a choice swirled beneath the surface. When her parents died, her maternal grandmother was still alive and begged to take her in, but no one listened to an illiterate old Cherokee woman. Grandma Cloud died two years ago without Sarah Anne having seen her again after their final parting when she was ten.

As November slid into December and consistently cold weather arrived, plans for Christmas celebrations consumed the Littlewoods and their staff. Adelia alternated between bouncing excitement in anticipation of her favorite brother's arrival and sudden, inexplicable terrors. Some nights, she awoke screaming, but could not or would not tell what caused her fear. On those occasions, Sarah Anne flew to Adelia's room in hopes of quieting the child before her father could hear the screams.

With the parents' rooms on the opposite end of the very large wing, the plan met with success. Another emotional outburst might just push

Mr. Littlewood over the edge in making good his threat of the asylum. Adelia did not deserve such a horrifying fate. She was a difficult, complicated child, but she needed love and support, not abandonment and isolation. Whether Adelia's fears were based on something real, misunderstood, or imagined, Sarah Anne was unsure. There were times when the unwelcome thought that the child might be unbalanced popped into her head. She pushed it down as quickly as it appeared. Thinking Adelia insane was neither edifying nor helpful. The only real certainty was that Adelia needed her desperately and Sarah Anne was determined not to fail the child.

The day the Littlewood sons were to arrive, paroxysms of excitement drove Adelia. She waltzed from the hallway banister with its view into the foyer to her bedroom windows with a view out over the front lawns and driveway to the schoolroom where Sarah Anne insisted lessons continue on schedule. In late afternoon, the child's vigil was rewarded.

Adelia grabbed Sarah Anne's hand. "He's here. Come on. We have to be in the hall to greet him when he comes through the door." Tugging all the way, Adelia dragged Sarah Anne down the stairs until they stood on the bottom step. Adelia squared her little shoulders as straight and tall as a soldier on watch.

The door swung open to reveal a group of six young men, some of whom were presumably friends brought by Adelia's brothers to alleviate the boredom of holidays in rural Georgia. Sarah Anne's gaze unwittingly searched the newcomers' faces. Her heart rate kicked up a tick as she caught sight of John Edgar van Beek striding into the foyer at the back of the group. She dropped her gaze before he could observe her notice of him. His comings, goings, and doings were something she must put out of her mind. He was not for her nor she for him. Their positions declared it thus.

Adelia tugging on Sarah Anne's hand distracted her from her depressing ruminations. The child hopped up and down as she pointed with her free hand. "There he is. See him? Jacob's the one in the front in the brown tweeds. Isn't he handsome?"

Before the question could be answered, Adelia's grasp tightened until her nails dug into Sarah Anne's palm. She flinched and glanced down at the child. Anxiety replaced the joy that only a moment before had made the little girl's eyes dance and glow. Sarah Anne followed Adelia's gaze back to the group chatting casually as they made their way into the foyer. She could see no one who might elicit such a reaction.

CHAPTER 18

Sarah Anne bent down and whispered in Adelia's ear, "What's wrong?"

The child looked up with real distress darkening her eyes. Rather than answer the question, she simply shook her head and continued to cling. Her attention was riveted upon the new arrivals as they clustered in the foyer. Sarah Anne's gaze swept over the young men for a second time. Jacob, whom Adelia had pointed out, stood restlessly beside what must be guests. He appeared anxious to be done with the more formal aspects of rudimentary hospitality. A slightly older man, who bore a remarkable resemblance to Jacob, lounged against a wall at the edge of the group. He must be the older brother, Oliver. In the center of the group, John Edgar van Beek gestured toward the paintings above the library door as the three unidentified young men looked on attentively, nodding sagely at whatever it was he was saying. A cousin, two brothers, and three strangers. Who among the group had skewered the little girl's heart with daggers of fear? Not Jacob, that was clear. But who? It was impossible to tell from Adelia's reaction which of the young men so unsettled her.

With John Edgar in full cry and acting as host, Jacob tore himself away from the group and made a dash for the stairs. He scooped Adelia into his arms, lifted her above his head then clutched her to his chest. "My little Lamb-chop, have you missed me?" He nuzzled her while she giggled and wrapped her arms tightly about his neck.

Adelia leaned back and searched her favorite brother's face. "You've gotten whiskers. They're scratchy."

"So I have. At twenty-one years of age I'm actually past due for them. I still forget to shave when I'm in a hurry. I almost missed the train this morning, but I ran to catch it because I couldn't bear to be away from you a minute longer than necessary."

Still in her brother's arms, Adelia shot Sarah Anne a satisfied grin. Jacob looked at Sarah Anne for the first time. His eyes widened then a rueful smile played across his lips. "I apologize for my rudeness. You must be Adelia's new governess." He extended his hand and bent slightly at the waist. A little jolt of current passed through Sarah Anne when her eyes met his. "Jacob Littlewood at your service."

Taking his hand, she replied with enthusiasm, "Sarah Anne Mercer. It's a pleasure to meet you. Adelia has talked of nothing but your visit for weeks. We are very glad you made the train."

He gave her a curious glance at the word we. "That is, um, kind of you."

Oh dear. Heat rose in her face. She had done it again. Violating social expectations had always been at the top of Aunt Edith's list of Sarah Anne's failings. The expression on Jacob Littlewood's face shouted her latest faux pas though he would probably be far too polite to ever say so. She should not have included herself in the declaration of pleasure. She was learning quickly that people from up north were more formal than what she had grown up with in a tiny village in South Georgia. She placed mental checkmarks next to social dictums. *Do not speak in a familiar manner with strangers,* adding a note of her own, *especially not your employer's son and his society friends.* Furthermore, *do not exhibit unladylike excitement—ever.* Aunt Edith and Wesleyan College had done their best to instill the social graces, but Sarah Anne knew she had been a wayward pupil at best.

To cover her embarrassment, she put on her brightest smile and asked, "Did y'all have a pleasant journey?"

Again, an expression that seemed to fall somewhere between surprise and censure flitted across Jacob's handsome face. "It was . . . tiring. We arose before dawn and I missed breakfast."

Instead of returning his attention to Adelia or his guests, he maintained eye contact. Sarah Anne knew she should say something—anything—decorum dictated a response, but her brain froze. She normally babbled when unsure of herself or a situation, but now nothing, not a single syllable came to mind. Confusion and embarrassment dueled within her. His gaze held a note of curiosity and something else she could not identify. Whatever she saw there, she was sure he thought her a complete fool, a naïve, unpolished yokel. At that moment, Sarah Anne agreed with his silent assessment. She was saved from further unspoken criticism and embarrassment by movement behind him and a hand appearing on his shoulder.

"Jacob, I see you have met Adelia's charming teacher." John Edgar van Beek nodded to Sarah Anne. "Miss Mercer, you look a picture today." To Jacob, he continued, "While dancing attendance on these lovely ladies would prove delightful, your father requires us. He is waiting in the library."

The young men turned and strode across the foyer, but at the library door, they stopped and looked back. Both handsome faces met Sarah Anne's gaze. John Edgar grinned with unabashed, somewhat inappropriately intimate admiration. Jacob was harder to read. Perhaps speculation best described his expression. Flustered, she lowered her lashes, but not before she saw Jacob give John Edgar a disgruntled look. John Edgar had hinted at competition between himself and the Littlewood brothers during the luncheon they shared on her first visit to Ripon House. A little flutter stirred in her heart, but she quashed it. Members of the Littlewood family were not for the likes of her.

Hearing a throat clearing behind her, Sarah Anne glanced over her shoulder. Eliza had slipped up without being noticed. She gave Sarah Anne a weak smile. "Miz Littlewood say can you come to her room now?" In a low whisper, the maid leaned in and added, "She ain't in a good mood. Be careful." Taken aback, Sarah Anne nodded slightly as a sense of alarm curled through her. Had they found her replacement so soon? Was she to be dismissed just as Adelia had come to depend on her? Taking the child's hand, she turned away from the scene in the foyer and led the way up the staircase.

While they trouped across the house toward Mrs. Littlewood's room, Sarah Anne reflected upon Eliza's courage in issuing the warning. Apparently, her determination to treat the young maid with kindness and respect was creating a bond of sorts. Sarah Anne hoped so for she desperately needed friends in this confusing household.

Once she came to live in, she had quickly learned that Ripon House ran in the English custom. Benson and Mrs. Bogard, the butler and housekeeper, were at the top of the service hierarchy, Mrs. Littlewood set the tone and communicated expectations, and Mr. Littlewood ruled over all. It was brought home to her daily that a governess was neither servant nor member of the family. She floated somewhere between those two worlds in near isolation. She spent her days with Adelia as her main human contact. After putting the child to bed at night, she took her evening meals at the small table in her bedroom. If she had anything that might be considered a sitting room, it was the schoolroom with its comfortable armchairs in the window bay. Though her accommodations were comfortable, it was a lonely existence.

When they arrived at Mrs. Littlewood's room, Sarah Anne and Adelia stopped for a moment as though in silent agreement. Sarah Anne glanced down at the child's upturned face. Fear and silent pleading glowed in the child's eyes. She must have heard Eliza's warning, too. Sarah Anne gave Adelia's hand an encouraging squeeze and plastered a cheerful smile on her face. Squaring her shoulders, she knocked on the door.

"You may enter."

Sarah Anne and Adelia stepped carefully across the Aubusson carpet, coming to rest by Mrs. Littlewood's chaise. "You wish to speak with us, ma'am?"

"No, not Adelia." To the child, she said, "Go to the schoolroom. Miss Mercer will be with you shortly."

A spasm of anxiety clutched Sarah Anne's midsection. Now would not be the time for one of Adelia's tantrums. Giving her hand an additional squeeze, she smiled down at the child and nodded encouragingly. "I won't be long. And if we finish your history lesson in time, perhaps George will saddle Merrybelle and Tulip for us."

When the door closed, Mrs. Littlewood said, "In addition to the young men who arrived today, we expect more guests within the week. Your Sundays away from Ripon House will end until all of our guests have departed. They will be here until the twenty-third. Send your regrets to your uncle and aunt."

Relief mixed with irritation flooded Sarah Anne. No replacement had been found, but being addressed in such an imperious manner was galling. "But, ma'am, my aunt has a gathering of friends and neighbors this Sunday and is expecting my help with entertaining."

"While I doubt your aunt's maid will help entertain, we are paying her so that your assistance is not needed. I will not have Adelia unattended while we have guests. Important people will be arriving shortly, including our elder son's future parents-in-law and his fiancée. This is a most advantageous match. Nothing will be allowed to interfere. Do whatever you must to keep my daughter under control and out of sight as much as possible. When she must be present among our guests, she is to be seen and not heard."

"Would it—" Sarah Anne began.

Mrs. Littlewood glared from beneath raised brows. "That will be all. Go to my daughter and see that my instructions are followed without delay."

Disappointment, anger, and unexpected relief all swirled and mingled through Sarah Anne. She treasured her Sundays at home in St. Anne where life as she understood it continued in an unbroken stream. But those Sundays presented their own complications. Adelia cried piteously and begged to go St. Anne. Sarah Anne spent her early Sunday mornings trying to keep the child's hysterics from being heard by her parents, often having to resort to reminding Adelia of her father's threats to send her away. The parents were adamant that their daughter would not visit St. Anne.

The guilt and heartache Sarah Anne felt at leaving the sobbing child was compounded by Adelia's near hysterical joy when she returned. Assurances that the separation was only a matter of hours did nothing to sooth the child's anguish. At least these scenes would not occur for the time being. Though it pained her to acknowledge it, Mr. Littlewood had some foundation for his threats of the asylum. Adelia's clinging had grown so that it now bordered on the abnormal, especially for a child nearly eight years old.

CHAPTER 19

Following Mrs. Littlewood's edict that Adelia be out of sight as much as possible, Sarah Anne kept the child occupied with lessons and riding during the weekdays and Saturdays, but Sundays were a different matter. On Sarah Anne's first Sunday at Ripon House she discovered the Littlewood's unusual habit required of the entire household. Mr. and Mrs. Littlewood had given no evidence of religious devotion, but they insisted the Sabbath be kept a Holy Day of rest. As such, no activity was to take place unless absolutely required for keeping body and soul together. What this really meant was that while the servants went about their usual work, members of the family and their guests had no choice but to lie about in mind-numbing idleness. Acceptable employments included reading, playing sedate melodies on the drawing room's pianoforte, and conversation. Even venturing out for a restorative walk was frowned upon before two o'clock. Since Adelia was neither to be seen nor heard during these long, restrictive afternoons, Sarah Anne found her job more challenging than usual.

"I'm bored. I don't want to read anymore. Can't we do something else?" Adelia's whine filled the schoolroom.

Sarah Anne glanced at the watch pinned to her bodice. "By the time we gather our wraps from our rooms, it will be acceptable to go out for a walk. How does that sound?"

Adelia' s upper lip curled. "I'd rather ride Merrybelle."

"I'm sure you would, but you know the Sabbath rules as well as I do." In truth, Sarah Anne would have loved nothing more than a canter on the beach on Tulip, the sweet little mare George had assigned to her. It would have been a wonderful diversion in an otherwise tedious day. Seeing Adelia's lips begin to quiver, the first sign of a tantrum in the making, Sarah Anne kept her voice neutral and casual. "I'm afraid it's a walk, a nap, or continue reading." Watching the child out of the corner of her eye, she continued, "Oh, and I don't suppose drawing would violate the rules, so there's that as well. The choice is yours."

Adelia tapped her jaw with her index finger, distracted from the rising tide of her emotions by choices. Sarah Anne had discovered the word's magic early on in their relationship. "Okay. A walk. How far can we go?"

"As this is a relatively small island and it is early yet, I suppose as far as we wish. I'll keep a check on the time. Beach or woods?"

"Woods I think. Today is pretty windy."

With admonitions that they return no later than five, the pair headed for the woodland path. At the edge of the Ripon grounds, they spied Eliza just ahead of them.

Adelia skipped up behind her. "We're going for a walk. Where are you going?"

The little maid stopped and turned. She seemed surprised and smiled hesitantly. "I'm going to see my family."

Adelia's eyes grew large with disbelief. "Are you going in a boat? The dock's in the other direction." Eliza glanced at Sarah Anne like she feared she was being accused of wrongdoing.

This interrogation could not be allowed to continue. This was clearly Eliza's afternoon off and she had business of her own. Sarah Anne took Adelia's hand. "If she says she's going to see her family, then that is where she is going. It's rude to interrogate people."

Adelia's face screwed up in disbelief. "But nobody else lives here. My father owns the whole island."

This time, Eliza raised one brow and spoke with more confidence. "That he do, Miss Adelia, but you ain't the only folks who lives here."

Sarah Anne knew one family remained on the island because Uncle Zach treated them occasionally. It would be interesting to know why they were allowed to stay, but the information was not forthcoming and she would not embarrass Eliza by asking.

Sarah Anne smiled warmly. "We should be getting on with our walk. We won't keep you from your family any longer. Enjoy the rest of your afternoon."

She turned to lead Adelia in the opposite direction, but the child wouldn't move. Instead, she looked up at Eliza and asked, "Can we come with you? Please?"

Appalled and embarrassed, Sarah Anne did not try to keep the edge from her voice. "Adelia, it is beyond rude to invite oneself to another person's home. Now say goodbye."

Not to be deterred, the child continued, "Are there any children where you are going?"

A spark of understanding flashed in Eliza's eyes. "Thay usually is."

Adelia jerked her hand from Sarah Anne's grasp. "Would they play with me?" Her voice trembled with pleading.

As pitiful as Adelia appeared, a stop had to be put to the self-centered behavior and disobedience. "Adelia, that's enough. Eliza has a right to spend her afternoon with her family without intrusion." Sarah Anne grabbed Adelia's hand prepared to drag her in the opposite direction if needed.

Instead of throwing a tantrum, a single tear rolled down Adelia's cheek. "I never get to play with other children."

Eliza looked from Adelia to Sarah Anne. She appeared to make a decision. "Wait, Miss. It'll be okay."

"Eliza, we can't impose on your family. What on earth would they think?"

"Y'all come on." Eliza nodded. "I told Momma and Daddy how nice you are. They want to meet you." Her invitation sounded sincere.

Sarah Anne dithered. It was unlikely Eliza's parents would be pleased when their daughter turned up with her employer's child and governess in tow. Still, to refuse such a kind, genuine invitation seemed ungracious. It took courage for Eliza to speak as she had. The state of relations between the races being what they were, social calls were almost unheard of. Then there was the issue of Adelia's parents. They most likely would be horrified that their child had visited in such lowly quarters. Sarah Anne gave Eliza a searching look that was answered with an encouraging nod and a smile. She glanced down into Adelia's upturned, pleading eyes and made her decision. If she were to be replaced shortly anyway, how much would it really matter that she and Eliza gave Adelia a taste of a normal childhood?

The walk to Eliza's home took them to the very tip of the island. The little dogtrot log house stood near the beach facing the bay and the mainland. Eliza's parents, siblings, and nieces and nephews welcomed Sarah Anne and Adelia graciously, but did not fawn. Their behavior indicated they in no way felt subordinate to the folks of the manor. Once the adults were settled on the porch and the children were playing in the yard, another surprise arrived in the form of George. It turned out he was Eliza's uncle. The company spent a couple of very pleasant hours on the porch talking, laughing, and telling stories of Oglethorpe Island and the families who once lived there. Sarah Anne learned things she did not know about how Mr. Littlewood acquired the island.

He bought it up in secret deals with local families, some of whom had lived there for generations, including mixed-blood squatters, former slaves, and the descendant of a Revolutionary War general who had been given the island as a reward for his service—mostly people with nothing to lose in selling out or being paid to relocate and a lot to gain with the generous price being offered. The general's descendant was land poor, especially after the Civil War. The townspeople had used the island as their private hunting and fishing domain as far back as anyone could remember, a condition of the general's will. This is why the townspeople were so angry about the sale. Though very interesting, all of the information still did not explain how Eliza's family managed to remain in their ancestral home.

As Sarah Anne gazed out over the water, she noticed mist beginning to rise. A little spasm of alarm trickled through her. She rose and spoke to her hosts. "This has been a wonderful visit. Thank you so much for sharing your home and stories with me. Your gracious hospitality has turned a dull afternoon into an entertaining one, but I think I'd better get Adelia home before we are fogged in." She gestured at the mist now curling around the bases of trees and crawling toward the house.

George rose as well. "Eliza and me best be going ourselves. I'll walk y'all home, if it's all right with you, Miss Mercer."

Sarah Anne looked gratefully at him. "That would be most welcome. Getting lost in the fog would be a bad end to a pleasant day."

As they followed the path back to Ripon House, the mist crowded in on them until visibility fell to only a few feet ahead. The normal woodland sounds became eerily muffled and non-directional. The island took on an otherworldly appearance and feeling. Adelia clung to Sarah Anne's hand and emitted a soft gasp.

Just ahead of them leading the way, George looked over his shoulder. "Don't be scared. Ole George know the way and won't let nothing bad happen."

In an attempt to distract herself and the child, Sarah Anne asked what both of them wanted to know. "How is it your family still lives on the island?"

Eliza answered from behind them. "My daddy, he a smart man. He got Mr. Littlewood's money, but he got a contract, too. He and Momma can stay in their house for the rest of they lives. After they gone, the house and land go to Mr. Littlewood for sure."

Eliza's father was indeed a smart man. He managed a feat of skillful negotiation with a titan of industry. Sarah Anne smiled over her shoulder. "That's quite remarkable. I hope your parents live for a very long time."

Caution flashed in Eliza's eyes and her gaze dropped to the path beneath their feet. "Yes'm." Her voice was quiet and formal, as though the camaraderie of the afternoon had suddenly evaporated.

Puzzled by the girl's coolness, Sarah Anne studied Eliza. Had she said something wrong or offended the little maid in some way? No, that couldn't be it. Eliza creased the fabric of her long gingham skirt, looked up toward the house, and then immediately lowered her eyes again. Sarah Anne followed the path of Eliza's gaze and understood. They were now at the edge of the Ripon garden. The house was shrouded in mist, gray upon gray, a wraith rising up from the earth. Its eyes glowered down dark upon them save for one window where a faint glow shone through. A figure stood backlit, his face concealed in shadow. He appeared to observe their progress across the lawns. The floor of that wing was reserved for the bachelors of the house. As she watched, the man's gaze began to feel sinister. Perhaps it was because he failed to acknowledge them. He just stared. No gesture of recognition. No movement of any kind. Simply watching.

At her side, Adelia pressed so closely that Sarah Anne nearly tripped. She had to do a quick double step to prevent falling in a tangle of legs and feet. Instead of moving away, Adelia simply fell in behind Sarah Anne while still clinging to her hand. A shudder passed from child to teacher. As they drew closer to the house, the figure stepped back from the window and the drapes closed. All was now dark on that side of the house. A shiver ran down Sarah Anne's spine like a haint had just walked on her grave.

CHAPTER 20

The need is becoming an undeniable imperative, but I must wait. Here in this isolated backwater it would be too obvious.

I am too easily recognized as an outsider, as the other. Of course, I have always been "the other" even with those who think they know me best. It would give exquisite pleasure to reveal my true nature to those self-satisfied, sanctimonious cretins. One day they will know and be humbled, damn them.

But she didn't think of me as such. She came willingly to the garden in the weeks leading up to that day. She had walked out with me of her own accord. She actually thought one such as I would stoop to court one such as she, a governess, no better than a glorified servant.

Why was I so stupid? Creating an Event with one who knew me was my one mistake, but it could not be avoided. Once the desire came on me, I could not stop. The more she struggled, the more excited I became. When she screamed, what choice did I have? Stupid, stupid little bitch.

No, I was the stupid one. I was a moron who allowed an unnecessary error to put himself in jeopardy.

CHAPTER 21

Approaching the open library door, Sarah Anne caught a gasp before it escaped, but there was nothing she could do to stop the butterflies fluttering beneath her dress bodice. The men of the family were gathered around the fireplace, but only one caught and held her attention.

"A Christmas ball? Must we? I suppose the usual gaggle of debutants and their anxious mamas will be in attendance." John Edgar van Beek smiled at his cousins and uncle over a whiskey glass as he placed an elbow on the mantel. He lounged against its marble surround as though he, and not his uncle by marriage, owned Ripon House. The golden threads of his brocade waistcoat caught the firelight, emphasizing the elegant cut of his tailcoat and the manliness of his figure.

Mr. Littlewood paused in the act of cutting the tip from a cigar and glanced up at his wife's nephew with an indulgent expression. From the depths of the best armchair, he replied, "Your Aunt Alva insists, I'm afraid. Oliver's future in-laws are invited. I am, of course, pleased he has the good sense to make such a fortuitous match but Alva is in her element. With Oliver settled, she now has set her sights on an advantageous match for Jacob, a Miss Frobisher of Pittsburgh, I believe. Her father is in oil and steel." He paused long enough to bestow an ironic smile on his younger son before adding, "Despite her delicate health, my wife rises to such occasions with the strength of ten men." When mentioning his wife's health, one corner of Mr. Littlewood's lip curled upward, hardening his features. Jacob's face flamed like the crown of a maple in full fall splendor.

Sarah Anne paused in the library door and placed a hand on Adelia's shoulder. Mr. Littlewood had requested she bring the child for his weekly interview before the adults went in to dinner. Interview was something of a misnomer, more like an inquisition really. A shudder passed through Adelia, who'd stepped close enough for her shoulder to brush Sarah Anne's hip. The little girl had good reason to tremble. Her father did not appear to be in the most congenial frame of mind. Coming back later definitely seemed the best plan. As Sarah Anne took a step back, John noticed the movement.

"Ah, the governess and the pupil." He smiled warmly and might have said more had his uncle not shot him a thin-lipped glance.

Jacob and Oliver stood in greeting. Mr. Littlewood did not join his sons in the courtesy, but merely glanced at Adelia and frowned. "Don't just stand there. Enter." He motioned them forward with an impatient jerk of his hand. "How many times must I tell you not to lurk?" The child seemed to physically shrink in the blaze of her father's glare. He was clearly in a foul mood.

Sarah Anne steeled herself against the rising tide of her own emotions. She mustn't let her desire to retain her position outweigh her obligation to Adelia. Whatever new indignity her employer had in store for his daughter, Sarah Anne must do all in her power to lessen the blow. Drawing a slow breath, she led her charge across an expanse of oriental carpet while the men observed their progress. Each set of eyes held a different expression. Oliver flicked his gaze over the duo then resumed his seat and returned his attention to the newspaper he had abandoned upon standing. John stepped away from the fireplace, grinned, and waggled his eyebrows from behind his uncle's chair. Sarah Anne fought down a giggle. She should be angry with him or at least irritated, but she wasn't. To distract herself, she glanced at Jacob. The younger son's smile brightened as her gaze met his. From what she had seen of him thus far, Jacob appeared to be a pleasant, but unremarkable young man. He lacked John's glamor and sophistication and his brother's august demeanor and burgeoning power as their father's heir apparent. Being a few years younger than the other two, he could not be faulted for these deficiencies. Nonetheless, he paled in comparison. She watched the three equally handsome faces of the young men, and considered how different they were in personality and disposition.

Without warning, Adelia stepped behind Sarah Anne while clinging fiercely to her hand, nearly sending both of them tumbling to the floor at Mr. Littlewood's feet. Doing a quick double step to keep them upright, Sarah Anne looked into the disgruntled face of her employer. She clenched her hands behind her to prevent their trembling. "I'm sorry, sir. I seem to have become rather clumsy of late." Silently, she prayed the man had not seen the real cause of her stumbling. Mr. Littlewood's frown deepened as he set his sights upon his daughter. Sarah Anne's prayer was not to be answered.

"Adelia, it seems you are now an impediment to Miss Mercer's health and safety. Step out and make an accounting of yourself." His tone held no levity or kindness. Moreover, concern for his employee's safety seemed the furthest thing from his mind. Adelia's hand trembled in Sarah Anne's despite the strength of her grip. Sarah Anne averted her gaze to avoid Mr. Littlewood's detecting the fire that must surely be shining in her eyes. Did the man really take pleasure in intimidating a child of seven? From what she had seen thus far, the answer would appear to be in the affirmative.

Adelia moved as directed, but remained silent. After several moments under her father's unyielding scrutiny, a single tear rolled down her cheek. Mr. Littlewood's disgruntled expression deepened. "Lost your tongue, have you? Apologize to your governess."

All of Sarah Anne's protective instincts rose as she attempted to intervene. "Sir, it was not Adelia's fault. My heel caught in the hem of my skirt."

"That is a lie. You may mean well, but you are not helping. The child must take responsibility for her actions. Do not interfere again." Returning his attention to Adelia, he continued, "Apologize."

Eyes swimming with tears looked up at Sarah Anne. "I'm sorry." Her voice was only above a whisper.

"That is not sufficient. Again and loud enough for all to hear."

"I'm sorry." Her voice, while louder, cracked with emotion.

Mr. Littlewood slapped the table beside his chair, setting the objects d'art and lamp rocking. He leaned forward until he was nose-to-nose with his daughter. "For what? Say it, me gel!" Had his tone had physical form, it would have ripped open a deep wound.

Sarah Anne could bear no more. "Mr. Littlewood, really, I must object. If there is an offended party, and I assure you there is not, it would be I. Please—" She was not allowed to complete her request.

"Oh, you object, do you? I suppose you object to the salary I pay you, as well? Perhaps you wish to leave my employ immediately?"

An agonized wail filled the room. "No. It was my fault. I'm sorry. I'm so very sorry. Do not send Sarah Anne away. I'll be good. I promise. Please, Father, please." Adelia sobbed in earnest. It was the first time Adelia had used Sarah Anne's Christian name.

Sarah Anne bent beside the child and pulled her close. She whispered, "Be calm. Crying will only make it worse." To her employer, she said, "I'm very happy teaching Adelia. She is intelligent and quick, a teacher's ideal student. Perhaps you would like to hear of her progress?" Anything to change the direction this conversation had taken.

"Progress? Highly unlikely, but make the dog do her tricks if you must." At the word dog, Adelia could no longer keep her sobs under control.

"Father!" Jacob's shout rolled around the library. "Adelia is just a little girl, a child. How can you be so cruel to your own daughter?" He knelt and put his arm around his sister's heaving shoulders.

Stunned, Sarah Anne looked from father to son, searching for something to say that might calm the situation. Nothing presented itself. The two men stayed locked in a battle of wills. Neither speaking. Neither breaking eye contact. After an eternity, a crack appeared in Mr. Littlewood's demeanor. His eyes softened and the anger drained from his face. Finally, he said, "You are right. That was a dirty thing to say to the child. Please accept my apology."

Sarah Anne was uncertain to whom he apologized since his gaze had wandered to a point above the fireplace mantel. One thing was clear, however. There was more to Jacob Littlewood than first impressions might allow. When Mr. Littlewood shifted his gaze again, it was to look upon his younger son with abject contrition. With the gesture, another thing became clear. Jacob's opinion mattered a great deal to Mr. Littlewood because Jacob was his father's favorite child. An uncomfortable silence settled over the room.

Movement near the fireplace caught Sarah Anne's attention. John stepped forward with a gleam in his eye. Beaming down upon his relatives, he snapped his fingers. "I have just remembered something I meant to pass on. A friend wrote with the latest news we are missing whilst in the wilds of rural Georgia. It seems the Arrington-Smiths and their daughter will not be accepting social engagements for the present due to a death in the family meaning we will be short a young lady if we go forward with this Christmas ball. However, a solution to the problem is in this very room. Miss Mercer, you had a dance master at your college, I believe?" Sarah Anne froze in appalled silence while John raced on. "Yes, you did. I remember our discussing it. I propose that Miss Mercer attend the ball to fill the gap."

Mr. Littlewood, who had lifted his whiskey glass to his mouth during John's antics, coughed. Before his father could recover his voice, Oliver frowned and growled, "Impossible! We can't have a servant at Mother's ball."

Jacob grinned at his cousin and before his brother could say more interjected, "Excellent notion! By all means, Miss Mercer must attend and she is not a servant. She is our sister's teacher." Four sets of male eyes turned her way. Flames crept up her throat and spread across her cheeks. Two of these young men seemed determined to get her relieved of her post. Did they not understand the position in which they placed her, or did they simply not care?

Mustering what little equanimity she still possessed, she said, "While it is kind of you to suggest it, I cannot. Mrs. Littlewood has been very explicit regarding my duties during the guests' stay." Sarah Anne had not told Adelia exactly what her mother had said and did not intend to divulge the information in this particular setting. She would not give her employer the satisfaction. "My place is with Adelia."

John moved to the center of the group. "Nonsense. One of the maids can tend her. What say you, Uncle?"

"Mrs. Littlewood has given her orders. They should be obeyed."

An earnest expression settled over Jacob's features. "Oh, Father, what can it hurt to allow Miss Mercer to join the festivities for a few short hours? Actually, it would be a kindness to me and to Miss Frobisher. Mother can plan all she wants, but I have no intention of giving anyone reason to believe my interests lie in Pittsburgh. They do not and never will. My friend Breckenridge, on the other hand, would be delighted to squire Miss Frobisher about. Inviting Miss Mercer to the ball will increase my chances of avoiding wrong impressions leading to dashed hopes and recriminations."

"Not very gallant, my boy, but honest." Mr. Littlewood gazed upon his younger son with affection. "Are you sure you cannot be persuaded to develop an affection for Miss Frobisher? An alliance with Frobisher Holdings would benefit everyone, including you."

"Father, she is a nice enough girl, but she isn't for me nor I for her. Sooner or later, she and her parents will see that. She has her sights set on life as a New York society bride. I, on the other hand, hope for a rural existence. I mean I know I will have to work in the city, but I want my family life to be in the country, Long Island perhaps."

John spluttered as he simultaneously laughed and choked on his whiskey. "Long Island? Surely you jest."

"What's your objection to Long Island?" Jacob sounded genuinely confused.

Incredulity shone in John's eyes. "It's just so . . . so decidedly rural."

"Preciously." Jacob turned to his father. "So you must see I really cannot allow Miss Frobisher to entertain false hope. That would not be the action of a gentleman."

Mr. Littlewood sighed and drew deeply from his glass. After several beats, he said, "I suppose that settles it, then." He looked up at Sarah Anne. "Miss Mercer, you will find a suitable member of staff to mind Adelia for the duration of the Christmas ball."

Oliver's face was a study in affronted upper-class sensibility. "Father, you can't. Mother will be furious."

"Your mother will do as I bid her and so will all of you." His gaze took in each of them, including Sarah Anne. "That is all. Take the child away. This has been a tiresome evening thus far."

Panic wrapped steely fingers around Sarah Anne's heart as they departed. She was a passable dancer, but a suitable ball gown was far beyond her means. An unwelcome image reared its head. She stood alone on the edge of the dance floor dressed like a farmer's wife on Sunday morning while the other ladies waltzed by in rich silks and satins. Their flowing skirts caught the light of the chandeliers in a swirl of color and grace, an attitude she would never be able to achieve. Her hands itched to grasp John Edgar van Beek firmly by the throat. While his intent was kind, his interference had placed her in an impossible position.

CHAPTER 22

"Ain't you feeling okay, Miss?" The maid Eliza peered through the bedroom door.

Sarah Anne jumped at being caught off guard. She dashed away the tear rolling down her cheek, embarrassed to be seen in an attitude of weakness. "I'm perfectly well, thank you. Is there something you need?"

Eliza looked confused then hesitated before saying, "It's just that Miss Adelia, she say you wasn't feeling too good and maybe I should see about you."

The child never ceased to amaze. The fact that Adelia showed concern for someone other than herself touched Sarah Anne to the point tears threatened again. They were the product of anger, frustration, and unexpected kindness. She glanced down and pretended to pick a piece of lint from her skirt.

When she regained her composure, she replied, "I believe Miss Adelia may have noticed I am none too pleased at being forced to attend the Littlewoods' Christmas Ball."

"Cain't you dance?"

"Oh, I can dance well enough, but I have nothing remotely suitable to wear. I do not cherish the thought of being the ugly duckling among all the well-dressed swans."

Eliza smiled. "You won't never be a ugly duck. You too pretty, Miss." As if caught being too familiar, Eliza dropped a quick curtsy. "If you forgive me saying so."

"You have nothing to be forgiven for. Thank you for that sweet compliment. Now if you will excuse me, I have to consider how to solve my problem." Thoughts of her inadequate wardrobe dragged her spirits even lower.

Instead of leaving at Sarah Anne's dismissal, Eliza lingered in the doorway. "Thay might be a dress you could have."

Sarah Anne glanced up in surprise. Now where would Eliza get a ball gown? "If anyone in St. Anne had ever been to a ball, I might be able to ask for a loan, but that's not possible."

"No, Miss. I mean get one from here."

"I can't ask Mrs. Littlewood to loan me one of her gowns. She would probably fire me on the spot."

"Won't be borrowing exactly. She give me some dresses she finished with. She say give them to my family, but what my mother and sisters gonna do with fancy clothes? You want to look at what she give me?"

"That is very kind, but I doubt Mrs. Littlewood would approve of me showing up in her dress."

"Maybe you can change it somehow."

"Thank you, but I think I will have to make do with what I already have." Sarah Anne fought to keep the catch out of her voice. Eliza's kindness only compounded her misery. The maid hesitated and looked like she wanted to say more, but ultimately dropped a curtsey and left. Soon her tread sounded on the stair.

Alone at last, Sarah Anne blew out the lamp and turned her chair so it faced the window. Sometimes sitting in the dark helped her think. As she stared into the night, the tears she had held in check flowed in streams down her cheeks and dripped from her chin onto the bodice of her dress. Giving in to despair would not solve her problems, but the release of tears acted as a catharsis that calmed her inner turmoil. There had to be a solution. It might be to simply wear her Sunday dress and defy anyone to think less of it. Whatever she came up with, it would hold little importance in the end. She was neither of the family nor a valued guest. Putting so much emotion into a dress was a foolish waste of time and energy. Just because John Edgar and Jacob appeared to want her to attend, it would mean nothing in the long run.

Sarah Anne propped her elbow on the side table and leaned her chin on her upturned palm, watching with gloomy interest while the grounds surrounding the house took on a grayish shroud. The day had been unseasonably warm and now fog crept in from the sea. The speed with which such liquid air could move never ceased to amaze her. Interplay between light pouring through the first-floor windows and the mist made eerie shadows of familiar things.

She sat mesmerized while the urns and benches on the terrace below her window were transformed into hulking, unrecognizable forms. Suddenly, someone walked onto the brick pavers, parting the earthbound cloud with long strides. At the edge of the terrace, the figure turned and looked up directly at Sarah Anne's window. By height and build, it appeared to be one of the young men, but they shared so strong a family resemblance it was impossible to tell which one. While his lower half stood in a pool of light that stretched from a library window, the illumination did not reach his face. The fog obscured his features. Whoever he was, the gentleman stood hipshot with one hand thrust into his tuxedo jacket pocket.

Perhaps he was taking a moment's escape from the library's oppressive atmosphere. Mr. Littlewood kept the rooms he inhabited overly warm for most people's comfort. As Sarah Anne watched, the gentleman continued to gaze at the second-floor window even as he lifted a glass to his lips. He lingered in that attitude for several moments before something or someone in the house drew his attention. He dashed away the glass's remaining contents and with one last glance upward, crossed the terrace and disappeared.

A wave of uncertainty washed over Sarah Anne. There had been something vaguely disconcerting about the man's posture as he looked at her window and tossed away the last of his drink. It was as though he might have been angry or disgruntled in some way. If she were the object of his scrutiny, then it was definitely discomforting for it felt intense, almost possessive. But of course it was nothing. How could it be otherwise? It would have been impossible for him to have seen her sitting there in the dark. Imagination run amuck again.

Sarah Anne grabbed her fanciful thinking by the nape of the neck and shoved it firmly into the deepest recess of her mind. The problem of a ball gown was more pressing at present than the mystery of which young man had gazed up at the second floor windows. She rose and trudged across the room where she flung open the chifforobe to better consider her fashion dilemma.

A couple of days later, Eliza appeared at the schoolroom door.

"Pardon, Miss. Miz Littlewood says to come to her room now. I'm supposed to stay with Miss Adelia while you're gone." The maid and child exchanged conspiratorial glances.

Now what were they up to? Those two seemed to know something Sarah Anne did not. Anxiety became her companion as she traveled the length of the house. Perhaps her employers had found a replacement for her or maybe she was to be let go due to John's plans for the Christmas Ball. He was an interfering fool who may have cost her this job. So why wasn't she angrier with him? She felt more anger at Oliver for his insufferable arrogance than at John for what might be his costly interference. A twinge of shame pricked her conscience. She worked hard to ignore the answer to no avail. She might be able to control her words and actions, but her emotions had a mind of their own. John's handsome face danced before her inner eye. He was all any woman could ask—talented, handsome, affable, prominent family, rich—but not for her. Clearly, she was the greater fool.

It must be the ball invitation because dismissal due to a replacement would surely come from Mrs. Bogard, as had her hiring. Parting would be difficult. She would return to St. Anne a defeated disappointment, but it would be worse for Adelia. The poor baby would have to start over again in trusting a new governess and she did not adapt well to change. As George so aptly phrased it, Adelia was indeed a delicate child. Sarah Anne's heart beat a little faster as anger welled up. Adelia deserved better than her father's belief that she was unbalanced and his threats of the asylum. Another teacher might not understand the little girl and that would lead to disaster.

When Sarah Anne came to rest at Mrs. Littlewood's door, she drew a deep breath. She reviewed her recent words and deeds and could find nothing untoward or inappropriate, nothing with which to castigate herself. If need be, she could defend all with confidence. It was not her fault John Edgar had insisted she attend the ball. Squaring her shoulders, she exhaled slowly and knocked.

"Enter." Her employer's tone sounded quite neutral.

Better to get it over with and face the tiger in her den. Sarah Anne opened the door and glided across the carpet with as much dignity as she could muster, coming to rest beside Mrs. Littlewood's chaise. "You asked to see me?"

Adelia's mother raised one eyebrow and ran her gaze over Sarah Anne. "I suppose you have a ball gown?"

Sarah Anne blinked a couple of times. "No, ma'am. I don't know where to get one. It would be better if I did not have to attend the ball. I would prefer to remain with Adelia."

"The matter at hand is not what you would prefer, but rather what you have been instructed to do. My husband's desire may be ill advised, but he wishes you to attend, so attend you shall." Mrs. Littlewood paused and cast another look over Sarah Anne. "That leaves us with what you will wear. I do not intend the visual effect of the evening to be marred by you dressed as a farmer's daughter. I have asked my maid to select a few options from among my older gowns. Is there someone who might make alterations for you?"

Sarah Anne did not answer. Shock for once stilled her tongue.

"I said, is there someone who does alterations in that godforsaken little village where your family lives?"

Sarah Anne forced her frozen tongue to action. "I'll find someone. Are you sure this is what you want?" Being blunt when agitated was another flaw Aunt Edith had worked hard to eradicate without much success.

"Of course it isn't what I want. Are you deaf or are you a simpleton? It is, however, my husband's wish." Mrs. Littlewood slammed her palm against the table next to the chaise setting a teacup clattering in its saucer. "Oh why did I ever let my husband persuade me to come to this island? We have missed so many seasons in New York and now it has come to this."

Mrs. Littlewood's eyes narrowed. "Do not think because you have found a champion in my nephew it in any way changes your position in this house. Furthermore, we have already begun advertising for someone more willing to be parted from the depths of rural Georgia. I am confident that shortly your services will no longer be required. For the present, see that you attend my ball suitably attired." With a wave of her hand, Sarah Anne found herself dismissed.

So, it was both, the invitation and her replacement. As tears threatened, Sarah Anne bit down on the flesh of her lower lip. She would not allow Adelia and Eliza to see how troubled she was by this conversation. She would remain strong and do what she could for the child until she was dismissed. After that, she had no idea what she would do.

CHAPTER 23

Eliza tied the laces at the back of Sarah Anne's gown, stepped back, and admired her handiwork. "You gonna be prettier than all them other ladies."

Sarah Anne smiled. "Thank you so much. I could never have gotten this dress ready on my own. You are a genius with a needle."

"My momma taught me. She made all our clothes when we was children."

"She's an excellent teacher. And thank you for staying with Adelia. She can be a handful, but she likes you."

"Miss Adelia's gonna be just fine with me. Well, if you don't need nothing else, I'll go now."

A wave of affection washed over Sarah Anne as she watched Eliza leave for Adelia's room. She sometimes forgot how young the little maid was until she remembered the Sunday afternoon those two sat on the schoolroom floor playing with Adelia's dolls. The weather had been too stormy for walking out, so Adelia insisted that Eliza play with her. Although Eliza must be around fifteen, she clearly enjoyed changing the dolls' clothes and pretending they were in a fashion parade. The memory brought a smile.

Sarah Anne turned and studied her reflection in the dresser mirror. A small kerosene lamp on an upraised shelf cast a gentle glow over the cornflower blue silk of the old-fashioned ball gown. It possessed none of the newest trends like the narrower silhouette and a bustle, but the flowing skirt, fitted bodice, and off-the-shoulder neckline complemented her figure, showing her shapely bosom and narrow waist to advantage. Blue had always highlighted the creaminess of her skin and brought out the glow in her dark hair. The cut and workmanship were superb. The label said Worth of Paris. She had heard of the maker, but had never seen one of his creations in person before now. It was simpler in decoration than many gowns of its era, but the single rows of pink rose buds that edged the neckline and swirled from waist to hem made the garment a work of art. Maybe she wouldn't be an ugly duckling after all.

Placing one final pin in her hair to anchor a wayward strand, she breathed deeply and headed for the second-floor ballroom. The ball was well underway in the enormous space, which anchored the two wings of the house, so she hoped her arrival would go unnoticed. She stopped just short of the entrance and surveyed the guests.

Ladies in the latest fashions swirled in the arms of gentlemen dressed in white tie and tails under enormous chandeliers. Gilded metal arms lifted multiple kerosene lamps turned low, their light playing through hundreds of crystal prisms. The effect of the lighting upon rich silks and brocades created a dreamlike scene straight out of a fairy tale. Sarah Anne drew a deep breath and slipped into the room. Finding an empty corner, she stationed herself against the wall behind a group of guests. While they laughed and chatted with great animation, her greatest desire was to make herself as inconspicuous as possible.

To her horror, her stomach growled loudly and three gentlemen on the edge of the conversation turned her way. Quizzical expressions shone in their eyes before good manners reasserted themselves. No doubt they wondered what this girl unadorned by jewelry and in an out-of-date dress was doing attending the ball. Flames crawled from her throat up to her hairline. In her rush to get Adelia settled for the evening and get changed into her ball gown, she had not eaten. Nodding to those eyeing her, she fled toward the side room where the supper buffet had been set up.

Glancing around, she saw no one of her acquaintance. She had not been introduced to the young men who came with John, Jacob, and

Oliver nor the guests who had been arriving all week. It was just as well. What topic of conversation would she possibly find to interest these northern strangers? Their lives and experiences would be completely foreign to her and hers to them. She could not remember a time when she had felt so alone in a crowd.

In Ripon House, she inhabited an in-between world—neither servant nor family nor guest. The ambiguity of her position did not stand in such sharp relief during her normal duties because Adelia consumed her time and attention, but tonight the contrast between herself and everyone else was so great that she could not keep the loneliness at bay.

Dwelling on the negative would not help or change her circumstances. At least she might enjoy an exceptional supper. Wandering around the buffet table, she marveled at the enormous number of offerings. Fish, fowl, game, shellfish, beef roast, and too many salads and sides to name covered the table end-to-end. Selecting grilled oysters, tomato aspic, celery, and olives, she found a small table in a far corner. As she was about to take her first bite, a shadow loomed over her plate. She looked up into John Edgar van Beek's smiling face.

"May I join you?" Before she could reply, he slid out the chair opposite.

She smiled and tried to appear nonchalant. "Of course." He must not detect the excitement presently taking hold. Distraction was in order. "Have you materialized out of thin air? I did not see you when I entered the room." Fool. Why hadn't she thought of something else? Now he would think she had been seeking him out.

He did not answer immediately but chuckled while he held her gaze. "That's because I didn't want you to see me." He leaned in and took her hand. "You are such a winsome creature when you think no one is looking. You lose that schoolmarm expression and become a wholly different person. I didn't want to disturb the effect, so I stayed out of your view."

The intimacy of his voice coupled with the way his eyes held hers unsettled Sarah Anne more than she could bear for him to see. She withdrew her hand from his, broke eye contact, and glanced toward the buffet table seeking something—anything—to change the direction of the conversation. "I don't think I've ever seen so much food in one place. How do they do it?"

John Edgar settled back in his chair and lifted a brow. "When you're rich as Croesus it's not difficult. You place your orders and tell the merchants when and where to deliver. You then threaten to take all future custom elsewhere if the wilds of rural Georgia are beyond their capabilities. I believe the beef arrived from Savannah yesterday and the oysters from Brunswick this morning. Simple, really."

The quality of his tone implied he did not share his relatives' ability to entertain in such style. Envy and irony were not a particularly attractive combination, but in John they failed to change his effect upon her or mar the attraction she felt. She said a silent prayer for deliverance before she made a complete fool of herself.

In seeming answer, a familiar figure headed their way. Sarah Anne latched on to the moment. "Oh, look. Your cousin Jacob is coming over. Perhaps you could bring another chair for him."

Looking none too pleased, John dragged up a third chair, placing it against the wall so that he would be between his cousin and Sarah Anne. Jacob grinned and moved the chair next to Sarah Anne even though it meant he would not be able to reach the table. "Move over, Cousin. You have commandeered enough of Miss Mercer's time."

It seemed Jacob was not the milquetoast she had first taken him to be. That he wanted her attention both flattered and alarmed her. If Adelia's mother disliked John's admiration of Sarah Anne, what would she say about her son dancing attendance on a near servant?

Not to be bested, John leaned forward and opened the folded rectangle dangling from Sarah Anne's wrist. "I see you have not yet filled out your dance card. I claim your first dance, and the second, and possibly the third. Now let's see. Where are we in the program? Ah, yes." He proceeded to take the little pencil attached to the card and began scribbling his name.

John got only as far as the second line when Jacob intervened. "Not so fast, Cousin. I claim her third and fourth." Four lines in the card were filled in before Sarah Anne could politely stop them.

Alarmed and flattered beyond measure, she wrested her card from beneath Jacob's fingers and tucked it into her glove. "I do not believe Mr. And Mrs. Littlewood had any intention of my dancing when they insisted I attend the ball."

Jacob grinned and took the hand that hid the dance card. "Oh, but there you are wrong. You forget you are acting as my savior from the spectacle of disappointed hopes and the subsequent recriminations sure to follow." He pointed through an open archway to the ballroom where a gentleman whirled by with a pretty, young blonde in his arms. "In fact, you are doing both myself and my friend Breckenridge a good turn. He's very enamored of Miss Frobisher there. I, on the other hand, am not in the least interested despite the entreaties of both my parents. Have you forgotten it was I who insisted you attend?"

Yes, she had forgotten. She was so flustered by the attention being paid her by John and Jacob, the reason for her invitation to the ball had completely slipped her mind. At the opening strains of a waltz, Jacob looked at his cousin. "I believe this is your dance. Perhaps you should take your position on the floor."

John extended his hand to Sarah Anne. "Indeed, you are correct." Bending at the waist, he said, "Shall we?"

Sarah Anne placed her hand in John's, but glanced down at Jacob. He must have sensed her distress for he smiled reassuringly and nodded. Without uttering a sound, he mouthed the words, "It will be all right."

John led her onto the dance floor and taking her hand from the crook of his arm, pulled her into a waltz position as they waited for the music to begin. Sarah Anne concentrated on controlling her breathing, but there was nothing she could do about the thumping of her heart. The touch of his hand resting on her waist created a rhythm all its own. With luck, John would not feel it through the bodice of her gown. Being held so closely in his arms made her lightheaded. Shocked by her reaction, she concentrated her attention on a violinist tuning his instrument. She had always believed herself above such foolish inclinations.

The music began and they were off in a whirl of candlelight and Strauss. Despite her better judgment, she began to enjoy the strength of his arms and the grace of his body as he guided her among the other dancers. Was this what falling in love felt like? It was difficult to say for she really had nothing against which to measure what she felt.

John whispered in her ear. "Are you all right? You look like you have been mesmerized. Open your eyes."

She didn't realize she had closed them. Her lashes flew up while her cheeks grew warm. She looked up into eyes filled with humor. "I'm sorry. I don't know what came over me. I guess I'm a little overwhelmed by the evening."

An expression of mock horror filled his face. "And I thought it was I who brought about that state. You have wounded me, dear lady, but we will speak no more of it." His smile dissolved, replaced by an inscrutable expression. It was as though a chilly breeze had suddenly passed between them.

Surprised and disappointed, Sarah Anne studied him from beneath her lashes. Her words were not meant as an insult, so why did it seem as if he had taken umbrage? Since the day of their first meeting in the attic and his insistence that she take luncheon with him, something had always felt a little off in his words and demeanor. Perhaps he simply enjoyed toying with her and none of this would mean anything tomorrow when the reality of her position reasserted itself. Dammit. He always managed to keep her slightly off-kilter. One minute he seemed to imply he found her deeply attractive and the next he was rather aloof. Could it be the nature of his social status? Was this how wealthy Yankees acted? Who knew? She certainly did not. Giving in to tears would feel good, but pride forbade it. She sucked a bit of the flesh of her inner cheek between her teeth and clamped down as a distraction.

They completed their two appointed dances in silence. She did not know what to say and he had withdrawn into a place deep within himself. With relief, she watched Jacob approaching, the light of anticipation shining in his eyes. He tapped John on the shoulder before the last strains of the second dance had died away.

"These next two are mine, Cousin."

John released her to Jacob without a word and walked away. Sarah Anne glanced at Jacob while her face burned with anger and embarrassment. Jacob watched his cousin's retreating back with a furrowed brow. "That was unconscionably rude. I am so sorry, Miss Mercer. I can't imagine what can have come over my cousin."

Sarah Anne gave him a weak smile. "I think I offended Mr. Van Beek in some way, but I'm not exactly sure how."

Jacob shrugged. "Pay him no heed. He has been moody since birth, or so all the family say. I've always found him good company, but my brother has never warmed to him even though they are more of an age. Still, John can become gloomy and withdrawn at times. I am sorry you had to see that side of him."

As her embarrassment and confusion subsided, gratitude and peace took their place. "Thank you for speaking so frankly about a member of your family. I am relieved knowing I may not be completely at fault and that perhaps I have a friend in you."

Jacob's eyes widened in surprise. His expression took on a crestfallen quality. "Yes, I suppose I am your friend, if you wish to think of it that way."

Dammit, dammit, dammit! Now she had gone and insulted Jacob by assuming they could ever rise to the level of friendship. She was a hopeless mess where these folks were concerned. Rich Yankees were definitely beyond her ken.

As the music began, she concentrated her gaze over Jacob's shoulder, trying to avoid any further awkward conversation. To her horror, Oliver stalked toward them with a determined expression. She would die of embarrassment if he sent her from the floor in front of all these people, even if they were strangers. As God was her witness, this was the last time she would ever attend a social function with people like this.

Oliver drew abreast his brother and tapped him on the shoulder. "The parents wish a word, ole boy. Better go to them at once."

Anger flashed in Jacob's eyes. He released Sarah Anne, bowed slightly, and turned on his heel. She watched him go with a mixture of irritation and trepidation. She turned to Oliver mentally daring him to leave her standing alone on the dance floor. It would mean losing her job, but her pride would not allow that level of disrespect. She had about had enough of the arrogance and self-centered behavior that apparently came with great wealth. Irritation turned to anger as she stared at Oliver. He looked amused for a moment, then extend his arms and they were off.

"Did you think I would leave you to make your way from the dance floor alone amid all of these people? That would not be the act of a gentleman even if you are a servant." They whirled on without additional conversation, but Sarah Anne's body stiffened with rage.

When they reached the supper room entrance, Oliver stopped abruptly and led her off the floor. "I see your champion, John, headed our way. I am sure you will enjoy his company more than mine." Oliver nodded rather than even pretending to bow and strolled away as John sauntered to her side.

The man was all smiles again. He pointed to an area nearby where the Littlewood parents sat upon gilded chairs resembling thrones. Jacob stood before them.

"My younger cousin seems to be in some difficulties with Aunt Alva and Uncle Jed. By the looks of things, he is receiving quite a dressing down. I believe its source may be laid at your door." John chuckled and offered his arm. "Shall we partake of additional refreshment? You really must taste the caviar. It is excellent."

When Sarah Anne stood rooted in place, he glanced down at her in amusement. "Oh, come now. Surely you did not entertain hopes where the boy is concerned? Trust me. My relatives will never allow it. Besides, if one such as Miss Frobisher cannot tempt him, I am not sure who can.

I, on the other hand, have and continue to be tempted. Very tempted, indeed."

Enough. If falling in love meant she must tolerate such impertinence, she would have none of it. Sarah Anne stood her ground and narrowed her eyes. "You, sir, are insufferably presumptuous. I have no designs or hopes where anyone in your family is concerned. Believe me when I say I know my place. There is no way I could miss it. I'm daily reminded of my lowly station amongst such exalted personages as yourself and your relatives. Furthermore, I would never consider any of you remotely suitable." She wheeled around and ran headlong into Jacob.

He caught her in his arms to prevent them tumbling to the floor. She shook herself free and shot him a blazing look. The expression on his face caught her off guard. If he wasn't who he was, she might have suspected he had heard her words and been cut by them, but he was a Littlewood and she must not place any store by what these people thought or did. One minute they pretended to take an interest in you and the next they put you in your place. As she headed for the ballroom door, she heard two male voices calling for her to please return. She did not give them the satisfaction of looking back.

The sound of rapid steps just behind her made her want to scream in fury. What new torment did these people have in store? She wheeled around to find John and Jacob on her heels. John wore a contrite expression while Jacob's was more one of confusion.

John spoke first. "You have my abject apologies. Please do not leave the ball on my account. As I have mentioned, I sometimes become agitated when I am trying to impress someone whom I admire. It makes me act like an arrogant ass."

Shooting his cousin an angry look, Jacob interjected, "By all means, please don't leave. You're an ornament to the evening. All of the fellows say so. They've badgered me all evening for an introduction, but I've deflected them out of selfishness. Besides, you still owe me two dances." He blushed and his words stumbled to a halt. He tilted his head, squared his shoulders, and grinned. "I'm glad my law professors didn't hear those ridiculous efforts at persuasion. They might not let me graduate. What I'm trying to say is I would be honored if you stayed. Your presence means more than I can say. Will you at least allow me this dance?" He offered his hand.

Sarah Anne studied Jacob. He seemed sincere. Perhaps she was the one who should apologize, but she was danged if she would. These people thought they owned the world and here on the island they pretty much did, but that did not mean she must abandon all self-respect. Jacob returned her gaze with one that communicated both supplication and an appropriate measure of self-possession. With an absence of arrogance, he made clear his desire for her to stay. Her anger melted away. He really was a nice boy.

She glanced at John, who wore a tight smile. He bowed slightly and said, "Yes, please do grant my cousin's request for this dance, but promise to honor me with the next."

She allowed Jacob to take her in his arms and they whirled away across the room. While they swayed to the music, she considered the two men. John was exciting and maybe dangerous where her heart was concerned, while Jacob was dependable, kind, and gentle. Both of them were attractive in such different ways, but Jacob paled somewhat in comparison. And neither was for the likes of her, so dwelling on their attributes was a waste of time. Better to seek distraction in a suitable topic for light conversation.

As she searched for a neutral subject, they danced into view of the Littlewood parents. When the older couple caught sight of their son and his dance partner, their eyes widened and their expressions darkened. Daggers of resentment and alarm flew in Sarah Anne's direction.

CHAPTER 24

The gliding couples, the strains of a waltz, the soft light from the chandlers, the offerings in the supper room, the odors of bodies doused with perfumes, the overly warm room—all of these elements are as familiar to me as my own face, but in this place they feel slightly distorted. Perhaps it is the isolation of the Georgia coast or those among the usual crowd who are not in attendance, or maybe it is the unexpected attendee.

She had tried to demure when commanded to attend, but we paved her way and we were right. She is an ornament to the occasion. The older style of her dress may be out of fashion, but it suits her well. The color highlights her dark hair and eyes. The generous neckline displays her shoulders and décolletage to advantage. She moves with a natural, unaffected grace that puts the young ladies of the 400 at a disadvantage. When we dance, she fits in my arms like no other. Perhaps she is the one who will save me.

I see her attractions are not lost on our companions. They are gathering ready to pounce at the first opportunity.

CHAPTER 25

Once the other young men saw Sarah Anne dancing, Jacob and John Edgar had no choice but to make introductions and her dance card filled up very quickly. Her dance partners seemed impervious to the stares and glares of the older guests, the other young ladies, and the Littlewoods. When Jacob claimed his next dance, Sarah Anne caught more than one group of ladies following them with their eyes then bending their heads together in whispered conversation. A smile flitted across her features. Gossip had haunted her since childhood. Her questionable heritage had given the old biddies plenty about which to speculate. She had become rather impervious to its hatefulness, but when she glanced at Mr. and Mrs. Littlewood, a prickle of warning shot through her. Their disapproval was unmistakable. Jacob must have seen his parents' frowns as well, for he whirled her away so the older couple was no longer in her line of vision. He smiled down at her, his eyes filled with tenderness. Her trepidation at the thought of incurring her employers' wrath melted away in the warm glow of unexpected admiration and the strength of his hand pressed against her waist.

John, not to be bested by his cousin, stepped in as soon as the conductor lowered his baton at the end of the dance. The music started again and they floated in a dream of melody and magic.

Despite her anger with both of them earlier in the evening, their apologies, solicitude, and charm soon turned ire to excitement. Her pulse beat a little faster each time one of them partnered her around the floor. She had not realized that it might be possible to fall in love with two men at the same time, but her heart did not discriminate when they held her. Danger lay in those arms, but caution be damned for just this little while. Just for tonight, just for this one magical night, her heart would be allowed to have its own way. In the morning, reality would return with its imperative to marshal her emotions. For now, she would give in to the pleasure of swirling under soft lighting with two handsome men who competed for her attention.

It was near midnight when Oliver tapped John's shoulder. "I say, Cousin, haven't you and my brother commanded enough of Miss Mercer's time? Give other fellows a chance."

John's right brow rose nearly to his hairline. "I thought you would be paying continuous court to your intended." He glanced across the room toward that young lady who could be seen tapping her foot and shooting Oliver a blazing look. "She doesn't appear the type to take being left to fend for herself with good grace."

Oliver followed John's gaze. "Agatha is quite all right. She complained of a headache and wanted to sit this one out. I left her in the tender care of her mama."

John grinned and winked at Sarah Anne. "Then I leave Miss Mercer to you, but be forewarned. Neither your brother nor I will take kindly to any attempted dalliance. Her happiness and wellbeing are our paramount concern." John made a flourish of bowing while he took Sarah Anne's hand and kissed it. To her horror, a giggle bubbled up, which she managed to quell before it escaped.

Oliver held out his hand and drew her into the dance position. Though he had been civil, if not exactly animated in John's presence, he became positively taciturn and stiff once they moved in time to the music. He pushed her mechanically around the room until they drew within his parents' sphere. He stopped dancing abruptly and took her elbow.

"Mother wishes a word."

Sarah Anne's pulse kicked up a notch. Here it came—her dismissal. And all because she had done what she had been instructed to do. How capricious these people were. Well, maybe it would be for the best. She was becoming far too attached to Adelia.

But then the memory of the child's last breakdown arose. Sarah Anne had ceased to think of those events as tantrums because they were far more than that. She had hoped to take a half-day to visit Aunt Edith, whose health suffered with the cold, damp air of winter. When Adelia learned of the plan, the resulting scene had been so upsetting and wretchedly pathetic Sarah Anne had not gone after all, but sent word she would not visit until Christmas Day.

Sarah Anne removed her elbow from Oliver's grasp and clamped her arms at her side. Allowing these people to see how her hands shook would be unwise. Besides, pride dictated a confident attitude. She stepped forward without a backward glance and presented herself before the dais upon which the Littlewoods sat in all their state.

"You wished to speak to me, Ma'am?"

Mrs. Littlewood's unsmiling countenance peered at Sarah Anne. After several beats, she said, "You have entertained the young men long enough. The maid needs to go to bed. She has an early start to her day tomorrow. You must return to your charge immediately." With a snap of her fan, she turned to her husband. "It really is quite close in here. Perhaps we should have a window or two opened."

Having been thoroughly dismissed, Sarah Anne made her way toward the entrance. This time no one called after her or ran to beg her to return. At the door, she paused and looked back. John danced with one of the snooty girls who came for the house party with her parents, distant Littlewood cousins. He saw Sarah Anne and nodded, but his expression contained little warmth. Only minutes before he had been charming and jovial. He couldn't be angry with her for dancing with Oliver or for leaving the ball. Neither had been her choice. Maybe he disliked his partner of the moment. Whatever the reason for his shift in mood, it could not be laid at her door.

Beside a potted palm near the entrance, she stopped, turned, and looked wistfully at the scene of the ball still in full swing. The dancers carried on with their graceful circling of the floor. Small groups stood about laughing, flirting, and talking. Servants edged along the wall bearing trays loaded with delicacies to replenish the supper buffet. It would go on into the wee hours, but not for her. Even so, it had been the most nearly perfect evening she had ever known. Other than a few moments of misunderstanding and uncertainty, it had been magical and she had difficulty tearing herself away. John drew near, but this time he winked and made a funny face over the head of his dance partner. Sarah Anne felt her cheeks glow as she returned his smile. John's partner caught their exchange and seared him with a withering smile of her own.

Sarah Anne tore her eyes away from the couple as they whirled away. Her gaze swept the crowd once more. Across the room, she located Jacob standing before his parents. The set of his shoulders revealed great tension, perhaps anger. His parents' faces communicated they were no happier than he. Mr. Littlewood spoke in the most emphatic manner while his index finger jabbed at Jacob. No doubt Papa Littlewood was expressing the extent of his displeasure at the attention Jacob had shown a mere servant. Mama Littlewood observed the confrontation with a brittle smile and eyes that darted to her guests and back, no doubt concerned about appearances.

As Sarah Anne watched the display, sympathy for Jacob welled up. He had been nothing but kind to her during his stay. His flame did not shine as brightly as his cousin's, but he really was a nice boy. How such a gentle nature had flourished in this family was a mystery. As to his mother's concerns, worry about her employees' needs was probably the furthest thing from the woman's mind this evening or at any other time, but Sarah Anne would not find fault with that little pretense of a moment ago. At least she still had her job. For the time being, she would try to look upon the Littlewoods with the charity they so often failed to show others. She would do it for Adelia's sake.

A group of ladies nearby commenced giggling behind their fans and casting glances at Sarah Anne. They clearly thought her dismissal from the ball humorous, or maybe they were making fun of her out-of-date gown. That was exactly what she had expected from people like this and why she hadn't wanted to attend in the first place. The bubble of her pleasure burst, punctured by the darts flung by those women. The magic disappeared.

Suddenly, she couldn't get away fast enough. Turning away, she made for the bedroom wing. The *tap-tap* of her slippers echoed as her speed increased. The need to put distance between herself and those people—the ones still dancing, eating, gossiping, arguing, breathing, existing—exploded within her. Life in this house was immensely more complicated and difficult than anything she had expected. She would take her earned time off on Christmas Day. Adelia's parents would simply have to deal with the fallout.

She had to have a break from the madness in this house.

CHAPTER 26

Christmas Day arrived cold and cloudless, a perfect day on the coast. Sarah Anne had thought she would be in St. Anne for the entire day, but learned too late that she would be granted only a half-day. She had hurriedly embroidered initials on handkerchiefs that Aunt Edith sent over by the ferry at the last minute. Her fingers still bore the marks where the needle had pricked them in her haste. Although she had no idea what was expected of her, she still couldn't imagine Christmas morning without the exchange of gifts. Not that she expected to receive a gift like a member of the family, of course. Perhaps it was incorrect of her to have gifts for her employer and his family. Life was just so confusing in this house. Time had not allowed the preparation of gifts for any of the servants beyond Mrs. Bogard, the butler Benson, and her friend, Eliza. Uncle Zach had sent something special that he thought the child would like. Sarah Anne looked at the little stack of packages piled on her bed and sighed. It wasn't much, but it was the best she could do in the circumstances.

She glanced at the clock perched on the fireplace mantel. Dread reared its head, which she stamped down with resignation. It was time for Adelia to join her family beside the big tree in the main drawing room. With luck, Eliza had been able to get the child ready. No loud wails or arguments emanated from the other side of the connecting door. Surely that was a good sign. Dressing the child was one duty blessedly not required of Sarah Anne. She plastered a bright smile on her face, crossed to the connecting door, and opened it.

Adelia sat in the middle of her bed still in her nightgown, her mouth turned down in a determined pout and her arms wrapped around her knees. Eliza stood beside her looking frustrated and distressed.

"Please, Miss Adelia. Your mama and daddy want you downstairs right now. You got to get up and get dressed."

Adelia dove under the bedcovers followed by a muffled cry. "I'm not going downstairs. You can't make me."

Sarah Anne met the maid's eyes and nodded. "Leave her to me. I'm sure you already have extra work with the guests in the house. You don't need this added to your load." Eliza flashed a grateful smile before she fled the room.

Sarah Anne's pulse pounded. *Not today of all days. I only have a half-day with my own family. Please, Lord, help me get this girl up and downstairs without a scene. Just this once.*

Tears of frustration and disappointment threatened to mar Sarah Anne's outward façade of calm. She sat on the edge of the bed and pulled the covers back. Adelia was rolled in a ball with her face hidden behind her knees. Sarah Anne laid a hand on the girl's shoulder, but the child jerked away and rolled to the far side of the bed.

"No, no, no, no!" The child's wail filled the room. "I don't want to go downstairs."

Sarah Anne dropped her hand into her lap and observed the bundle at the edge of the bed. Adelia's thin shoulders trembled with each ragged breath she drew. Instead of being in the throes of a tantrum, terror might better describe her attitude. But what did this child have to be afraid of on such a beautiful Christmas morning? Mr. Littlewood believed his daughter to be unbalanced in her mind. At times like this, Sarah Anne was inclined to think he might have a valid point. This was decidedly abnormal behavior. She searched for the correct approach. Sensitivity and finesse were required. And if those failed, downright bribery might work.

"Darling girl, your parents will be very disappointed if you miss opening gifts. I wonder what Santa has brought you. Surely, you want to see."

The child peeked around her knees and scowled. "Santa Claus is not real and my parents won't miss me. They never do."

"But they asked specifically that I bring you down this morning. Besides, if you don't come downstairs with me, you won't see what Uncle Zach sent for you."

Adelia stopped her quivering and sat up. "Uncle Zach sent me a present?"

"He certainly did. He said he couldn't let Christmas pass without sending his best girl something special." Uncle Zach would never understand how just the mention of his name worked magic. He was too humble and much too practical.

The child cocked her head to one side and her eyes narrowed with suspicion. "What is it?"

"You'll have to open it for yourself downstairs. It's something from his office."

Adelia considered her options for a moment. "All right. I'll go downstairs, but promise you will stay with me the whole time. Do not leave me with them. Promise!"

"I promise." Guilt stabbed Sarah Anne. Adelia did not know about the half-day in St. Anne. "Let's get you dressed and then you can help me take my gifts downstairs."

"Did you get me anything?"

"Of course. It is a little gift, but I worked on it myself. I hope you'll like it."

Surprise widened the child's eyes. "You made it, so I will love it and keep it for ever and ever." Adelia spoke as though it was a foregone conclusion that could never be in doubt.

Sarah Anne had to turn away to hide tears welling up. The innocent proclamation touched a place deep within the core of her being. Adelia was a bundle of contradictions—one minute obstinate and self-centered, the next passionately affectionate, but always clinging whatever her mood. She dreaded telling the child about her departure. It was only to be for a few hours, but Adelia would probably take it badly, giving her father one more reason to threaten the asylum.

Sarah Anne went to the wardrobe and threw back the doors. "Which dress would you like to wear?"

Dressed and arms filled with packages, Adelia followed Sarah Anne down to the drawing room. The family, Oliver's future bride, and his future in-laws were already gathered in front of a crackling fire. All the other guests had departed the day after the ball. The little group seated before the fire presented a visually pleasing vignette. In any other household, this might have been a happy scene where a little girl could expect a warm reception. The tree rose to a height above even the tallest head. Candles on the tips of its branches shed a golden glow over the ornaments covering its great girth. The ladies' costumes were worthy of a society wedding or High Mass on Sunday. The gentlemen were impeccably turned out in bespoke morning suits. A formidable gathering, indeed.

Sarah Anne drew a calming breath and steeled herself for the hour or so of agony that being among these people might bring. She glanced over her shoulder at Adelia and winked. The child did not crack a smile. Knitted brows and the forlorn set of her small face confirmed the trepidation she felt.

Mrs. Littlewood noticed Sarah Anne and Adelia in the doorway. Uncharacteristically, she held out an arm, motioning her daughter into the room. Only then did the child smile. With a look of triumph, she swished past Sarah Anne, placed her load of packages on an empty chair, and went to her mother.

As Sarah Anne followed, she felt a prickle at the nape of her neck. Glancing toward the trio perched upon the settee closest to the fire, she found Agatha, Oliver's intended, glaring at her and making no attempt to hide her antipathy. Why this girl had taken such a dislike to someone to whom she had not even been formally introduced was a mystery, one that Sarah Anne decided to ignore. She had enough mysteries surrounding her position in this household without adding another.

"Adelia, dear, what are those things you put on the chair? Perhaps they were intended for the servants' area?" Mrs. Littlewood never missed a chance to make other people feel like they were less than she.

Adelia, bless her, scowled at her mother. "Those are Sarah Anne's gifts to the family. There are two for me, one from her and one from Uncle Zach. I know we will appreciate her efforts. The gifts are handmade." Such mature, corrective words from one so small.

"Yes, well then. I suppose we should see what she has made." A snicker came from the direction of the settee where Agatha's hand hid a smirk. Mrs. Littlewood cut her eyes at her future daughter-in-law and froze the girl with a flick of her brows before continuing, "But first, see what is under the tree for you."

Adelia tilted her head to one side. "No, I think I want to see what Uncle Zach sent me."

"I asked you to look under the tree first. Please do as you are asked." Sharpness had entered Mrs. Littlewood's voice.

Adelia locked eyes with her mother. "And I want to see Uncle Zach's gift."

Alarmed by the altercation building between mother and child, Sarah Anne moved to intervene, but a hand slamming against a table stopped her and made the gathered company jump in unison. "Oh, for God's sake. Do as your mother says. And do not refer to your governess's relation as uncle. He is Dr. MacAllister to you." Mr. Littlewood's roar filled the space.

Chastened, Adelia raced to the tree and grabbed the first package she saw with her name on it. Torn wrappings revealed a lovely china doll's head. "She is very pretty. Thank you, Mother and Father. Now may we have Sarah Anne's gifts?"

Oliver bestirred himself and placed the newspaper he had been reading on the table beside his chair. Leaning forward, he cast a knowing glance at Agatha, who returned a conspiratorial smile. "It looks like she will give us no peace until the packages are distributed."

Standing by the chair upon which the gifts rested, Sarah Anne's face filled with heat. This was not how she had envisioned the morning going. She had thought she would simply slip her gifts under the tree for distribution once she had gone to St. Anne. She couldn't decide if Adelia knew the situation she was creating or if she was simply reverting to the little girl she actually was. The child ran from person to person until all of the gifts had been distributed. She then knelt on the carpet and tore into the package that was shaped differently from the others.

"Look, it's a magnifying glass. I love it! What did Sarah Anne give everyone?"

Agatha held up her hand-embroidered handkerchief. "I'm not sure you should have bothered, Miss Mercer. We can all purchase far better than this by the dozens."

To her horror, tears threatened. Humiliated, Sarah Anne looked at the ceiling and willed the tears down her throat. If only she could flee the room, but she was trapped by her responsibility to Adelia and her position. Movement across the room drew her attention. John rose to his feet, his face a study in outrage.

"That is completely uncalled for, Agatha. You may be able to buy lovely things, but you have neither the talent nor the brains to produce them yourself. I, for one, will treasure Miss Mercer's gift. My shame is that I do not have something suitable for her, but I plan to correct the omission, if she will allow it."

"Oh, please!" Agatha's mother turned to Mrs. Littlewood. "A better brought up young lady would know giving gifts to one's employers' family members, especially the gentlemen, is highly inappropriate. What her motivation could be is certainly of concern. Is this really the kind of person who should be teaching your daughter?"

This time, Jacob stood. "Mrs. Smythe, perhaps things are done differently here in the South. I am sure Miss Mercer's intentions were completely innocent of any ulterior motive. In my experience, her behavior in all things is above reproach. I cannot say the same for others present."

Agatha and her mother both gasped and glared at Sarah Anne's defenders. Bless them. They meant well, but they had damned her by overly fulsome praise when faint praise might have served her better. Mrs. Smythe was right. She should have known better than to give gifts to her employers.

Oliver rose from his chair and sauntered over to where his brother and cousin were standing. Fixing each person in the room with an expression that conveyed authority, he joined the confrontation. "Brother, I have no idea to whom you refer. Everyone here, with one notable exception, has displayed remarkably excellent manners given the situation."

Jacob shot Oliver a withering glance, but did not respond to his brother's verbal barb. John, standing slightly behind his relatives, gave Sarah Anne an encouraging smile before commenting, "I believe Miss Mercer has been granted the first half-day off since she began working at Ripon House. Perhaps she would like to be with her own family. George has the motor craft ready."

Sarah Anne felt Adelia before she saw her movement. The girl wrapped her arms around Sarah Anne's knees from behind. "No, no, no. You can't leave me here. Take me with you. You promised you wouldn't leave me."

Mr. Littlewood jumped from his chair to standing faster than a man his age had any right to move. With two strides, he stood beside Sarah Anne and reached around her to grab his daughter by the arm. Hauling the child to her feet, he bent down and pulled her to within an inch of his nose. "You, me gel, will do as you are told. If I must beat sense into you, a good hiding it will be. I was afraid of my father's strop and by God you will be afraid of mine."

For once, Adelia displayed common sense. She stopped wailing, but her body trembled and her eyes rolled like a terrified animal's. Sarah Anne had once seen a schoolmate go into a fit. Just before she fell, the girl looked exactly the way Adelia did now. This could not be allowed to continue, her blooming job be damned.

"Sir, my aunt and uncle adore Adelia. They would be thrilled if she came with me. Please. Let her come to St. Anne with me."

Without thinking, she placed her hand on her employer's shoulder. He shook out of her grasp and straightened. "Get her out of my sight. When you return, we will have a serious discussion about your future in this house. I am not at all convinced you have been the correct influence for a child as disturbed as this one."

Sarah Anne surveyed the room. Shock shone from each face in the startled eyes and mouths slightly agape. Mrs. Smythe physically leaned away from Mrs. Littlewood and placed her arm around her daughter's shoulders.

"May we be excused, sir?" Sarah Anne did not trust herself to say more. She clasped her hands behind her back so the others could not see them shaking and assume she feared for her job. Nothing could be further from the truth. They shook with rage.

"Be gone with ye, then."

Sarah Anne reached out to take the child's hand and froze. Adelia no longer stared into her father's face. Instead, she looked over his shoulder to where her brothers and cousin stood. Her eyes were wide with what could only be described as fear. Stunned, Sarah Anne grabbed Adelia's hand and escorted her from the room. As they trudged up the stairs to gather their coats, Sarah Anne reviewed the scene from which she had just escaped.

There simply should not be any reason for Adelia to fear her brothers or cousin, but something hovered in the child's mind. What? Sarah Ann shuddered. Was there a legitimate reason for her fear? Seemingly, she should be more terrified of her father, but that didn't appear to be the case. That Mr. Littlewood had proclaimed mental illness in the family was a faux pas from which the family might not recover. And it would serve him right. A father should never treat his daughter thusly. But was Adelia unbalanced as her father believed? Her fear of innocent relatives indicated the awful answer might be yes.

CHAPTER 27

"Are These Crimes Connected?" The headline fairly screams from this week-old copy of the *New York Herald.*

Damn, damn, dammit to hell. I made that blasted mistake at the beginning of my punishment of fallen women and now it has returned to haunt me. How could I have been so stupid to mistake a lady's maid out of uniform for a prostitute?

The article said the girl was running an errand for her mistress in one of the less salubrious parts of the city when she was attacked. Though the purpose of her errand was not fully disclosed, I suspect I know its true nature.

I thought when she approached me that the girl sought to sell her favors. Apparently, I was in error. The article hinted the maid became lost while searching for a certain pharmacy. I know the place. It is common knowledge in certain segments of society that the owner is not too particular about doctor's prescriptions accompanying requests for certain elixirs. The pharmacy's trade in laudanum is astonishing. Now, a damned meddling *Herald* reporter has decided to go on a crusade and has made a connection between my first Event and those that came later.

The reporter speculated the perpetrator must be a gentleman of the city. In print for all the world to see is the maid's description of my hands, young and without calluses. She perfectly described the suit I had worn as being of the finest woolen fabric and of elegant cut. Thank

God I did not speak to her and that my hat and the darkness of the evening had obscured my face and hair.

Wearing my own clothes and without gloves was my second mistake, but one I could not have avoided. I hadn't intended to attack that girl or anyone. Until the moment she approached, punishment of harlots had only been imagined. But then, something in her manner reminded me so strongly of the past that I became consumed. My rage, once ignited, had taken control and driven me to violence.

With this reporter making connections among the events of my vengeance, how long will it be before the police make the connections as well?

CHAPTER 28

Sarah Anne sat at her Aunt Edith's kitchen table in St. Anne mashing potatoes for the Christmas Day meal. Uncle Zach lounged in the chair across from her sipping coffee from a steaming mug. Despite having spent the night coaxing a recalcitrant infant into the world, he remained adamant that he would not retire until after the family had celebrated the day with good food and fellowship. At the wood-burning stove, Dorcas stirred the gravy with her ever-present shadow, Adelia, standing on a chair at her elbow.

As Sarah Anne watched the duo, the memory of the morning's scene at Ripon House played through her mind. It so unsettled her that she glanced at her uncle and pondered discussing her concerns with him. He looked tired and older than his years, but he was wise and understood people, including how children grew and developed.

A thump in the doorway behind them made her jump. Aunt Edith's wheelchair rolled up to the table.

"Give me those potatoes. You need to enjoy this little bit of time you have off." When Sarah Anne hesitated, Edith continued, "Don't be insulting. I can still use my arms."

Sarah Anne smiled ruefully as she gave Edith the bowl. "I know better than to doubt your abilities. I guess I'm distracted by something that worries me."

When Sarah Anne did not elaborate, Edith arched a brow. "And so what is it?"

Sarah Anne picked up her own mug and drew a sip of tepid coffee while she decided how much to tell her aunt and uncle. Perhaps the whole story would be best. Between the pair of them more common sense and compassion existed than in the rest of the world combined. "Adelia, that's enough cooking for now. Please help by setting the table and then go read in our room. I'll call you when it's time to put the food on the table."

Instead of objecting or having a tantrum like she might have at Ripon House, the child smiled sweetly. "Okay. Should I continue with Jane Eyre? I really like the story."

Sarah Anne nodded. "It's an excellent choice."

Once Adelia was out of earshot, Sarah Anne leaned in and lowered her voice. "I'm really worried about her." She described the tantrums, the clinging, and the unspecified anxiety that seemed to govern the child's behavior and consume her mind. She ended with, "Her father says she's mentally unbalanced and it just breaks my heart. He seems so determined, but I'm not convinced. Sometimes she seems just like other little girls. What do you think?" She looked from her uncle to her aunt.

Before they could answer, Dorcas slammed her ladle against the spoon rest on the stove and whirled around, one fist on her hip. Since moving in full time, Dorcas had become a de facto member of the family accustomed to speaking her mind. "Ain't nothin' wrong wit de chile. She scaret. Anybody wit half a brain kin see it."

Sarah Anne's head snapped back as the shock of those words hit her like a slap in the face. Dorcas, who in reality had spent very little time with Adelia, understood something Sarah Anne had dismissed as irrational or imagined. Dorcas had very little formal education, but Sarah Anne had always been in awe of her cool head and great common sense. She saw so clearly where others faltered.

What Dorcas could not tell them was the source of Adelia's fear or why it seemed to have something to do with Jacob, John, and Oliver. Try as she might, Sarah Anne could see no reason for the child to fear her relatives. They were well educated, polite, well brought up young men—all three. Of course, each must have a negative trait or two. They were human, after all. There was not one thing about any of them to make a child afraid. Sarah Anne couldn't say she actually liked Oliver. He and his intended had not treated her very well, but her bruised feelings counted for naught in the situation. She shot Uncle Zach an inquiring glance. He stroked his chin as though deep in thought. He often remained quiet while considering a problem.

Finally he nodded. "I agree, Dorcas. There's nothing wrong with Adelia that good parenting and a feeling of security can't fix. Has she said anything to you about being afraid?"

"She don't have to. It been clear from de first time I seen her holdin' on to Sarah Anne like she done. Now she know us, she ain't been clingin', has she?"

Sarah Anne blinked, once again taken by surprise. She had been so consumed with worry she had not considered things from only the St. Anne angle. Dorcas was right. Adelia had become a completely different child once the ferry landed at the mainland dock. It was only in Ripon House where she behaved in the manner that prompted her father to threaten the asylum.

As the day progressed through dinner and the sharing of gifts, Sarah Anne observed Adelia closely, looking for any sign of abnormal behavior. She saw none. It was only when the child was in her own home that she became so distraught and nonsensical, especially around her brothers and cousin. The last thought stabbed Sarah Anne in the heart. She choked back a gasp.

Aunt Edith rarely missed anything going on around her. Taking Sarah Anne's hand, she said, "There's something you haven't told us, isn't there?"

Sarah Anne wanted to melt into the floor until she disappeared completely. Her cheeks flamed at the truth she did not want to admit to herself, much less her aunt and uncle. However, once Aunt Edith's suspicion was aroused, she could rarely be deterred.

Sarah Anne drew a long breath and began a description of her predicament. She ended by saying, "So, I think I may be in love with two men. I don't know how I could let this happen, but there it is. And the worst part is they're my employer's son, Jacob, and his nephew, John. They have both been so nice and kind. It's hard not to have feelings for them. How could I be so lacking in control?"

Aunt Edith tilted her head and smiled ruefully. "Because, sweet girl, the heart has a will of its own. Knowing something with your mind is very different from knowing it with your heart. I don't have much advice to offer when it comes to controlling your heart, but I would remind your head of an old saying. *All that glitters is not gold.* No man is the paragon a girl in love thinks he is. Remember that when you're putting these young men on pedestals. They're rich Yankees accustomed to getting whatever they want. They're not one of us."

Sarah Anne fought back tears. She knew what Edith said was right, but she was surprised at how much it hurt being forced to acknowledge the truth. For someone who prided herself on never crying, tears were becoming a too common occurrence. Adelia was not the only one adversely affected by the atmosphere at Ripon House. The place possessed a threatening, depressing quality like a medieval torture chamber transplanted to the Georgia coast.

Dread at the thought of returning welled up in Sarah Anne. As much as she hated abandoning Adelia, maybe it would be for the best if the Littlewoods had found her replacement. Perhaps this job was beyond her capabilities. She became a teacher because she wanted to help children, but was she helping Adelia?

Nothing in her life so far had shaken her self-confidence like working for the Littlewoods. There was also the issue of Jacob and John. Would she be able to resist their attention and control her emotions? Her head swam with unresolved questions.

Their time in St. Anne ended far too soon. It seemed like they had just arrived when George knocked on the door to escort them to the motor craft. After tearful hugs, Sarah Anne and Adelia followed George to the dock. The sun hung over the treetops as they made their way across the bay. The closer they got to the Oglethorpe Island dock, the more withdrawn Adelia became. Her face transformed into a study in anxiety. Overcome by emotion, Sarah Anne put her arm around the child's thin shoulders and pulled her under her arm.

Adelia leaned in and buried her face in the folds of Sarah Anne's coat. "I wish we could stay in St. Anne forever." Her voice was just above a whisper.

Sarah Anne's only response was to kiss the top of the small head then quickly look toward the horizon. She didn't trust herself to speak.

CHAPTER 29

Sarah Anne glanced at the tall case clock in the foyer while she hurried down the main staircase. She had slept badly after their return from St. Anne last evening and awoke with a thick head and the muscles at the base of her skull knotted. Now she was late to breakfast with her charge nowhere in sight. Please, Lord, let the child be in the morning room.

Sarah Anne wasn't sure she could manage a protracted search. Passing through the morning room door, she was relieved by the sight of Adelia seated on the sofa with a copy of the *New York Herald* spread across her lap. The child was making remarkable progress in her academics and had developed a strong interest in current events. It was rewarding to see her so engrossed in reading. Sarah Anne smiled at the thought.

But as she crossed the room, Sarah Anne witnessed a dramatic and most unwelcome change in her pupil's expression. Coming to rest behind the sofa, she read the headlines over Adelia's shoulder. "*Are These Crimes Connected?*" *Eight women attacked in as many months. NYC may have a madman running loose.*

The article spoke of crimes no child should ever read about much less understand. It was clear from the haunted look in Adelia's eyes her comprehension was unerring. Sarah Anne reached over and grabbed the newspaper, but Adelia held on. A tug-of-war ensued.

Realizing she had reacted unthinkingly to the shocking headline, Sarah Anne released the paper. A more reasoned approach usually worked better with the child. "I can see you're upset. Let's talk about what you read."

Instead of replying, tears filled Adelia's eyes. She jumped up from the sofa and casting a troubled look over her shoulder, fled the room. The sound of feet flying on the staircase met Sarah Anne as she ran to catch up. By the time she clamped eyes on Adelia again, she was standing in the doorway to the girl's bedroom. A lump under the counterpane indicated that Adelia hid there.

Sarah Anne crossed to the bed, sat on its edge, and massaged the muscles at the base of her skull. She rolled her head and shoulders. The tension in them loosened somewhat. Marshaling her emotions, she drew the covers back and mustered a more soothing tone. "Please tell me why you're upset. I want to help you. Was it something you read in the newspaper?"

Adelia neither looked at Sarah Anne nor replied. If anything, she pulled her knees tighter against her chest. Fetal position best described the ball she had made of her body.

Sarah Anne ventured her hand on a shoulder. The child's body trembled beneath her touch. "Please. Tell me what's wrong." The only response was muffled sniffling.

A wave of frustration surged through Sarah Anne. She didn't need a struggle this morning. Her energy was at an ebb. This was simply enough of such behavior. "Adelia! Sit up and tell me what your problem is. Now!"

A wail rose from the ball on the bed, but slowly she unfolded her legs and did as she was bidden. When she was finally upright, her eyes held a baleful glare, but her lower lip quivered, her body trembled, and tears streamed down her cheeks. Guilt replaced Sarah Anne's anger. She mustn't take her discomfort out on Adelia. This was just a seven-year-old child. Whether the source of her fear was legitimate or irrational, anger was not an appropriate response to her distress.

Sarah Anne adjusted her expression and her tone. "I'm sorry I yelled at you. That was wrong of me." She held out her arms and Adelia scooted into them. With a rocking motion, Sarah Anne continued, "Please tell me what has you so upset. I really want to help."

Adelia drew a ragged breath. "But you can't help. That's the problem. Nobody can help because nobody wants to."

Confused, Sarah Anne held the trembling body away from her so she could see the child's face. "But I care. I want to make it better. Are you afraid? Tell me what it is."

For a moment, it seemed Adelia would answer the questions, but then terror filled her eyes. "No. Father said I must never say such things. If I do, he will send me to the asylum. I can't tell! Don't you understand?" Her voice ended in a wail of pain.

Sarah Anne pulled the child against her chest and held her in a firm embrace. She was still no closer to knowing whether Adelia had reason to be afraid or was simply irrational and highly-strung, but one thing was clear. The child believed her father would send her into the oblivion of an asylum. The thought rekindled Sarah Anne's anger, but it was no longer directed at Adelia. What could she have said that angered her father enough to threaten putting her away? This episode began when Sarah Anne discovered the child reading the article. She must read it for herself. In the meantime, the child needed distraction.

Sarah Anne released Adelia and stood up. "I want you to stay in your room and read. I am going to send Eliza to sit with you while I run a quick errand to the kitchen. When I return, I'll have a picnic basket. Since the weather has turned warm again, I think we should have a picnic on the beach. I'm going to ask George to accompany us. Would you like that?"

The little blonde head bobbed up and down. "But we haven't eaten breakfast. Mother will be angry."

Sarah Anne had been so focused on the child's emotional outburst, she had forgotten about the meal. Glancing at the watch pinned to her blouse, she said. "We'll have a European breakfast. When they eat outdoors, they call it al fresco. In France, they have pastries, buttered bread, jam, and maybe boiled eggs for breakfast." Sarah Anne went to the bell cord and gave it a yank. "Get your book out and I'll be right back."

"No." The cry split the quiet air. "Don't leave until Eliza gets here."

Once Adelia was settled with Eliza by her side, Sarah Anne made a quick trip to the kitchen, placed her order for the breakfast basket, and then rushed to the morning room. She found the newspaper where they had left it. She picked it up and folded it, planning to read the article later when she was alone. Analyzing its contents might shed some light on Adelia's emotional state. As she ran her fingers along the final crease, the door opened and Oliver strode in.

"I say. Is that my copy of the ***Herald***? Benson said my ridiculous little sister made off with it this morning." His tone held anger and something Sarah Anne could not quite identify. "I have need of it."

He advanced across the room with his hand outstretched.

"Of course. I'm sorry." Sarah Ann remained in place. "I thought perhaps everyone was finished with it."

His face turned stony. "You should have asked before presuming. Furthermore, a child should not read this paper. It leans toward the salacious. I am surprised you allowed Adelia to see it." His words were curt and his tone harsh. This morning's rudeness made him even less likable than his behavior on previous occasions.

An idea occurred that made Sarah Ann's stomach twist. The unidentified quality appeared to be a state of nerves. Something about Adelia having read the newspaper or the contents of the paper itself unsettled Oliver. A shiver ran through Sarah Anne creating a slight tremor in her hands. What did rich, well-placed Oliver Littlewood have to be nervous about? He had made an advantageous engagement and he was his father's heir apparent. As far as Sarah Anne could tell, Oliver was the Littlewoods' most favored fair-haired boy. More than ever she wanted to know what was in that article. She could risk asking for the paper when he finished with it, but if he inquired as to why she wanted it, she would have to prevaricate. Instinct told her to keep Oliver in the dark about Adelia's reaction to the article.

He came to rest beside the sofa, his hand still extended. She made a quick decision as she relinquished the paper. "May I have it when you've finished?"

Annoyance darkened Oliver's eyes. "What possible purpose could you have in wanting it?"

Sarah Anne gulped and blurted out the first thing that came to mind. "I saw the headlines and my interest was piqued." She smiled and lifted one shoulder in an offhand way. "We don't have a lot of excitement in the schoolroom."

Oliver gave her a superior once-over. "You show a shocking lack of decorum in wishing to read such. It is hardly a subject in which young women should take an interest."

Her cheeks flamed. "You're right, of course. I apologize."

"I should think so. I may have a talk with Father about this unseemly interest." He turned on his heel and stalked from the room.

She watched his ramrod straight back retreating and again wondered why he had seemed nervous. Maybe she had misread his reaction. Yes, that had to be it. She must not let her dislike of the man color her judgment. And yet, he took the newspaper with no intention of letting her have it when finished. His reaction felt excessive given the situation. She was an emancipated adult free to read whatever she chose whether Oliver Littlewood liked it or not. In addition, she had never given the family any reason to accuse her of inappropriate guidance in Adelia's education. None of this made sense. But whatever Oliver's motivation, she was still no closer to getting her hands on the paper.

Drat it. She would have to finagle a look at the article another way. Perhaps she could enlist Eliza's help. Newspapers were sent to the kitchen once they had been thoroughly read by all interested parties. Maybe her friend could fetch it from the kitchen before it got wrapped around day-old fish and other scraps.

Kitchen. Breakfast. Picnic. She had almost forgotten her promise to Adelia. Cook would be furious if her food went to waste. Sarah Anne scurried upstairs to gather her charge and then took the backstairs two at a time.

Adelia's feet sounded from behind. "Wait. You're going too fast."

"I'll wait for you in the kitchen. It's a beautiful day. Let's not spend any more of it inside."

In the end, Eliza was able to procure the newspaper for Sarah Anne. She eagerly read it by her bedroom fire late in the evening after Adelia was in bed. She read it twice, but could find nothing that touched the family. As to whether all of the crimes described were related seemed a possibility. Certainly the ones committed later in the summer and early autumn were almost identical in their details, but none of the women had been able to give any information that might lead to the perpetrator's identity. As Sarah Anne mulled the article's contents, a troubling thought resurfaced. Something beyond the violence described had clearly upset Adelia, but for the life of her, Sarah Anne could not see what it might be.

Sighing deeply, she placed the newspaper on the table beside her chair. Staying up half the night worrying would help no one, so the matter might as well be put aside for the time being. Furthermore, there was nothing to be gained at present from questioning Adelia again.

• • • • •

In the gloom of an early January afternoon, Sarah Anne stood with arms crossed over her stomach gazing from the schoolroom's bay window. The house felt very empty now that all who did not permanently reside at Ripon House had departed. While she would not miss most of the guests, there were two in particular who invaded her thoughts no matter how hard she tried to push them out. Jacob and John commanded space in her heart and mind and there was little she could do about it.

Compounding her loneliness, winter had finally made an appearance, spreading its wet and bitterly cold breath over the island preventing venturing out. Her contact with the adult world had returned to conversations with servants about the child's needs. Mr. Littlewood instructed Sarah Anne to keep Adelia out of the way with the exception of breakfast. Eager to return to the solitude of his library, he spoke only briefly to his child during those meals then closeted himself away behind closed doors. Mrs. Littlewood, exhausted from entertaining, remained in her room ensconced upon her chaise. Sarah Anne's isolation felt complete.

Surveying the scene below her window, an involuntary sigh escaped her slightly parted lips. Other than the near black of the live oaks' leaves, everything was either brown or gray. And depressing. A sudden longing for the familiarity of St. Anne settled over her and her eyes stung with unshed tears. To keep them at bay, she pinched the webbing between her thumb and index finger. On this dreary day in this equally dreary house the simple coastal cottages with their light filled rooms called to her soul like a mother with open arms.

As she continued to observe the beige winter lawn bordered by equally brown salt grass and dark tree trunks, it seemed as though Ripon House's atmosphere had crawled out through the windows and doors to envelope the entire island.

The state of mourning had returned, although what the house grieved for was unclear. Perhaps it missed the joy of a happy family, but that was ludicrous. A happy family had never lived in this house as far as she could see. The only bright spots in the otherwise dismal period were that the Littlewoods had yet to find Sarah Anne's replacement and Adelia's mood had brightened considerably. In fact, the child's emotional state improved almost as soon as the train carrying her relatives pulled out of the station.

Sarah Anne glanced at Adelia and smiled. The child appeared calm and happy curled up in one of the bay window armchairs poring over a volume of Jane Austin. Maybe they had turned a corner. Maybe, just maybe, she was going to be all right. A shudder passed through Sarah Anne as she remembered Mr. Littlewood's threat of the asylum. Her primary goal had now become ensuring the permanency of this improvement.

Movement in the doorway caught Sarah Anne's attention. Eliza entered with a knowing smile curling her lips and her hand outstretched. "You got some letters, Miss Sarah Anne."

Puzzled, Sarah Anne took the offering. Aunt Edith's latest letter arrived only yesterday and she was Sarah Anne's only correspondent. She glanced at the postmarks. New York City. A jolt of anticipation shot beneath the white cotton lawn of her blouse. Turning each letter over, she discovered no additional indication as to who the sender might be, but the handwriting on the front of each was markedly different.

Sarah Anne tucked the letters in the pocket of her navy gabardine skirt to be read when she was alone in her room. Adelia had abandoned her book for the more interesting prospect of unexpected correspondence. She watched Sarah Anne with interest.

"Thank you, Eliza. Did you need something else?" Sarah Anne disliked taking a superior tone with her friend, but having Adelia's curiosity piqued would not do. After Eliza dropped a quick curtsey and turned to leave, Sarah Anne cast a corrective gaze upon her student. "Have you finished the chapter?"

Adelia ducked her head back to her novel, but Sarah Anne could have sworn she heard a little giggle emanating from the depths of the armchair. The afternoon dragged until it was finally time to tuck Adelia in. For once, she didn't beg for just one more story. Maybe she understood that Sarah Anne was anxious to get to her letters. Adelia could be so infuriatingly babyish at times and then suddenly surprise with an understanding far beyond her years.

Alone at last, Sarah Anne sat in the middle of her bed with the lamp on the bedside table turned as high as it would go. The letters were both alluring and fearsome at the same time. One envelope was thicker than the other. It rested in a dent on the counterpane like a self-satisfied cat that had licked the cream from the top of the milk jug. The writing on the front was precise with letters that leaned slightly left. The hand that had imprinted her name and address demonstrated care in the measured dotting of the *i* and the crossing of the *t*.

The other envelope, while thinner, weighed only a little less than its mate due to the heavy, high-quality paper with which it was made. Its script was not exactly sloppy, but was written in a more carefree, less disciplined style. Her name had extra flourishes at the end of each word and the loops of the letters bent to the right. She picked it up, tore open the flap, and found the signature. It was from Jacob.

She devoured his single page and read it a second time. There was a brightness and optimism that signified his youth and position. He wrote of mundane things and about his life as a law student, making no attempt to venture into the realm of emotions. If his purpose was to woo her, he went about it in a less than romantic manner. He had not asked permission to write to her, no doubt assuming she would welcome his attention. Fury that he had been correct took hold. Her anger was not directed at him, however, but at herself for being so easily swayed.

She put Jacob's letter aside and picked up the fat envelope. She lifted the flap and turned it upside down. A flurry of newsprint fluttered onto the bed. The letter bore the valediction and signature of John Edgar van Beek, making her heart skip a beat. He had mentioned staying in communication, but she never once believed he would follow through. Eagerly, she went to the beginning.

• • • • •

My Dearest Miss Mercer,

I hope you do not think me overly brazen in what I am about to convey. I intend no offense. It is my greatest wish that you believe me when I say I have only the highest regard and respect for you. You are a young lady beyond comparison and one whom I hope to meet again. Having returned to my daily routine in New York, I find it holds far less satisfaction than it once did. I fear I must place the blame squarely at your door. In truth, you have bewitched me. The image of your dear face is never far from my thoughts. It is a face of which dreams are made.

Now that I have completely abandoned all pride and have lain my heart at your feet, I have something to offer that you may find of interest. I learned from my tiresome cousin, Oliver, that he prevented your reading accounts of certain crimes committed here. Why he should be so overbearing is beyond understanding, but he can be an odd individual when he so chooses. He has been thus since childhood. It may have to do with his being the first-born. He was certainly overly indulged as a child. Whatever his motivation, I have determined to thwart him in his purpose. To that end, I have enclosed all of the articles written by myself and my competitors at other newspapers. I hope I am doing the right thing. I believe you will find my work informative without the prurient speculation of my colleagues. If you find offense in my gesture, please accept that I am only doing what I thought would please you. My cousin made your position less happy during the Christmas holiday and I wish to offer this token as a small recompense.

Until we meet again, I remain your most devoted servant,

John Edgar van Beek

• • • • •

A bubble of pure happiness rose beneath her breastbone, sending ripples of warmth and pleasure throughout her midsection. If it was possible to tingle with joy, then she must be glowing. She couldn't remember ever having experienced such sensations. Could this be what it felt like to be in love? While her head reminded her that this must be the extent of their relationship, her heart rejoiced in what they had.

Smiling to herself, Sarah Anne returned the letter to its enclosure. Scooping up Jacob's missive and the newspaper articles, she practically skipped to the chifforobe where she hid all beneath her small clothes for later examination. John had not only sent her his affection, but possible clues to the source of Adelia's problems. He was a man to be treasured.

CHAPTER 30

Hellfire and damnation! May this rag of a newspaper and its overly inquisitive reporter burn in hell like the fire now consumes the cheap newsprint.

My face shows clearly reflected in the window's night darkened glass. How gaunt I am beginning to appear. My fear of discovery and the most recent details reported in the paper are taking their toll.

I should never have given the bitch that damned coin. I took it on a whim. She had admired the collection and I wanted something to convince her of my admiration. Another mistake.

I had never before, not once, been required to pursue a woman. When she pretended shock and accused me of theft, I had little choice in what followed. The bitch should have been grateful for my attention, but instead she fought me. It was actually she who had instigated the Event. The stupid trollop should have given herself to me and been grateful that I would stoop to offer my attention to one such as she, one not much above the station of servant. Now her body has been found and her identity is broadcast for all to see.

Good lord. I am sweating despite the coolness of the evening. I must get a grip on myself. I must maintain control. Yes, it is the secret to my success. I have always been in charge. The choices were mine, not the whores'. In any event, why would anyone suspect me? I had no real connection to the woman.

CHAPTER 31

Sarah Anne shoved aside the newspaper articles John had sent. Although they described a series of brutal rapes, she could see no connection to Adelia whatsoever. The child's life was as far removed from the world of prostitutes and their patrons as one could get. While John merely reported the facts, a rival reporter had made a case suggesting the crimes were linked in some way, but the police seemed unmoved by his arguments.

Instead, the New York City Police Commissioner insisted that prostitutes could not, in fact, claim rape due to the nature of their business. That a business transaction had turned rougher than the women anticipated was of no consequence. Indeed, it was an occupational hazard for fallen women.

Sarah Anne's lips thinned as she shook her head. What a misogynistic ass the commissioner was. He clearly had no concept of what it was to be a woman without education or means of support. Farm laborers and factory workers barely earned enough to keep body and soul together. If those workers happened to be women, they earned even less. Just thinking about it made her want to beat some sense into the man. Pounding the bed pillows as a substitute would be a satisfying occupation, but she picked up her watch from the bedside table instead.

The right corner of her mouth lifted in a self-deprecating curl. No more time to contemplate the injustices of the world for she was already late in attending to Adelia. She crossed to the connecting door and peeked into the adjoining bedroom. Adelia still slept. She looked so peaceful and angelic Sarah Anne didn't have the heart to wake her. It would make little difference if the child arose now or in half an hour or so. Adelia possessed a facility for learning that surpassed her almost eight years. For Sarah Anne, having the chance to eat breakfast alone before beginning the school day didn't come often.

She met no one on the backstairs as she made her way to the kitchen. Perhaps Cook wouldn't be too angry if she asked for a plate of eggs, bacon, and toast to be eaten in the servants' dining area. She daren't go into the dining room without Adelia. The odor of coffee and bacon drifted into the service hall as she reached the bottom of the stairs making her mouth water.

The morning beyond Ripon House's walls was heavy with low, rain-engorged clouds ready to deliver themselves of their burden at any moment. Since no one had thought to light the single wall scone in the service hall, Sarah Anne tread carefully toward the beam of light coming through the kitchen door.

Low voices greeted her as she entered Cook's domain. Two of the housemaids, Lila Jane and Sookie, gasped as they bent over the worktable with a newspaper spread before them.

"You sure it's her?" Sookie glanced doubtfully at her companion.

"If you could read, you'd see for yourself. It's her, all right. Has her name right here." Lila Jane jabbed an index finger at a line on the paper.

"I'm glad they ain't asked me to go up north. I'll quit before I go to that place."

"And where would that be, Sookie? Lila Jane?" Mrs. Bogard's voice rang with authority and impatience. Both maids quickly stepped back from the table, their gazes glued to the floor. "That's what I thought. Be about your duties. The dining room needs attention. Miss Adelia has not yet eaten."

The maids scurried from the kitchen leaving Sarah Anne alone with the housekeeper and the kitchen staff. Unfortunately, her relationship with the housekeeper had improved little since their chilly encounter the day Sarah Anne first arrived at Ripon House. They had settled into a pattern of speaking to one another only when needed. Since Sarah

Anne spent all of her time with the child, contact with her nemesis was blessedly limited.

After watching the maids until they were out of sight, Mrs. Bogard turned her attention on Sarah Anne. "What may we do for you, Miss Mercer? Mr. Littlewood noticed that you and Miss Adelia did not come down for breakfast with him. Is the child ill?"

"No, Adelia is quite well. She's still asleep. She had a nightmare in the middle of the night and had trouble going back to sleep. I decided to not wake her just yet."

"Her father may be displeased with your decision, but that is your affair." With that, Mrs. Bogard turned on her heel and marched away. The echo of her steps in the service hall grew fainter as she hastened toward the front of the house.

Sarah Anne stood by the worktable shifting from one foot to the other working up the courage to speak to Cook, who hovered over her stove sampling and stirring the contents of several pots. Stalling for time, she glanced down at the newspaper and her breath caught in her throat. The title of an article screamed a name she had heard so often she felt she knew the woman. She grabbed the paper and tucked it under her arm. She would read it when she was alone. Whatever other information the article might reveal would make little difference to the impact the central fact would have on Adelia. The child's welfare was her first and foremost concern. The article's title read "Body Discovered Believed to be a Miss Margret Ballard."

"Hey, what're you doing with my paper? I need it to wrap the scraps. Put it back." The cook stood with a ladle poised above a stockpot, a scowl darkening her face.

"May I keep it long enough to read an article that's caught my attention?"

Cook cocked her head. "Caught your attention, did it? I guess it's caught just about everybody's attention in this house. Read it and give it back before George takes the trash for burning."

Sarah Anne smiled and nodded her thanks. Taking a few steps toward the center of the kitchen, she gathered her courage. Cook was not a person with whom one trifled. Her temper was legendary, but so was her cooking. Much was forgiven a woman who could produce elegant meals for twenty in the wilds of rural Georgia.

"Would it be possible to have my breakfast in the servants' dining area? I'll take Adelia to the dining room after I've eaten, if it's all right with you."

"I guess you expect me to cook something just for you?"

Oh dear. Of course the breakfast cooking was finished and preparations for other meals were underway. "Maybe I could serve myself something from the dining room and bring it back here?"

Inexplicably, Cook laughed. "You should see your face." She slapped her thigh before continuing, "Don't be ridiculous. I'll cook something for you. You're good to the child, so I'll be good to you. There's some around here like me and George who see how things are with that sweet baby."

Sarah Anne couldn't speak. George's affection for Adelia was common knowledge, but she had no idea the formidable cook felt the same. Humbled, Sarah replied softly, "Thank you. You are very kind."

Settled at the long table in an alcove next to the kitchen, Sarah Anne unfolded the paper and started reading.

• • • • •

New York Herald

January 20, 1891

The body of a lady believed to be one Miss Margaret Ballard of this city, lately governess to the daughter of industrialist Mr. Jedidiah Littlewood, was discovered on Blackwell Island on the morning of Friday last. A vagrant scavenging the shore made the discovery. It is not known how she came to be on the island. She was not an inmate of any of the island's facilities and was not known to have business there. Foul play is strongly suspected as the bodice of her dress was torn down the front from throat to waist. The remnants of a rope were found tied around her ankles and her windpipe was crushed further indicating that the lady met with an untimely end.

Upon examination, Manhattan Coroner, Dr. Ferdinand Eidman, believes that Miss Ballard may have been assaulted in the most immodest manner possible before being throttled and deposited in the river. The condition of the body indicates she had been there for some time, possibly as long as two or more months. Identification was made possible by a letter found in the pocket of her skirt, which her attacker must have overlooked in his haste to dispose of her body. An odd detail of the crime was the antique coin found tucked inside the glove of her left hand. Thus far, it has not been determined how the coin came into Miss Ballard's possession or if it has some bearing on her death.

Given the facts, it seems the craven attacker of women who haunts our city has moved on to murder most foul. While Miss Ballard may not have shared the occupation of earlier victims, the manner of her death indicates she is the latest in this series of attacks. Police Commissioner McLean may see no connection among these crimes, but it must be asked. Why should women, even those of the lowest class, not expect to travel abroad in the evening without fear of being attacked? Has our city sunk so low, become so calloused that we refuse to protect some of our most vulnerable citizens?

• • • • •

Sarah Anne folded the paper again and pushed her chair back. As much as she dreaded the thought of an interview with her employer, it was her duty to ascertain how best to deal with the discovery of Adelia's beloved Margret. She couldn't speak to the child without her parents' permission, but with the servants aware of the situation the chances of Adelia overhearing something untoward increased. After making her way to the front of the house, she stopped outside Mr. Littlewood's library. Angry voices emanated from the other side. She drew a calming breath and knocked.

"Enter." His voice telegraphed his mood.

Sarah Anne steeled herself and opened the door. Mrs. Littlewood stood beside her husband, her face a study in distress and something else that Sarah Anne could not identify. She had clearly been crying. Both Littlewoods looked at Sarah Anne with angry eyes, but she didn't believe the anger was directed at her. They seemed lost still in the depths of whatever they had been arguing about.

"Sir, Ma'am, have you seen the paper and the information regarding Miss Ballard?"

"Come in and close the door." He waited until she stood before his desk. "We are aware someone has been discovered who may or may not be Miss Ballard. We choose to believe it is not. We maintain that she is with her paramour, alive and well. It is all anyone needs to know."

"But sir, the servants already . . ." A chop of his hand silenced Sarah Anne.

"The servants will do as they are told. This topic is not to be discussed again by anyone in this house. Disobedience will result in dismissal." His gaze lit upon the paper folded under arm. "Is that the *Herald*?"

"Yes, sir."

"Give it to me."

He did not wait for Sarah Anne to hand it over, but moved around to stand in front of his desk. He extended his hand to receive the offending tabloid. Instead of looking at it, he marched to the fireplace and tossed the newspaper into the flames where it was consumed within moments.

"That is the end of the matter. You are dismissed."

As she left the room, Sarah Anne glanced back at her employers. Mrs. Littlewood dabbed at her eyes with a handkerchief while her husband stared straight ahead with a thunderous expression.

Sarah Anne closed the door and leaned against it for a moment. Her head spun with the Littlewoods' reactions to the news. She had expected Adelia's father to be brusque and unwelcoming, but his complete dismissal of facts and refusal to believe the obvious were perplexing in the extreme. Something was terribly wrong in this house.

CHAPTER 32

Sarah Anne made her way back to her bedroom and sat on the edge of the bed. She had not received the guidance she hoped for from the child's parents and they had made it clear none would be forthcoming. After gathering up the newspaper articles, she folded them, shoved them back into the envelope in which they had arrived, and hid the packet in her chifforobe with her undergarments. It was doubtful her employers would appreciate her having them in her possession. Returning to the bed, she slumped again on its edge.

Mr. Littlewood may think the matter of Miss Ballard was a closed subject, but every word of the article describing her murdered corpse was burned into Sarah Anne's memory. No matter what Adelia's father said, the *Herald* reporter appeared correct about the crimes being connected and in his conclusion that Margret Ballard had fallen victim to the depraved rapist—a rapist who had turned killer. Well, Mr. Littlewood could not hide from the facts forever, though his pigheaded refusal to acknowledge them was infuriating.

Sarah Anne's fingers drummed against the counterpane. If she didn't need to succeed in this job so badly and if she wasn't so worried about Adelia, she would just walk away from all of it. She would return to St. Anne and take up the life she dreaded while she applied for the positions she had dreamed of. But she could not desert the child now. Adelia had come to depend on her for the affection and stability her parents refused to provide. The Littlewoods had much to answer for in neglecting their child and for refusing to face the reality of Miss

Ballard's disappearance. When the killer was caught, the truth would be revealed whether they liked it or not. The truth . . .

Sarah Anne sat up straight and grabbed the bedpost as her heart and mind raced. Details of the crimes and of her interview with Adelia's parents tumbled together until they created a troubling whole.

Oh God, that had to be it. It was the only logical explanation for Mr. Littlewood's attitude toward the murder of his former employee. Yes, it had to be. Someone in the Littlewood family knew the identity of the rapist. Then her stomach flipped and bile rose in her throat. There was another possibility. Someone in the Littlewood family *was* the rapist. And by extension, one of Adelia's relatives was a murderer as well.

Her hand flew to her mouth as she choked back a gasp. Oh please, don't let it be so. John Edgar and Jacob's faces floated before her mind's eye. Her heart filled at the very thought of them. It couldn't be one of them. She couldn't be attracted to a murderer. Falling in love with two men was complicated enough. Surely she would have recognized evil if it had been present in one of them.

Sarah Anne's lips thinned and her eyes narrowed. Oliver, on the other hand, was another matter altogether. He was arrogant enough to think he could get away with anything. He was also disdainful of anyone he considered beneath him. And she didn't like him, not one little bit. Oliver as criminal. What a satisfying thought. Then guilt shot its arrow straight through her. Just because she disliked the man didn't make him a rapist or a murderer.

Sarah Anne shook her head. No, probably none of her solutions were correct. Her imagination was running free again leading her to jump to conclusions. She had completely overlooked the most likely reason for his views. Mr. Littlewood was simply trying to shield his family from the stigma that would attach itself if a member of the household were the victim of murder. The innocent were often punished by society for circumstances beyond their control. Hadn't some of the old biddies in St. Anne shunned Mrs. Alcott and her children after Mr. Alcott ran off with that woman from Waycross? Of course Adelia's father would want to protect his family from such a fate.

While his behavior was odd, he was doing what he thought proper and she had no right to judge him for it.

Sarah Anne started to rise from the edge of the bed then plopped back down and stared at the pattern on the carpet beneath her feet. But that explanation raised an entirely different issue. If he was simply protecting his family from scandal, why did Adelia act so strangely when her brothers and cousin were visiting? Her father maintained she was unbalanced in her mind.

Sarah Anne could not accept it. Adelia was highly-strung and easily upset, but she wasn't insane. At least Sarah Anne prayed her analysis was correct. Although she had read a little about the subject in college, she had no real training in alienation. The field was so new that she had only encountered the subject in her senior year. Wesleyan did not even teach the subject as a course or offer it as a major area of study. It would help to know more, but there were no sources presently available and no one she could consult other than Uncle Zach. He agreed the child was deeply troubled and neglected by her parents, but otherwise a normal seven-year-old.

She leaned against the bedpost and sucked her lower lip between her teeth. The possibilities she'd conjured only led to greater alarm, not less. Insanity, knowledge of terrible crimes, or a murderer in the family—each explanation brought hopelessness, grief, and despair.

"What's the matter? You look upset?" Adelia's voice sounded small and anxious.

Sarah Anne had been so lost in thought she had not heard the connecting door between the bedrooms open. Standing in the doorway in her nightgown with her sleep tousled blonde tresses and huge blue eyes, Adelia looked like a frightened angel who suddenly found herself flung to earth without warning. Sarah Anne's heart swelled with affection and the realization she was breaking one of the cardinal rules of teaching. One should never allow oneself to become too attached to one's students. A teacher was not and could never be the parent. Still, it was far easier to know something with one's head than with one's heart and Sarah Anne was already a lost cause where the child was concerned.

She opened her arms and the little girl flew into them. Kissing the top of the child's head, she said, "There's nothing wrong. It's a perfect day and you're a perfect girl. Let's get you some breakfast and then think of something fun to do."

Sarah Anne could not face the prospect of academics. She needed distraction from the overpowering emotions her questions engendered. None of the things that had happened had been part of her plan—staying in St. Anne, being a governess in a drab old dungeon of a house, being attracted to two men beyond her reach—none of it was what she had dreamed of. And yet, she did not regret this path. She had never felt so needed and adored in her life. Adelia had entered her heart and taken up residence with the fierceness of a bear cub clinging to its momma. It was unlike anything Sarah Anne had ever expected in the teacher/pupil relationship.

Adelia drew back and considered the proposal with glowing eyes. "No schoolwork today?"

"No. You're already far ahead of your peers."

"Something fun? Like what?"

"Oh, I don't know. Maybe go search for buried treasure in the attics?" It was the best she could do on such a cold, blustery day.

"You mean like in *Treasure Island*?"

"Yes, just like in *Treasure Island*." Someone else would have to solve the mystery of Miss Ballard. All Sarah Anne could do was protect Adelia with every ounce of her strength and will.

CHAPTER 33

Sarah Anne stood at her bedroom window gazing out upon an island that seemed to be shrugging off winter like a grubby, too small coat. Spring comes early to the coastal South and this year proved no exception. After the damp, bluster, and cold of January and February, March had settled into a more peaceful attitude and coaxed the azaleas and dogwoods into their full glory. The rising sun's rays, filtered by low tree branches, played along the tips of the salt grass at the edge of the garden and caressed the blossoms that lined the stone terrace. The light's quality predicted a glorious day, but the beauty and calm of the morning contrasted starkly with Sarah Anne's emotions.

She glanced at the envelope in her hand and ran her finger under the flap, but stopped before she withdrew the two pages she had already read more times than she cared to remember. The postmark showed it had been mailed from New York City two months ago and the message closed with *Warmest Regards, John Edgar van Beek*. Another from Jacob lay in the open drawer, but letters from Jacob and John only came sporadically now and were handed over to her under the disapproving glare of Benson, the butler. Sarah Anne should have been relieved that the young men were losing interest, but she found it depressing and dispiriting. She was clearly more attached to them than was good for her. She fingered the flap and then tucked John's letter back into its resting place atop its fellow. No need to continue torturing herself with *what ifs* or *might have beens*. Looking at the positives might improve her mood.

On that note, Adelia seemed so much better these days. Perhaps the improvement in the child's behavior and outlook was permanent. Sarah Anne prayed the storms of the past were banished for it had been months since Adelia had thrown a fit. In fact, there had been no untoward incidents or moments of discord since the turning of the year. Although peace and harmony reigned, a small voice of warning set Sarah Anne's nerves on edge. Intuition said that the calm would not last and that a battle of wills and raging emotions hovered just over the horizon. Maybe her unease lay in knowing that Adelia's eighth birthday loomed and thus far no preparations of any kind had been mentioned. Even Jacob seemed to have forgotten because no package had thus far arrived. It was disappointing and seemed unlike him.

The best she could do if the family continued their pattern of neglect would be to make a day of celebration for the two of them. Maybe Mrs. Bogard would allow Eliza to join them for an hour. Adelia loved the little maid and declared Eliza to be her best friend. Being a child of great privilege had not guaranteed the friendship and companionship of other children. In fact, it seemed to have the opposite effect as children never attended the house parties her parents gave and Adelia had not been allowed to return to St. Anne since Christmas Day. The child was lonely and craved someone with whom to play. Eliza filled the void when she was able.

There was little Sarah Anne could do about Mr. and Mrs. Littlewood's treatment of their child, but despite all that was not right in the family, Adelia had improved so much Sarah Anne did not risk leaving the island to attend Easter service with Uncle Zach and Aunt Edith. They were disappointed, but Sarah Anne refused to indulge any guilt on their account. It was her uncle, after all, who placed her in the position of having to choose between family and work responsibilities.

Sarah Anne stared at nothing in particular in the garden beyond her window while she absentmindedly toyed with the fringe on the curtain. It wasn't fair to lay blame for her situation completely at her uncle's door, however, it was he who had beseeched that she stay in St. Anne and not accept the job in the mountain community so far from home.

That was part of the problem. She still thought of the north Georgia mountains as home and she longed to return, even though she left them when she was ten and had not been back, not even when her maternal grandmother died. Sarah Anne swiped at tears threatening to escape, leaned her head back to send them down her throat, and slammed the door on what might have been. Dwelling on impossible dreams would not change her situation nor improve her day.

After washing and dressing, Sarah Anne opened the connecting door between the bedrooms and peeked in at her charge. Adelia lay on her back with eyes wide open staring at the ceiling. At the click of the knob, her head turned toward the door. Sarah Anne's heart fell. Storms were gathering. The expression in the child's eyes was a sure indicator that peace had deserted her.

Plastering on a cheerful façade, Sarah Anne called out, "Up, up, up, sweet little pup." Her singsong rhyme did not have the desired effect.

Adelia's face turned stony. "Why did you call me a dog?" The child looked and sounded too much like her mother in that moment.

"I'm sorry. It was not what I intended." Sarah Anne adopted a soothing tone. "It's something my mother used to say to me when I was little. I thought you might like it. Sort of our special signal."

"Well, I don't. I'm not a puppy and I'm not little. I'll be eight tomorrow." Adelia's voice was cross with the effort of holding back tears.

Perhaps a neutral approach would be better. "Of course. I was foolish to think a grown-up girl would like something so silly."

"Stop treating me like a baby." Her wail bounced off the walls. "And don't try to make me eat breakfast. I'm not hungry." The child was clearly not to be comforted.

"All right. I will treat you as requested." Sarah Anne's expression shifted from soft to firm. "The day has begun. Get up and get dressed. We have lessons waiting." The child deserved sympathy, but rudeness must not be tolerated. She locked eyes with Adelia in the day's first contest of wills. Hopefully it would be the last.

Several moments elapsed before a small quiver shook Adelia's bottom lip. Then a single tear rolled over each cheek. "Nobody cares that tomorrow is my birthday. Mother and Father always have parties for Oliver and Jacob, but they never remember me. Ever. Why don't they love me?"

Sarah Anne's heart broke open and all of the sadness she had felt as a child washed over her anew, but with an unexpected dimension. So now then, which was worse? To lose parents who showed you every day that they loved you dearly or to have living parents who demonstrated at every turning that they did not care you existed? In the moment, it was difficult to say.

Sarah Anne went to the edge of the bed and held out her arms. Adelia flew into them and sobbed. Kissing the top of the golden head, Sarah Anne said, "I was going to save this as a surprise for tomorrow, but I'll tell you now, if you wish."

The sniveling lessened and Adelia peeked up from the folds of Sarah Anne's blouse. "A surprise? For me?"

"Yes, for you, silly. Brush your teeth and wash your face while I make sure the arrangements are complete. I'll send Eliza up to help you dress. Tomorrow will be a special day. I promise."

On the way to the housekeeper's rooms, Sarah Anne prayed she had not promised more than she could deliver. Mrs. Bogard had never been her biggest fan. Asking a favor could easily be met with rejection and derision. She paused and gathered her courage before knocking.

"Come." Irritation colored Mrs. Bogard's voice.

Sarah Anne opened the door and stepped inside, trying to strike an attitude somewhere between supplication and self-confidence.

"Oh. It's you. What is it? As you can see, I am extremely busy."

Perhaps a simple, direct approach would be best. Sarah Anne nodded and said, "I apologize for intruding, but I need your help."

Mrs. Bogard gave Sarah Anne the once-over. Surprise shone in her eyes. "What can I do for you?"

"It's not for me, exactly. It's—"

With a wave of her hand, Mrs. Bogard interrupted. "Then who?"

Sarah Anne squared her shoulders and made a decision. "May I speak plainly with hope of discretion on your part?"

Mrs. Bogard eyed Sarah Anne. "Perhaps. Out with it."

"Tomorrow is Miss Adelia's birthday and no preparations have been made for celebration or even acknowledgement unless you know something I don't." The housekeeper's face softened and she shook her head. Sarah Anne continued, "I'm hoping you and the staff will help me make the day special for the child. She is despondent and feels no one cares for her. Unfortunately, I must say I agree. Mr. and Mrs. Littlewood are unaccountably thoughtless where their only daughter is concerned. It's beyond understanding, but it seems to be the way things are."

Setting her pen aside, Mrs. Bogard frowned. "I will pledge my discretion to you in this matter and now I must ask the same of you, Miss Mercer."

"Of course. Thank you."

Mrs. Bogard's eyes narrowed. "You have placed your finger squarely on the crux of the problem. There was talk at the time of her birth, but I put no countenance in it. Whatever the truth may be, it was clear Miss Adelia was an unwanted pregnancy and is now an ignored child. Her mother, when she thinks about the child at all, sees Adelia only through the lens of her own needs. I sometimes think Adelia's fits of temper are simply her way of gaining the attention that is hers by right. The staff has always tried to make up in whatever small ways we are able for what she lacks from her family. You have done better than I anticipated. What may we do to help?"

Sarah Anne blinked in disbelief at having discovered a soft side to her nemesis. Perhaps she had misjudged the woman. A guilty memory of how she had spoken to the housekeeper upon their first meeting skittered across her mind. Maybe their shaky start had been partly her fault. Yes, she had been less than gracious. She could blame it on being nervous and unsure of herself, but it had put them on a wrong footing and for that Sarah Anne was now heartily sorry.

She put on what she hoped was an endearing smile and made sure her voice held a contrite tone. "Thank you so much. And I want to apologize for how we started off. I hope that maybe we can be friends from now on."

For a moment Mrs. Bogard actually looked flustered, then she regained her composure. Clearing her throat, the housekeeper said, "I am not sure friendship is possible given our respective roles within the household, but I believe we might work together for the child's good. Now, what is it the staff may do to help prevent disaster tomorrow?" Despite her proclamation, Sarah Anne could have sworn a small smile softened Mrs. Board's features before it disappeared into the locked safe of her iron control.

The day of Adelia's birthday dawned clear and mild, perfect for what was planned. As she and Eliza spread the picnic blanket under a live oak at the edge of the garden, Sarah Anne watched Adelia out of the corner of her eye. The little girl sat on the grass under the tree playing with a carved wooden doll Eliza's father had made for her. Its jointed limbs moved smoothly as she dressed and undressed it. When Sarah Anne first saw the doll, she prayed the child would appreciate it. It took time and skill to produce the carved braided hair and the lovely painted face. Eliza and Sarah Anne had made clothes for it with material scraps provided by Mrs. Littlewood's maid. She was probably the best-dressed doll in all of Georgia. Adelia had taken one look and declared she had never had such a wonderful gift. She cradled it in her arms and cooed to it, calling it her most loved, special girl. The expensive china dolls lining a shelf in her bedroom seemed to have been forgotten. When the picnic had been eaten and the candles and cake laid waste, George had a special ride planned that would take them over the entire island, including a secret place he had never shown anyone. Adelia was beyond excited.

Adelia had just blown out eight candles when Mrs. Bogard appeared, red faced and breathing hard. "Miss Mercer, you and Miss Adelia are required by Sir and Madame. He asks that you come to the library now."

Above the child's head, Sarah Anne shot the housekeeper a quizzical look. It was met with raised eyebrows and a slight shrug of the shoulders. Sarah Anne caught Eliza's eye. Uncertainty shone in the maid's eyes, as well. "Eliza, will you stay with the picnic while we are with Mr. Littlewood?"

Sarah Anne led the child into the house, down the service hall, and into the foyer. Trepidation increased with every step. Surely Adelia's parents would acknowledge the child's birthday. Mrs. Littlewood wasn't entirely without feeling for her daughter. The memory of the mother kneeling beside the child as she lay fainted from an extreme tantrum reassured Sarah Anne on that point. Still, it was the form the acknowledgement might take that was worrisome. Being called into The Presence, as Sarah Anne had come to think of these requests, never brought good news. She tapped at the door and was bade enter.

"You wished to see us, Sir? Ma'am?"

"Indeed. I have news that affects you both." Mr. Littlewood fixed Adelia then Sarah Anne with his gaze. "We have engaged a tutor to prepare Adelia for boarding school in the fall. As of June, your services will no longer be required, Miss Mercer."

Adelia's nails dug into the palm of Sarah Anne's hand and a tremor radiated from her small body. Sarah Anne glanced down. Fear froze Adelia's features in a mask of desperation and despair.

CHAPTER 34

My hands show well in the light of this lamp. One might even consider them works of art. The nails are perfectly shaped and my fingers are long and slender. They are young hands, strong hands, capable hands. Hands that could have performed surgery or played a sonata equally well, but they were not destined for those things. They—no, I—have discovered a higher purpose. The whores of the world deserve punishment and my hands mete out justice with a vengeance. But I feel all at sea.

The need to continue my work is growing. It has been much too long since the last Event. My desire rages at night, but with the discovery of that blasted woman's body, danger to myself lurks at every turning. How much longer can I avoid detection? It was a mistake to become entangled with Margaret. I should never have given her the damned coin. It left no other option but killing her. What other clue might I have unwittingly left?

I must gain release. I must achieve an Event soon or risk going insane. But where? When?

CHAPTER 35

Instead of pitching a tantrum, Adelia's body went rigid and her face turned the color of ginned cotton. In the next moment, her eyes rolled back until only the whites showed then she went limp and fell to the floor. Sarah Anne knelt beside the child while Mrs. Littlewood gasped and clutched her husband's arm.

Mr. Littlewood grunted in disgust. "Typical. She doesn't get her way, so she causes a scene." He turned to his wife and continued, "This is what comes of tainted blood. Getting her away cannot come soon enough."

Getting her away. Sarah Anne didn't like the implication. If they planned to send the child to boarding school, surely he would have phrased it differently. Or maybe Mr. Littlewood was simply referring to sending Adelia off to school. Rich Yankees had their own ways, many of which still remained a mystery.

Sarah Anne raised her eyes to Mrs. Littlewood, who said nothing and turned to look out the French doors. The woman was a disgusting excuse of a mother. Without waiting to be dismissed, Sarah Anne lifted Adelia and carried her from the room. None of what she had just observed was in the least normal. Something was very wrong in this family and she was determined to find out what. Adelia didn't deserve the treatment she received at the hands of her parents. And what did her father mean about tainted blood? Some confronting needed to be done and, by God, she would do it. She had less than three months before her dismissal. After that, it would be too late to help Adelia.

Anger burned through her, fueling a furious determination. Although her job was teaching academics, a more important task lay ahead. The child's happiness, maybe her life, was at stake.

Adelia's eyes opened when Sarah Anne placed her upon the counterpane. Sarah Anne sat on the edge of the bed, picked up one small hand, and rubbed it between her own palms. "I think it's time you told me what's going on, don't you? And don't say it's because I will be leaving you. People don't faint simply because they are being separated from a friend."

Tears filled Adelia's eyes and rolled down her cheeks. She shook her head and buried her face in the pillow.

Sarah Anne pulled the child into her arms and held her while the small body trembled. "Please tell me what's wrong. I can't help you if I don't know what's bothering you."

Adelia's voice floated up between sobs. "You can't help me. Nobody can. Father said I must never talk about it again."

"Talk of what? You can tell me. I'm very good at keeping secrets." Adelia heaved a great sigh, but did not reply. Sarah Anne held the child at arm's length and searched her face. "Other people believe your fits are put on to get your own way, but I think you are terribly afraid. I can see it in your eyes. Please tell me why."

Adelia's head dropped so that her chin nearly touched her chest. She drew a long breath and let it out. When she spoke, her voice was an almost inaudible whisper.

"When you mumble, I can't understand you." Sarah Anne put her ear near the child's mouth. "Can you say it again, please?"

"I think someone in my family killed Margaret."

Sarah Anne felt like she had been punched in her midsection. Adelia seemed to be on the verge of confirming everything Sarah Anne feared. "Why? How?"

"I can't tell anyone. Father said if I ever spoke of it again, he would send me to the asylum for sure. He said we do not have criminals in our family. He punished me for telling him what I saw and said I was disloyal to the family."

Oh, dear Lord! The child had been carrying the secret for months unable to speak of it to a single soul. No wonder she was an emotional mess. One of the people who should protect her and make her feel safe was the very one who had created the terror. What an infuriating circumstance.

"Tell me what you know." Sarah Anne's voice was harsher than she intended. She had to fight to keep control. The desire to grab the child and run away with her was almost overwhelming

"I can't. Father means it. He really does. I promised not to say. I won't and you can't make me." Adelia's whole body shook as hysteria tinted each word.

Confusion and desperation churned through Sarah Anne. Her most important job was to protect Adelia, but how could she do that when she had no idea what they actually faced? Sarah Anne made shushing sounds and stroked the child's hair while she considered her next course of action. As desperate as she felt to know what had happened, she had to marshal her emotions for the child's sake. For the time being, Adelia could be pressed no further without risking a full-on fit.

Sarah Anne pulled the child into her arms and held her until the shaking eased. Finally, she said, "Okay. I won't ask again for now, but you must promise me something. You must tell me if you feel afraid. You must let me protect you." Sarah Anne placed a finger under Adelia's chin and lifted until their eyes met. "Swear it." Adelia nodded.

The sound of a throat clearing drew Sarah Anne's attention. Eliza stood with her hands behind her back waiting to be acknowledged. "Mrs. Bogard said to pack up the picnic and bring it all inside. I put Miss Adelia's doll on her bed. Can I do anything else for you, Miss?"

Sarah Anne grabbed at the chance. "Yes, as it happens, I need to speak with Mrs. Bogard. Please stay with Miss Adelia until I return."

Before either girl could protest, Sarah Anne hurried through the door and down the stairs. If she couldn't force Adelia to tell what she knew, maybe she could get the information she needed another way. She found the housekeeper in her office across from the kitchen. Once inside with the door closed, she set aside her usual caution in Mrs.

Bogard's presence and came straight to the point. "Mr. Littlewood has hinted there is family history of bad blood in connection with Adelia. I think you know what he means. I need to know what it is."

Mrs. Bogard put her teacup in its saucer. "As you can see, I am taking my afternoon break. This is a most unpleasant interruption. I get very little time to myself." Picking up the teapot, she refilled her cup. "If you wish to interrogate a member of staff, I suggest you consult George. He probably knows more than he has ever been willing to share regarding Miss Adelia's origins."

Sarah Anne did not stop to speak, but turned on her heel headed for the stables. Shock sped her steps. Upon finding George in the tack room cleaning saddles, she blurted out, "Tell me what you know about why Adelia's father says she has tainted blood. Something is very wrong in this family and the impact on my student is unacceptable." Her voice filled the small space. Anger and fear colored her words and annihilated all discretion.

George stared at her for what might have been a full thirty seconds then placed the can of Neatsfoot oil on the workbench and wiped his hands on a towel hanging on the wall behind him. Rising from the bench, he moved to the door. When Sara Anne failed to follow, he turned around. "If you want to know about that time, you ain't gonna hear it where just anybody can walk up on us."

They exited through the back of the stable and followed a path leading away from the house. They walked through the woods until they reached a shack set in a clearing. The bay slapping against a bulkhead sounded in the distance. George opened the door and stood aside for Sarah Anne to enter. Fishing nets, crab traps, and empty crates lined the walls. One grimy window let in a shaft of late afternoon sunshine where dust motes floated. The dank, musty air and layers of dirt spoke of disuse, perhaps complete abandonment. It was certainly isolated. Sarah Anne sneezed as a shiver raised goose bumps on her arms. It was not a place she would want to spend time in unless she had to.

George closed the door and finally spoke. “Before I tell you anything, you gonna tell me what’s got you so stirred up.”

Sarah Anne searched George’s face while she decided how much to reveal. He had always shown great affection for Adelia, but his livelihood depended upon the Littlewoods’ good will. Would he keep secrets? She suspected he could be as safe as a bank vault when he chose. Since she expected him to reveal a deep family secret, she must first demonstrate she trusted him even if Adelia might view the revelations as a betrayal. Sometimes one simply chose the path that would cause the least harm or provide the greatest good, however imperfect.

After telling George what Adelia had revealed, all that she suspected, and about her June dismissal date, Sarah Anne ended with, “Adelia is terrified and I only have a couple of months left here. When I’m gone, she will be abandoned to whoever has her so frightened. I can’t bear it. I love that little girl. I need to know everything if I am to help her.”

George rubbed his chin for several beats before saying, “My, my. That a mess, sure enough. I always knew Miss Ballard wouldn’t of run off with some man. She was a good woman and a lady. No wonder our girl’s so scared. You sure you cain’t get her to say who she’s afraid of?”

“Maybe sometime, but not today. It’s taken all these months for her to trust me enough to tell what she has so far. It doesn’t seem to be a secret among the staff that her parents don’t care for Adelia. I suppose her mother shows some affection in her own peculiar way, but I would say her father doesn’t even like his daughter, much less love her.”

George didn’t speak for a moment then his eyes narrowed. “Who would you say Miss Adelia look like?”

“I’ve never given it much thought, but I suppose she looks like her mother.”

“Do you see any of Mr. Littlewood in her?”

“No, I can’t say that I do. But sometimes children don’t look a thing like their parents. Appearance can skip a generation or two.”

“But, you see, that’s the problem. Some folk say Miss Adelia look exactly like her father.”

Sarah Anne blinked and gasped. "Are you implying that Mr. Littlewood is not Adelia's father?"

George looked away without replying. The desire to jump up and shake him until he answered set her alight. Instead of giving in to it, she remained seated and followed his gaze to the ceiling where dust balls clung to the cobwebs strung between the rough sawn rafters. His eyes seemed to lose focus so that his internal struggle was almost palpable.

Finally, he drew a deep breath and nodded. "I don't suppose telling you what I know is gonna hurt nothing and it might help you with the child." He pulled his handkerchief from his pocket and spread it on the top of an old crate. "We might as well sit." When Sarah Anne was perched on the crate, he dragged over another for himself.

George placed his elbows on his knees and stared at the floor for a moment then looked at Sarah Anne with eyes that held deep sorrow. "Our sweet girl never had a chance with Mr. Littlewood. You see, he sent Miz Littlewood down here end of August the fall before Miss Adelia was born in the spring, but he stayed in New York 'til nearly Christmas. She was all high strung when she got here and just stayed in her room. Wouldn't come downstairs to eat or nothing. The maids said they could hear her crying sometimes. She was just real unhappy 'til the other one come.

Showed up one day bold as brass. Said he rented a house in St. Anne for the winter and it still hot as blue blazes down here. Him and her spent every day and most evenings together. Some days, she'd say she needed to go to town, as if there's anything in St. Anne for her. He had a boat, so she didn't need the ferry. By the time her husband got here she was getting big and her fancy man had done disappeared. You could hear them yelling all the way out to the stables. He say she a whore and the baby ain't his."

Sarah Anne's head spun with all George had revealed. "This explains a lot. Why didn't he divorce her? He certainly had cause."

George cocked his head, irony making a thin line of his mouth. "And have a scandal? No, he cain't have that. Miz Littlewood, she from a family that's a big deal up there in New York. Mr. Littlewood come from nothing back in England where he growed up. He made a lot of money, but he was still a nobody 'til he married her. He had the money, but she had the society family. Thay's only one thing he care more about than money and it's what his fancy friends think. He make out to anybody who matters that he be Adelia's daddy."

As they returned to the house, Sarah Anne's mind raced with all she had learned. Even if the child's imagination had created danger where none existed, the threat from the man whom she thought of as her father was very real. He possessed a very hard heart to blame an innocent baby for choices made by others. Adelia was not an easy child, but she deserved to be loved and cared for, not threatened with exile to the oblivion of an institution.

Rage coursed through Sarah Anne until her heart pounded and her breath came in short gasps. How dare those good-for-nothing, sorry excuse for parents treat their child so? By all that was holy, she would fight them. They would not know they sheltered an enemy within the walls of Ripon House, but that is what she would become in order to protect Adelia.

CHAPTER 36

The back garden of Number 625 Fifth Avenue is looking rather peaked since winter reappeared a couple of days ago, blown in as it was on the currents of a late cold spell. The tulip and daffodil blossoms have disintegrated under a dusting of snow and the city's chimneys are belching smoke eighteen hours a day turning the sky an ugly gray. The climate and atmosphere match my mood perfectly.

Margaret Ballard's sketched image stares from the front page of this rag. Another blasted article about her murder and her connection to the family. Best toss the paper in the fireplace where it will turn to ash before one of the servants catches sight. My thoughts race in rhythm with my steps on the library floor. The ghost of my single greatest mistake haunts me, playing havoc with my peace of mind.

Perhaps I am a masochist, but I cannot stop myself replaying scenes from that day. When I close my eyes, Margaret stands before me with her hand on the door in the garden wall. My hand on her arm halts her progress. She looks up at me in surprise, a touch of irritation marring her lovely features. When I present the coin to her, fear replaces the irritation. She opens the garden door and walks away. I am left with no option but to follow.

She actually rejected the gift. She ordered me to replace it and turned her back on me. Rejection and being ordered about like an underling is a state I do not tolerate. It was then my rage took hold and led to her demise.

There has been no Event since that day and the need for release is possessing me, taking on a life of its own. It demands all of my will not to venture into the night and hunt down a whore, but New York is on high alert. Extra police patrols have been shifted to the areas where I have done my best work.

I must—No, I will—find a way. After all, I always have.

CHAPTER 37

Sarah Anne glanced at the watch pinned to her blouse and quickened her pace. She had been gone from the house much longer than she should have. Her boots crunched on the crushed oyster shells of the back driveway as she broke into a near run. Figures peering from the schoolroom window told her Adelia and Eliza were anxiously awaiting her return. Pray her employers had not noticed her absence. Being dismissed now would spell disaster for everyone.

She slipped through the backdoor into the service hall to discover Mrs. Bogard blocking her way. The housekeeper took in Sarah Anne's flushed face and raised an eyebrow. "You've been gone too long, but I covered for you. Mrs. Littlewood sent for Eliza to fetch a shawl from her bedroom. I went instead. If asked, say you felt ill and had extended need of the water closet. Then you rested in your room to ensure it was something you ate at luncheon which did not agree rather than a contagious illness." Mrs. Bogard's words snapped to a halt and she leaned closer. "I assume George was willing to enlighten you regarding the child?" Sarah Anne nodded. "Good, now get upstairs and take Miss Adelia's afternoon tea with you. It's ready on a tray in the kitchen."

The mention of food made Sarah Anne's stomach growl, reminding her she had not eaten all day. Her head swam with hunger and with all she had learned. Feeling lightheaded and shaky, she opened the kitchen door, but stopped halfway into the room where she found the maids Sookie and Lila Jane hard at work on dinner preparation and gossip.

"Boarding school, my foot." Lila Jane punched bread dough in a bowl on the table and cut her eyes at Sookie. "They ain't gonna send the girl to school. They're sending her to the asylum more like. Her daddy done threatened it often enough."

Sookie's eyes grew wide. "You think it'll be over at Milledgeville or somewhere up north?"

Lila Jane shook her head. "God bless her if it's Milledgeville. My grandmother's sister was sent there when she was just ten years old. She had fits so bad they couldn't handle her at home. She died after about a year in that place. Grandma said they kept her sister locked in a cage the whole time she was there."

Sookie's intake of breath was audible. "Poor little girl and poor Miss Adelia if . . ." Her lips snapped shut when she caught sight of Sarah Anne standing in the doorway.

Sarah Anne picked up the tea tray from the hunt board and smiled at the girls. She hoped the maids understood she would not reveal the content or extent of their gossiping. They looked at her with neutral expressions then finally returned her smile. Thank goodness for small things. The girls seemed to know she meant them no harm and they clearly felt compassion for Adelia. At this point, Sarah Anne and Adelia needed allies wherever they could find them. She nodded at the maids, smiled again, and left the kitchen.

Rather than use the service stairs, she headed toward the front entrance and the grand staircase. Adelia's parents would be less likely to question her if they saw she carried a heavy tray laden with their daughter's meal. At least, she hoped that would be the case. As she entered the foyer from the service hall, the sound of angry hisses reached her.

Mr. and Mrs. Littlewood stood in the center of the entrance hall clearly engaged in some sort of confrontation. Adelia's mother held her husband's forearm in a tight grip while her upturned face, drained of color, created the impression of the powdery mask of an earlier century.

Her red-rimmed eyes indicated she had been crying. Desperation radiated from her every pore. Both parents hissed at one another until they sensed they were not alone then turned as a body to face the intruder.

Mr. Littlewood spoke first. "I see you have recovered sufficiently to return to your duties. Send the maid currently with Adelia to Mrs. Littlewood's suite with cold compresses and tea. I fear she is overwrought and must lie down."

He shook his arm to release his wife's grip and grasped hers instead. Together, they moved toward the staircase, but Mrs. Littlewood's halting steps communicated her reluctance to accompany her husband. At the foot of the staircase, Mrs. Littlewood rocked back on her heels making Mr. Littlewood stumble. She looked at Sarah Anne as though silently communicating a plea until her husband jerked her up to the first step and they began their ascent.

Sarah Anne watched their progress with a heavy heart. The argument had clearly affected Mrs. Littlewood. Whether she was angry or frightened was impossible to ascertain, but whatever the subject, the confrontation had left her depleted. Where Adelia's fate was concerned, that woman was the child's only hope. For once, she must put her daughter first if Adelia was to have any chance, but experience had taught Sarah Anne to prepare for the worst. She must have a plan. Would taking Adelia to St. Anne without permission be considered kidnapping under Georgia law? Pray she would not have to find out.

It was some days later that Eliza appeared at the schoolroom door. "Miz Bogard says you need to come to her office."

Sarah Anne rose from the school table and shot the maid an inquiring look over Adelia's head. Eliza rolled her eyes and shrugged. "She say I should stay with Miss Adelia cause you gotta to come right now."

Sarah Anne dreaded what awaited her and approached the housekeeper's domain with trepidation. Once admitted, she was surprised to find a tea table set for two. Mrs. Bogard smiled and waved at the chair opposite her. “Sit. I have news.”

As she took her seat, Sarah Anne felt as though she had tumbled down Alice’s rabbit hole and come face-to-face with the Queen of Hearts.

CHAPTER 38

The coals in the library's grate are sighing into crumbling to ash, but I shall not bestir myself to add more fuel. The days are growing warmer as spring settles into full bloom and still I have not found release. No, New York is still too much on high alert and the risk to myself too great.

It is time for the family to return to New York, but I have heard no word of their coming north. Just the opposite, in fact. For some inexplicable reason, they have decided to stay in Georgia and are demanding I come south. Perhaps returning to Ripon House is an opportunity I should consider.

Returning to the island will work in my favor far better than anyone might realize. I shall find safe release in that backwater. The yokel sheriff will never suspect a member of the Littlewood family and I am sure the whores in that hellhole are in need of my corrective touch. I will not make the same mistake I did once before. After all, I am not insane. My self-control will be evidence of my mental stability. And there is another completely separate attraction in Georgia, as well.

I have finally discovered a woman worthy of my attention, and by God, I will have her, social class and family notwithstanding. Her behavior has always been beyond reproach and without outward indication of what she might feel for me. That is appropriate and as it should be. It is times such as these when a gentleman must join the game and become its master. A woman beyond price must be wooed in a manner that in no way subjects her to gossip or ridicule. I will take care, but I know the truth. She may play at being disinterested, but she desires me as much as I am obsessed with her. I can admit obsession. It is not a sign of mental weakness. Only a truly sane, confident man can look his need in the eye and remain as calm as I.

CHAPTER 39

Mrs. Bogard filled Sarah Anne's teacup and then her own. After adding milk and sugar in copious quantities to her cup, she leaned forward over the table and spoke in a low voice. "Did you see anyone in the hall before you entered?"

Surprised by the apparent desire for secrecy, Sarah Anne shook her head and the housekeeper continued, "I have news which affects you and the child. The household is not returning to the city until June. This is most unusual. We should already have departed for New York and yet we remain. Benson overheard Mr. and Mrs. Littlewood discussing Miss Adelia in regard to your situation. Apparently, they agreed you will never set foot in the New York house, but for once, Mrs. Littlewood stood up to her husband. It was she who insisted they remain here until arrangements can be made."

Sarah Anne jerked back as her breath caught in her throat. She studied the housekeeper before asking, "What do they mean by arrangements?"

"I don't know for certain, but Benson and I fear the worst. Mr. Littlewood wants an excuse to put her away. I just know it. You must keep her calm no matter what happens."

"Mr. Benson is on our side?"

"Oh, yes. He feels very sorry for the little girl. He has daughters of his own and is appalled by how Miss Adelia is treated."

Sarah Anne stopped herself saying that it was hard to imagine the butler with children much less married. "An important ally like Mr. Benson is very welcome. Did he hear anything else of importance?"

The color drained from Mrs. Bogard's face as she looked away. "I hardly know how to tell you. It just breaks my heart to think it."

Sarah Anne grabbed the housekeeper's hand. "You must tell me if it affects Miss Adelia."

"Benson said the word Milledgeville came up, but Mrs. Littlewood became very agitated and began wailing, so he couldn't understand anything more. I take it that is not a very nice place."

Sarah Anne could hardly breathe. She swiped at angry tears trickling down her cheeks. "How could they? How could they do that to their child? Milledgeville is a horrible place where the inmates are kept in cages and worse." Only when her words ceased did she realize she had been shouting.

Mrs. Bogard seemed to wilt like a flower exposed to flames. "Oh, dear. I feared as much. Something must be done. The child will not survive such a place."

"No, she won't, but I am at a loss for how to protect her. If only Mr. Jacob were here. He might be able to stop them."

Mrs. Bogard straightened and seemed suddenly lighter. "In my upset, I forgot to mention it. The young men are coming down in two weeks."

"All of them?"

"Yes, all three. They will stay until the household moves back to the city."

Relief washed through Sarah Anne at the thought of Jacob and John's return. Surely they would help Adelia. Of course they would. They were the good fellas.

Sarah Anne traversed the stairs feeling happier than she had in weeks. Elation shouldn't be the emotion uppermost in her heart, but she could not help herself. Joy lifted her spirit and lightened her step. She couldn't deny her feelings for John and Jacob even though their interest in her appeared to have waned. As personally disappointing as it may be, the absence of romantic complications would be for the best because they could focus on Adelia's plight. Jacob could prevent his father making a disastrous decision regarding Adelia and John could share his theories of who killed Miss Ballard. If they could solve the mystery, perhaps they could get to the bottom of Adelia's emotional problems. Something was not right in the Littlewood family and John was in a position to know what it was. Together, the three of them would protect Adelia from her father's evil plan.

Warmed by the vision, Sarah Anne held back the smile that wanted to burst across her features as wicked thoughts popped into her head. Too bad the odious Oliver would be with them. It was surprising he was not required in New York to dance attendance upon his intended and her unpleasant parents. But maybe New York was becoming too uncomfortable for him. She immediately stamped out the uncharitable idea. She had no proof, none whatsoever, that Oliver was anything more than an officious boor.

Two weeks can drag as though burdened with a ball and chain when one is awaiting their passing in anticipation. Such was the case for Sarah Anne. She did not tell Adelia the boys, as she had come to think of them, were coming for fear the child would become overly excited and cause yet another scene.

The morning of the impending arrival, Adelia bounded into Sarah Anne's room. "Eliza said my brothers and cousin are arriving today. Did you know? Why didn't you tell me?"

Sarah Anne turned from the washstand and studied her charge. The child twisted the hem of her dress into a wad while she fairly danced on the carpet. Perhaps the truth would serve her best. "Because I was afraid you would work yourself into a fit and I see I'm not far from right. Straighten your dress and stand still. We have lessons waiting for us." Adelia's reaction to the news did nothing to allay Sarah Anne's fears about the Littlewoods or the child's future. Keeping to their normal routine seemed the best plan for the present. Once John and Jacob were settled in, she would figure out a way to enlist their help without drawing her employers' attention.

Just before luncheon, the clattering of activity in the foyer and male voices drifted up to the schoolroom. An extra heartbeat shuddered beneath Sarah Anne's bodice. She fought the desire to run to the balcony railing for a peek at the arrivals.

Adelia had taken notice of the sounds as well for she accidentally dropped her paintbrush onto the botanical illustration she was creating, sending watercolor splattering over the project. She lifted rounded eyes to Sarah Anne, but did not speak.

Sarah Anne gave the child an encouraging smile. "Do you want to greet them now or would you rather wait?"

Adelia's mouth became a thin line as she thought about her answer. Finally, she shook her head. "No. I need to start over with my picture of the island." She held the ruined project up for Sarah Anne's inspection. "See? I've messed it up. I want it just right for when I have to go back to New York. I hate the city. I wish I could stay here forever."

It was odd that Adelia had not rushed down to see Jacob as she had in the past. Perhaps she was upset with him for forgetting her birthday or maybe she wanted to avoid Oliver. The elder brother had never been particularly interested in or kind to the child. Sarah Anne certainly had no desire to be in his company. In fact, she could not prevent herself wanting to cast him in the role of criminal even though she had no reason other than instinct and animus. On the other hand, she would dearly love to see Jacob and John.

Sarah Anne's inclination was to say the project could wait, but thought better of it. The child was concentrating so hard on the watercolor of local plant life that the tip of her tongue protruded from the corner of her mouth. Sarah Anne had come to recognize her complete absorption in something as a sign Adelia was dealing with difficult emotions. It was almost as if the child was in a trance for she neither heard nor saw anything other than the object of her focus when in such a mood. Sarah Anne remembered what it was like to desperately need distraction as a child. She tilted her head as she studied her student. Something was preventing Adelia running to see her favorite brother, but Sarah Anne could not see a logical explanation.

She was still considering the issue when Mrs. Bogard appeared at the open door. Her face was flushed and her breath came in short puffs. Rather than speaking, she jerked her head toward the hall. Sarah Anne eyed Adelia who was still deeply focused on her painting before following the housekeeper.

Mrs. Bogard looked about before leaning in to whisper. "There is a terrible row in the parlor between Mr. Jacob, Mr. John, and Mr. and Mrs. Littlewood. It's about you. The boys want you at dinner, but Mrs. Littlewood is adamant on the matter. She has bent only as far as saying you should bring Miss Adelia down before her bedtime. I think it is the Littlewoods' intention that the young men have as little contact with you as possible. You are to bring the child down precisely at seven o'clock. And one more thing. Benson said the parents told Jacob and Oliver there is distressing news regarding their sister and decisions must be made before they return to New York." The housekeeper's voice caught as she shook her head. "I fear the worst."

A storm built within Sarah Anne until it felt as though her chest would burst open releasing a tornado of anger and anxiety. Adelia must be protected, but Sarah Anne could not accomplish her goal if she acted rashly. In the past, she would have rushed headlong into the situation and dealt with the consequences afterward. If she had learned anything during her time at Ripon House, it was that she must act and speak with discretion and forethought. She could no longer afford the luxury of acting impetuously.

She placed a hand on each of the housekeeper's shoulders and looked down into her eyes. "We can prevent harm befalling the child if we are willing to accept the risk. Will you help no matter the cost?"

CHAPTER 40

Mrs. Bogard's face drained of color.

A tremble passed beneath Sarah Anne's hands where they gripped the housekeeper's shoulders. She broke eye contact and remained quiet for several beats. When a flush of pink crept across the housekeeper's face, Sarah Anne decided to press on.

"Please, Mrs. Bogard, please help. I know you care about Adelia. Mr. Benson and George do also. As individuals, we are pretty powerless, but together we may be able to protect her."

She shook her head before responding, "I don't see how, but yes, I will do what I can. I will alert Benson. He may not be willing to act on your behalf, but he is a vital source of information. I cannot predict how George will react. You must ask him yourself."

Sarah Anne smiled and dropped her hands to her side. "Bless you. You are a treasure, Mrs. Bogard."

The housekeeper was a study in surprise tinged with pleasure. "I never thought I would hear such from you, but then I guess we've learned a thing or two about one another." As the tall case clock in the foyer began striking the hour, a sad smile creased her brow. She hesitated then patted Sarah Anne's arm. "Don't worry, my dear. We will take care of our girl. Now, I must return to my duties before someone marks my absence."

With mixed emotions, Sarah Anne watched her nemesis-turned-ally waddle away. Trusting the housekeeper had come with difficulty, but acting alone was out of the question. Pride was said to be a deadly sin. If such were true, she would never make it into heaven. Her pride had gotten her into trouble on too many occasions in the past.

Aunt Edith had despaired of a girl who thought herself the equal of anyone regardless of gender or social position. Humility, gentility, and submission were a Southern woman's calling cards in Aunt Edith's opinion, but she had failed in her mission to pound those qualities into Sarah Anne. Her pride would have to be kept in check if she had any hope of helping Adelia.

It was after luncheon that work in the schoolroom was interrupted for a second time. Sarah Anne stood at the window hoping for a glimpse of Jacob or John, folly to be sure, but an activity from which she couldn't dissuade herself. Fleet footsteps bounding up the staircase interrupted her vigil. The sound drew nearer and she turned as the two faces she most wanted to see appeared in the doorway, sending a warm glow throughout her. In contrast, Adelia sat stiff-backed with rounded eyes and downturned mouth. Whatever was wrong with the child, she communicated her displeasure without uttering a word.

Hoping to cover her pupil's distress, Sarah Anne scurried to the door. "Good afternoon, gentlemen. To what do we owe this pleasure?"

"We thought a visit to the schoolroom was in order since neither of you deigned to greet us when we arrived." Jacob leaned to catch a glimpse of Adelia. "Does my favorite sister no longer love me? Won't you come say hello, my little Sweet Pea?"

Upon hearing herself described thus, Adelia placed her paintbrush on its rest and joined the trio at the door. Instead of jumping into her brother's arms as she had in the past, she fairly hid behind Sarah Anne's skirts. Jacob shot Sarah Anne a quizzical look. She lifted her brow to communicate her own confusion over the child's rudeness.

Jacob bent down on one knee and peered around Sarah Anne. "I'm sorry I forgot your birthday. It was a terrible thing to do. Benson told me Miss Mercer had a lovely picnic for you with your friend Eliza. Would it make any difference if I told you I was cramming for my final examinations? I've graduated and will sit for the bar next month. Surely that's a fine reason for being forgetful."

Although the words were intended to make amends with Adelia, they also lifted Sarah Anne's spirits. He hadn't written because he had been overwhelmed.

Spying a gaily wrapped package held behind his back, Sarah Anne said, "I am wondering what you have there. Is it a present for me?"

Jacob grinned and winked. "I am desolate, but alas it is not. It's for someone else, but she doesn't seem to want to speak to me, so I guess I'll have to give it to some other little girl."

Adelia stepped forward, her mouth puckered up in a pout. "Don't speak about me as though I am a baby." Her expression and tone mimicked her mother, but her eyes softened. "Did you really bring me something?"

"I did, but you must give me a hug before you can have it."

Adelia jumped into his arms sending the gift tumbling to the floor. John picked it up and handed it to Sarah Anne. "It seems all is forgiven. Perhaps, Miss Mercer, you might give me a few moments after dinner so that I may make amends for my failures of correspondence. I, too, have an explanation, however feeble it might be."

Sarah Anne gazed into his eyes. Though she found his manner arrogant and presumptuous, whatever his excuse, she knew she would probably forgive him. "Of course. Perhaps after Adelia is in bed."

"Excellent. I will make my excuses to leave the table as soon as dinner is finished." He bent slightly and caught her free hand. Brushing it with his lips, he continued, "Until then."

Watching him turn and walk away stirred conflicting emotions. Social customs dictated she should be aloof until he had acquitted himself, and though somewhat angry, she could not keep excitement at bay.

The sound of a throat clearing interrupted her thoughts. Jacob was now looking at her with a quizzical expression. "I hope I too might have a word in the near future. Since my cousin will no doubt consume what time you will have after dinner, may I request tomorrow morning?"

Sarah Anne hardly knew how to respond. "I would be delighted, but my duty lies in the schoolroom."

"Of course. How inconsiderate of me. Perhaps I might send one of the maids to sit with Adelia tomorrow so you and I might spend a moment together. Would it be suitable?"

"I believe I could manage it. Please send Eliza. She is Adelia's favorite." Looking at the child, she continued, "You would like that, wouldn't you?"

Though she nodded in agreement, the child's face was inscrutable. Whatever she was feeling, it was not joy. Perhaps she was disappointed or jealous that Sarah Anne was to spend time with someone other than herself. A change of subject was in order.

"Adelia, I wonder what Mr. Jacob has brought you. Don't you want to open your gift?"

Opening the package and finding a complete assortment of artist's supplies returned Adelia to good spirits. As she skipped to the art table, Jacob took his leave.

The smile he bestowed on Sarah Anne held both warmth and affection. "Until tomorrow."

As she watched him follow his cousin down the stairs, she considered their visit. So, they both had been too busy to write. It was less than flattering. On the other hand, she well remembered what the final push before graduation was like and it must be much more so in law school. In addition, John's excuse may well be feeble, but he clearly must want her company for he had no other reason to visit the schoolroom.

John and Adelia had only the most limited affection for one another. In fact, one might say they merely tolerated one another. Of course, John did not seem to have particular patience with the child, but then she was difficult and became more so in his presence. If they only knew how lucky they were to have one another, but the Littlewood family relationships were out of her experience.

For that matter, it was odd Jacob's parents had not attended his graduation. The Littlewoods were unlike any parents she had ever known in their disregard for the important events in their children's lives. However strange the family dynamics, one thing was certain.

Time alone with Jacob and John would offer the opportunity she needed to enlist their assistance where Adelia's future was concerned. It would be hard to put aside the hope she harbored where the young men were concerned, but the child's situation must be paramount.

The remainder of the day dragged by as only time does when one is anticipating a longed-for reunion. In the afternoon, Eliza delivered a note from John requesting Sarah Anne meet him in the back garden at eleven o'clock, sending her spirits soaring. The time was not particularly convenient, but he could not have left his relatives any sooner to be sure. Lost sleep was a small price.

At the appointed hour, Sarah Anne made her way down the service stairs and out to a small gazebo near the stables. Her favorite place for reading and taking the air would be made even more special now. The thought of a midnight assignation made Sarah Anne want to giggle. When she entered the enclosure, John rose and offered her his arm.

"Shall we walk a bit? The dining room was very stuffy and I feel the need of the sea breeze."

They walked the path toward the boathouse in silence. When they were some distance from the house, John finally stopped and turned so that he faced Sarah Anne. "I fear you believe me to have grown indifferent due to my failure to correspond. I must apologize and make amends. Please believe that my feelings for you have only grown in my absence. If you will permit, I might say I have become devoted to you. Please say I am forgiven and you are not offended by my expression of affection."

Caught off guard by his forthrightness, Sarah Anne took a moment to consider her reply. Finally, she said, "I'm gratified by your declaration. I should be coy and tell you that you must not say such things, but it would be disingenuous and I hate dishonesty." She smiled and continued in a teasing tone, "You will be forgiven only if you tell me the reason for your silence."

John dropped his gaze then met hers with full force. "I have been on the trail of the criminal who has stalked New York these past months and I fear I may have uncovered his identity."

"Oh, my goodness. I never expected such a revelation. You are absolutely forgiven. Will you tell whom you suspect?"

"I will, but only because it affects you."

Sarah Anne drew back in shock. "Me? That's impossible. I've never been to New York and won't be going when the family heads north. They have made it abundantly clear."

John took her hand so firmly a tingle shot up her arm. "I hardly know how to say this. It is not New York you should fear, rather, it is Ripon House."

Sarah Anne's knees betrayed her. If John had not caught her elbow, she would have fallen to the ground at his feet. Recovering her equilibrium, she blurted, "But who? Who among you could possibly do such things?"

"You should know that in my capacity as an investigative journalist the police allowed me to read the transcripts of interviews with the victims. They contained descriptions not revealed to the public. I am sworn to secrecy until the man has been apprehended, but I cannot keep the promise where you are concerned."

"You are frightening me out of my wits. You must tell me now. Whom do you suspect and why?"

"The information to which I am privy involves certain articles of clothing worn by the assailant. The descriptions match jackets and vests I know for a fact belong to Jacob and Oliver. Since they use the same tailor, their clothes are very similar. In addition, there was an article found with one of the victims tying the crimes to this family."

Staggered beyond all reason, she stammered, "And . . . and do you suspect one or both?"

"I can hardly say, but if I had to select one, I suppose Oliver's personality fits better than Jacob's. Then again, how would Oliver have found the time to perpetrate these crimes? When not consumed with learning his father's businesses, he is dancing attendance on Miss Smythe. Jacob has seemed very frustrated in ways I must not describe to a young lady, but has rarely had his nose out of laws books this past year. I am confounded by these facts, yet I know the garments to belong to one of them. If, on the other hand, they worked in concert, it is conceivable both might be guilty."

Sarah Anne's heart felt as though it might rip its way from her chest. She could hardly think for the pounding of blood against her eardrums. Jacob could not be the fiend. He simply could not. She would have detected that in his character. Surely she would have. Oh, please let John be mistaken there.

Then, her eyes narrowed as she considered what he had told her. Something was missing in his explanation, something she could not quite put her finger on. Of the two he suspected, Oliver was certainly her choice. Her head spun until she was dizzy with the thought of a killer in Ripon House. Drawing a deep breath, she let it out slowly. She must get a grip. Giving in to silly feminine vapors would help no one, especially not Adelia or herself.

A sudden desire to get away came over her. She needed time to think, to sort out what John had told her. Could her instincts about people, and Jacob in particular, be so off kilter? She extended her hand, which he took. "Thank you for alerting me to the danger. May I depend on your protection for Adelia and me?"

John did not release her hand when she took a step back. "I will guard you with my life,"—his lip curled and a furrow grew between his brows—"but I see no reason for alarm where my little cousin is concerned. Why do you fear for her?" Even now, his did not hide his antipathy for the child.

Clearly, this was not the best time to mention Mr. Littlewood's threats of the asylum. Her need to get away from this conversation overtook her manners. "Another time, perhaps." Her words were brusque bordering on rudeness. "I must get back to Adelia. Please excuse me."

"I see I have upset you. It was not my intention, but you must understand my need to forewarn you."

"Of course and quite frankly, I am terrified. Now, I really must go."

"I will not allow you to return alone. The danger is too great." John tucked her hand under his arm and turned toward the house.

Although Sarah Anne had an inclination for solitude to process all she had learned, she saw the wisdom in his warning. Besides, she was too frightened to return to Ripon House unaccompanied. That damnable mausoleum possibly sheltered a killer. While her mind raced, they walked in silence until they reached the bottom of the grand staircase.

"May I call upon you tomorrow?"

"Yes, please do. I will feel better knowing you're near."

Tomorrow. Dear lord. She was to meet with Jacob in the morning. Her mind churned with everything John had revealed. How would she ever sleep?

But sleep she finally did. After hours of tossing and turning, she dropped into an exhausted slumber until Eliza shook her awake.

"Best get up, Miss Sarah Anne. Miss Adelia been awake for a hour and asking for you. She done had her breakfast, so I brought you some coffee and toast. It's on the tray over by the window."

Sarah Anne sat at the tray choking down the meal. Her head felt as though filled with clouds of cotton, but she had to marshal her thoughts. This was no time to be at less than her best. A knock at the door interrupted her brooding. When she opened it, Jacob greeted her with a smile. She studied him for a moment. His expression was guileless and filled with innocent eagerness. Nonetheless, she must be on her guard.

"You should not have come to my bedroom." A pinprick of guilt touched her when she saw Jacob's crestfallen expression. Her words had been sharp, rude even. Chalk it up to too little sleep and too much worry.

"I apologize for the liberty, but I simply couldn't wait any longer to see you. I have something to say to you. May I come in or will you step out into the hall?"

Again, she assessed Jacob's demeanor. He was either a very good actor or he bore no blame. Furthermore, his affection for his little sister was beyond doubt and they needed his help with his parents. "I have something I must tell you, as well." She glanced at either end of the hall. "Please come inside."

When she closed the door behind them, surprise and pleasure in turn flitted over his face. In fact, he appeared young, carefree, and full of joy. Relief flickered through Sarah Anne. He clearly had no knowledge evil was afoot. How much should she reveal? Sarah Anne made a quick decision as she placed a hand on his forearm. "Adelia is in danger. You must help us." Her words were harsh and abrupt.

His face turned to stone. "What on earth do you mean?"

Sarah Anne recounted all she had learned about his parents' plans for the child, including the overhearing of proposals involving the nightmare of Milledgeville, where Georgia housed its insane in appalling conditions. Jacob said nothing, but he looked at Sarah Anne as though she had just admitted to some horrible crime or might herself be mentally unbalanced.

Shaking his head, he said, "I do not believe you. My parents are not the ogres you paint them to be. Granted, Father has never shown Adelia much affection, but she has always been a difficult child. He is not a monster. I will hear no more of these slanderous accusations."

It was only after he stormed from the room that Sarah Anne remembered he had come to her with the intention of telling her something. Now, she would probably never know what he had wanted to say. She had anticipated his being upset by her revelations, but not the manner in which they had affected him. His anger had seared her with such intensity she was relieved when he left. He had accused her of lying when all she wanted was to protect his little sister. This wholly unexpected turn had caught her off guard and set her reeling. If he reacted thusly to a request for help for the little sister he professed to adore, what else was hidden beneath that glittering façade? The realization of the likely answer fairly broke her heart.

CHAPTER 41

The Atlantic breeze catching the fabric of my cravat, lifting it against my cheek, reminds me of the touch of a woman. I often shudder at my memories of female contact. A woman's caress should be gentle and given selflessly to those to whom she owes her devotion. Mothers have a duty to provide such loving contact with their children. Too bad my own mother had been a selfish whore who thought only of her own pleasure and needs. She had watched with nary a concern while her paramour had beaten me, mocked me, used me.

I was just a small boy trying to protect my mother's honor. It was a thankless task. As it turned out, she had no honor to protect. My father should have kept better watch over his house, but he was too involved elsewhere to see the viper in his nest until it was too late. But that life is over and I must bury those memories. I must collect myself. Everything I have ever wanted is within my grasp, but only if I plan carefully.

Riding on the beach today has given me some respite. Rolling breakers always soothe me. The way the sand sighs as the foam kisses it is the aquatic equivalent of a child's reaction to his mother's caress. It is a happy condition I have never enjoyed. I know my desire to punish whores has surely grown out of my childhood experiences, but in no way does this knowledge mitigate my need for release. In some ways, it increases my desire to create an Event. The next will be my last for I have found a higher purpose and my blood roils at the knowledge of all I hope to achieve. Despite this confounded agitation, I have reason for exaltation.

Soon she will know how much I adore her, how I am obsessed with her and our future together. Once she is mine, I will no longer need to create Events with strangers. She will submit to my desires as only a wife must. My Sarah Anne will fulfill her duties with joy. I have seen her yearning and it matches my own.

CHAPTER 42

A scream from the attic split the quiet of the schoolroom and sent Sarah Anne and Adelia flying to the hall. The cry from above was definitely Mrs. Bogard's. Unable to leave the child unattended in such circumstances, Sarah Anne could only wait in agitation as footsteps pounded on stairs from above and below. Within a moment, the housekeeper appeared on the attic stairs, her face the color of ginned cotton and her eyes wide as a hundred-acre field.

Coming to rest beside Sarah Anne, the housekeeper placed her hands on her knees and spoke between gasps. "Get Mr. Benson. Something horrible has happened." She nodded toward the ceiling.

Leaving the child beside Mrs. Bogard, Sarah Anne made it as far as the head of the staircase where she was met by not only the butler, but also all the men of the house. Mr. Littlewood pushed his way to the head of the group.

"For the love of God, what the hell is going on up here?" His eyes fixed on Sarah Anne in accusation.

"I'm sorry, but I'm not really sure. Mrs. Bogard seems to have made a discovery in the attic."

All eyes set upon the housekeeper. Having recovered some of her composure, she pointed above their heads. "Go see for yourselves what's up there. I'm taking Miss Mercer and Miss Adelia downstairs with me."

It was doubtful a servant had ever spoken to Mr. Littlewood in such a manner, but he did as he was bidden. The quality of Mrs. Bogard's voice communicated such urgency and terror it was impossible to ignore. Sarah Anne pulled Adelia back into the schoolroom doorway enabling the men to pass. When they disappeared, the housekeeper grabbed Sarah Anne's hand.

"Come down with me now. You and the child should not see what they will find."

Sarah Anne followed the housekeeper, but paused at the head of the stairs and glanced back over her shoulder at the entrance to the attics. She needed to know what had happened up there, yet dreaded the knowledge. Every instinct told her their lives were about to change forever.

When they reached the kitchen, the sound of buzzing bees greeted them. All of the female staff were gathered awaiting an explanation for the disturbance. Mrs. Bogard took charge.

"Get back to your duties. You will be informed of the situation when Mr. Benson deems it necessary." As she took in each of the maids with her sharp expression, she continued, "On second thought, no one is to go up to the third floor or to use the grand staircase." Her gaze swept the room, alighting upon Eliza. She crooked her finger and Eliza came over at once. The housekeeper leaned close to the maid and whispered, "See to Miss Adelia. Take her to my office and lock the door. Do not open it to anyone other than myself, Miss Mercer, or Mrs. Littlewood."

Amidst the confusion, Sarah Anne had completely forgotten Mrs. Littlewood's existence. Had she heard the cry? It was anyone's guess. Her rooms were on the opposite side of the house and two floors below. Although most people would wonder why the child was not taken to her mother with such turmoil afoot, Sarah Anne was grateful for the housekeeper's understanding.

After Eliza and Adelia were behind the locked door of her office, Mrs. Bogard caught Sarah Anne's hand and drew her into the hall while she whispered, "Come with me to the morning room. We won't be disturbed there."

Once they were settled side-by-side on the sofa, Sarah Anne cast an evaluative gaze over the housekeeper. "Let me get some tea or coffee. You are shaking from shock."

"No, I'll be all right in a minute. I just need to sit and calm down." After several beats, her breathing became more normal. "I must tell you what has happened." She took Sarah Anne's hand and held it firmly between her own. "You must take great care for we have a murderer in the house. Sookie has been killed and that is not the worst of it. I could see from the state she was left in she had been . . . I hardly know how to say it to a young lady."

Despite her growing horror, Sarah Anne spoke with determination. "Just tell me. I'm a doctor's niece and I studied biology. I know more about the physical side of life than most young women."

"Oh, my dear." Mrs. Bogard's voice broke with unshed tears. "The poor child was violated. That evil man choked the life out of her, tore the clothes from her body, and violated her innocence. To think we have such a villain in the house makes my blood run cold."

Sarah Anne did not want to believe it. In accepting what Mrs. Bogard said, she would acknowledge that someone she cared about might be a criminal or worse. It would be so easy to run screaming from the room, but it would do no good. Instead of giving in to her fear, she buried it beneath the steel of her resolve. "You're sure it couldn't have been someone from outside the household?"

"I wish it were otherwise, but I feel certain the man dwells within these walls. The doors and windows were not disturbed during the night. No one could have entered without notice. I saw all of the maids to bed last night and Sookie did not appear for servants' breakfast this morning. That's when I summoned George. I felt it best not to alarm the others needlessly. While he searched the grounds and outbuildings, I searched indoors. I'm not sure what made me think to search the attics. I suppose it is knowing that you and the child have played there. I wish I'd never gone up those stairs. The vision will haunt me to the end of my days."

Sarah Anne felt as though her heart had shattered for her worst fears had been confirmed. One of the three young men must be guilty, but which one? John had come close to accusing his cousins, but that in no way put him in the clear. Terror wrapped its claws around her heart and squeezed until her breath came in short gasps. If only she could give in and just leave this horrible house and all of its misery. But instead of fleeing danger, she must stare it in the face. She must hold her fear deep inside until it choked her if it was necessary to save the child.

Tension permeated the days following the discovery of Sookie's body. The sheriff and his deputy came and went at all hours without heeding either the Littlewoods' complaints or threats. Mr. Littlewood fumed and cursed, but the sheriff would not be dissuaded from his duty. Unlike her employer, Sarah Anne was not surprised for she knew what Mr. Littlewood did not. Sheriff Caldwell may appear a backwoods, ignorant yokel, but he had a steely regard for the law and upheld it without consideration to rank or position of the guilty. Still, after one week of interrogating the family and servants without mercy, the sheriff was no closer to solving the mystery.

Ripon House now lived up to Mayweather County's long held belief that the boil erected by the Yankee industrialist on their beautiful home island was indeed filled with festering corruption. Sookie's parents were brought in from their sharecropper's holding to claim the body, which added fuel to already smoldering coals of resentment. When the coals threatened to burst into flame, the sheriff ordered the ferryman to cease all passenger transport to the island unless personally authorized by him or his deputy. It was the only time Sarah Anne had ever heard white men calling for vigilante action to avenge the murder of a Colored and it would probably never happened again. Sheriff Caldwell might be a true guardian of law and justice, but he lived and worked in South Georgia.

The realities of her home region had never been lost on Sarah Anne. This defense of a Negro girl was a passing fiction. It just went to show how disliked Mr. Littlewood was in the county. He had made fierce enemies when he constructed Ripon House, but he seemed unfazed by their hatred if he even knew it existed.

As hard as she tried to keep Adelia from knowing what had happened, the task had been impossible in the end. The child seemed to have a sixth sense for secrets and had figured it out. Sarah Anne could not get the truth out of Adelia regarding who she feared or what she knew, but since the discovery, she had insisted upon sleeping in Sarah Anne's bed. Under ordinary circumstances this was something Sarah Anne would never have allowed, but their circumstances were about as far from ordinary as it was possible to get.

Sarah Anne had just tucked Adelia in and settled herself in a chair to read when Eliza slipped into the room. She drew near and whispered, "They want you in the library. They're all there and it ain't good. They told me to stay here until you get back."

Sarah Anne approached the closed library doors with her heart hammering. She drew several deep breaths before knocking.

Mr. Littlewood's voice boomed from the other side. "Enter."

As she approached, Mr. Littlewood made a chopping motion and all conversation ceased. The room's climate was absolutely electric with tension. Sarah Anne came to rest beside the fireplace where the five family members were gathered.

"You wished to speak to me, sir?"

"Would I have asked for you otherwise?" Her employer's voice dripped sarcasm. "Tell me where my daughter sleeps these days."

Sarah Anne sensed a trap, but saw no way out. "With me, sir. The events of this week have frightened her terribly."

"I see. And you have been unable to reassure her?"

"I'm not sure anyone would be able to do so with what has occurred. She is a child in a house where murder has been committed."

Mr. Littlewood's fist smashed down on the table next to his chair sending his whiskey glass crashing to the floor. "Don't you think I know what has happened under my own roof? But it does not affect the child. She is not in danger. This is clear evidence of her hysteria." He looked at each of his relatives with a sharpness that set Sarah Anne's nerves tingling. "This settles the matter. You may leave us, Miss Mercer."

Before Sarah Anne could take a step, Jacob was on his feet. His position prevented her exit. "Father, you can't mean this. Adelia is eight years old. Anyone with common decency would understand why a small child would be afraid." He looked to his mother for backing. "You must for once in your life stand against his cruelty. I have no idea why you let him treat your child as he does, but it will stop now or I will file a custody case claiming cruelty and neglect."

Mr. Littlewood emitted a humorless laugh. "And you would lose on day one if the case ever got to court. A man's family is his to command."

"Possibly, but just think of the delicious scandal. A man's own son accuses him of cruelty toward the family's youngest, most vulnerable member. The mother stands by and allows her husband to neglect their child. It would make excellent fodder for the gossip rags. Don't you agree, Cousin?"

All eyes turned to John, who did not immediately reply. When he did answer, Sarah Anne could hardly process his words. "I'm afraid I must agree with your father. Your sister has always been a troubled child and I believe the situation has pushed her over the edge into the realm of mental instability."

Sarah Anne could no longer hold her tongue. Rage consumed her. "How could you? How could any of you consider this? She's a wonderful child if only you would get to know her. But that's the problem. None of you knows the real little girl beneath the façade you have forced her to adopt." She held her entwined hands out in supplication. "Please, I beg you. Don't do this."

CHAPTER 43

No one, not even Jacob, answered Sarah Anne's plea. After looking at her in surprise, he stepped out of her way, allowing her to flee the room. He was no doubt astonished that a girl who needed a job would dare speak thusly to her employers. And as for John, she would gladly murder him for his despicable words.

Bile rose in her throat as her stomach rolled with the fury she had been unable to express. To hell with Jacob and John. To hell with all of them. As she ascended the grand staircase, she reached a decision. Adelia knew more than she had told. Tonight that would end. For everyone's sake, the child must reveal everything she knew or even suspected. Oncc shc had the information, Sarah Anne would then decide how best to proceed.

Entering their now shared bedroom, she did not even try to be quiet. The door banged shut under the force of her shove, making Eliza jump and waking Adelia.

"I'll be going now, Miss."

"No you won't. You'll stay and help me convince Miss Adelia to tell us what she knows about this murder and another in New York." Catching sight of the signs of an impending tantrum, she went to the bed, gathered the child onto her lap, and mustered the most soothing tone she could manage. "It's time to tell me everything. I can't keep you safe if I don't know what you're hiding."

Adelia's lower lip trembled and tears streamed down her cheeks. She buried her face in Sarah Anne's blouse and mumbled, "I can't. You know I can't."

There are times when the truth, no matter how painful, must be revealed. This was one of those times. Moving the child away from her until their eyes met, Sarah Anne recounted what had transpired in the library, finishing with, "So you must see your father will make good on his threat unless we can convince him otherwise."

"But I told him long ago. He didn't believe me and that's when he started talking about the asylum."

Sarah Anne tilted her head and fixed the child with relentless scrutiny. "Tell me exactly what you said to your father."

"I can't."

Distressed and driven by fear for the future, Sarah Anne sucked in a breath in an effort to maintain control. She wanted to shake the information from the child. Adelia's obstinacy would spell her doom. As inner turmoil grew, an idea presented itself. Maybe a good shaking might loosen the girl's tongue. To Sarah Anne's eternal shame, she did just that until Eliza caught her arm.

"Stop, Miss. You gonna hurt the child. Won't do nobody no good." Eliza placed her hand atop Adelia's golden curls. "Child, you got to tell Miss Sarah Anne what you knows. It's the only way."

Sarah Anne grabbed each of Adelia's shoulder, forcing the child to meet her gaze. Terror and despair looked back. That one so young should feel such emotions broke her heart, but they were so close to answers. Sarah Anne couldn't stop now. "Tell us what you know."

Between shuttering sobs, Adelia at last said, "It was Cousin John."

A writhing snake stirred in the pit of Sarah Anne's stomach. It slithered its way upward until it reached her throat. "What makes you accuse him?" She had not intended to shout at the child, but the harshness in her voice caused Adelia to tremble. Failing to keep her own emotions in check would spell disaster. She swallowed hard and softened her tone. "Forgive me. I'm not angry with you. I'm just really frightened for all of us. Please tell me what you know."

With huge, terror-filled eyes, Adelia whispered her truth. "He killed Margaret. They went out the garden door together. He came back and nobody ever saw her again. I told my father that Margaret wouldn't leave me without saying goodbye." Her voice cracked on the final word as she buried her face in Sarah Anne's lap.

Taking Adelia by the shoulders and gently pulling her upright, Sarah Anne asked, "And what else did you tell your father?"

Between sobs, the child finished her story. "I told him John had done something bad to her, but Father didn't believe me. That's when he said I was disloyal to the family and mentally unbalanced."

As much as Sarah Anne hated to agree with anything the sorry bastard said she could in a way see his point. Adelia had not actually seen John kill Margaret Ballard. It was instinct rather than evidence that made the child accuse her cousin of murder. On the other hand, John seems to have been the last person to see Miss Ballard alive. Policemen were always deeply suspicious of such persons.

Desperate for some mitigating circumstance that might resolve the mysteries without pointing to John, Sarah Anne asked, "Is there anything else?"

Adelia nodded. "I've spied on Cousin John many times. I sneak out of bed and wait until he retires to his room. I was afraid he would try to hurt you like he did Margaret. I watched for him every night. Even the night with Sookie. I saw him take her upstairs to the attic, but only he came down. It was just like Margaret. He killed them both."

Sarah Anne felt she might be sick. Dear God. No wonder the child was so much more volatile when the boys were at Ripon House. She was getting far too little sleep in an attempt to protect the one she loved. Through her tears, Sarah Anne glanced at Eliza then met Adelia's gaze once more. "My precious lamb. You've carried such a burden all by yourself, but no more. You are not alone." The maid nodded as she swiped tears from her cheeks.

Rage, terror, and heartbreak washed over Sarah Anne in equal measures, but brought with them an inexplicable calm for now she knew. The knowledge left her drained, unable to speak. She gathered the child into her arms and held tight as though their world was ending. And in a terrible way, it was.

CHAPTER 44

Wind created by the motor craft's speed cools, sweeping away all sounds other than those of the engine and the hull slapping the water. Droplets of spray mingle with sweat trickling from my brow. I have been an idiot and now I, not some whore, am the prey. The very thought of capture is an abomination.

Why did I not wait? Why? I have been a fool all because that damnable maid directed her dubious charms my way and I could not control myself. It was Margaret Ballard all over again. The kind attention. The gentle glances. The feigned laughter at my attempts at humor. Those two women snared me in their webs. They were like black widow spiders wanting to suck the life from me. In the end, they were intolerable.

But Sarah Anne is another creature entirely. She has not adopted their pretense and is all the more worthy for it. Our life together will be so different from what I have known thus far. We will disappear together. The mistakes of my past will not be repeated. She is not like my mother.

Poor Papa. He really had no choice. My whore of a mother shamed him with her indiscretion, with the lover she took when he was away. I will never know exactly how he discovered her betrayal, but discover it he did and she paid for it with her life. Papa did not know his young son had been awakened by raised voices and that I watched through the keyhole of Mother's bedroom door. The gunshots echoed throughout the house and blood soaked the carpet where their bodies fell.

Uncle Littlewood was the first of the family to arrive. He took charge and saw to it there was no scandal. He paid the staff for their silence and fashioned a believable story of my parents' deaths at the hands of an intruder. He took charge of my life, as well. Being passed from relative to relative in a never-ending rotation made for an interesting, if somewhat nomadic existence.

My extended family was not particularly kind. Whenever they were displeased, they hinted at my dark past and bad blood being behind my misadventures. Is it any wonder I preferred being at my boarding school and faced term breaks with dread? They were correct, however, in one thing. My mother's bad blood was the root of all the evil in my life.

But my life with Sarah Anne will not be tarnished by that sin. We will be happy. She is not my mother. I will return for her when they have forgotten about me. They will never know she has escaped with me to a new life.

CHAPTER 45

Sarah Anne stood at her bedroom window with her head pressed against the glass. The coolness against her skin helped ease the fever of her anguish. It seemed the nightmare would never end. Only yesterday the sheriff received a cable from New York. The police had connected the rapes and Miss Ballard's murder to John and it was clear Sookie's murder followed the pattern. Two detectives with an arrest warrant and extradition papers were expected to arrive within the week.

The events had torn the lives of Ripon House asunder and Sarah Anne's sorrow over the part she had played grew with each passing hour. Her failure to recognize John's true nature and failure to protect Adelia would be heavy burdens for a long time to come. Adding to her misery, she had taken the only possible path in sharing the information learned from Adelia, but the grief-stricken faces of Jacob, Mrs. Littlewood, and Oliver haunted her. They really had no inkling of what John was capable. They had loved him—no, still loved him—and their hearts were broken.

Making matters worse, he was on the run. No one knew his whereabouts so no one could rest easy. It had been a period of shocking revelations for the mother and sons, but Mr. Littlewood's reaction was wholly different. When informed of the extent of his nephew-in-law's criminality, he seemed unsurprised. His only comment was to ask what one expected of bad blood. If she had to guess, Sarah Anne would say he had known or at least had suspected John's guilt for some time.

Mr. Littlewood had much to answer for, but at the top of the list was his treatment of Adelia. Sarah Anne would never forgive him for forcing the terrified child to return to her own bed. The poor little girl cried until she fell into an exhausted sleep each night. Why would a man inflict such on a child?

It was all so very confusing, depressing, and tragic. Since her arrival at Ripon House, Sarah Anne had sensed something was amiss within the family, but she had no inkling it would involve such evil.

She had been a fool in so many ways. She would never forgive herself for being blinded by John's glittering aura. He had seemed a shining knight when they first met and his golden aspect only began to dim toward the very end. His glow had been extinguished, but at great cost. If only she had pressed Adelia for the truth sooner, perhaps Sookie would still be alive.

Her greatest regret, however, was that she had ever suspected Jacob. Her days at Ripon House were now numbered, but she took consolation in knowing he would protect his sister once she was gone. It tore her heart to think she would never see him or Adelia again. But their lives were too different, the worlds they inhabited separated by a chasm too wide to cross.

She jammed a fist into her mouth to muffle sobs she could no longer be held in check.

CHAPTER 46

Despite the night-cooled air, tension and excitement heat me from within. I have chosen well. The abandoned cabin stands on a patch of ground concealed by encroaching forest, the building itself nearly consumed by wild grape vines. One last rattle of the chain and lock on the door and then I am off. The child won't be found until we are away from the island then my beloved and I will finally be free of the brat.

I must admit I admire her devotion to duty, but that will dim in comparison to the love she will know for me. She will forget the girl soon enough once she has borne my child.

Gaining entry to the house and taking the brat were easy enough. Uncle gave me a key to the service door years ago and he never required its return. He surely forgot its existence. Slipping the cloth laced with ether over her face had insured a quiet exit. Despite the connecting doors between the bedrooms, my beloved's rest had not been disturbed. She slumbered on oblivious to her impending release from near servitude among cretins who did not know her value or appreciate her worth.

In truth, Jacob admires her, but he is just a boy. What can he possibly offer her in comparison to the life of adventure and travel I have planned for us?

All that remains is to aid my darling's escape from Ripon House. My plan is true, my cause just. She will rejoice when we board the boat bound for Brazil tomorrow evening.

CHAPTER 47

Sarah Anne struggled to breathe. She was smothering in dreams that had suddenly turned dark and frightening. She had to wake up, but her exhausted mind clung to the first good night's rest she had had in weeks. Slowly, slowly, she surfaced from the depths of slumber with a growing realization. A hand covered her mouth. Terror sent her heart racing. Her eyes flew open, but all she saw in the dark was a form bending over her.

The figure leaned closer and whispered, "Come with me, my darling. I am here to rescue you." The voice belonged to John Edgar van Beek.

This could not be happening. She must still be dreaming. She tried to shake her head to clear her mind, but the hand over her mouth pushed her farther back against her pillow. This was no dream. It was a waking nightmare.

"Remain calm, my sweet. You must be disoriented being awakened without warning. I apologize, but there was no other way. You will recover your wits in a moment and then you will rejoice." With his free hand, John gripped her upper arm and dragged her from the bed. "I have our steamship tickets in my pocket. Do not worry about packing. I will buy whatever you need once we are away from this desolate place."

Sarah Anne caught a glimpse of his reflection in the dresser mirror. The effort of hauling her bodily across the room contorted his handsome face turning it into an evil mask, frenzied with determination. Or perhaps he was simply insane. Either way, she was in deep trouble. She twisted and tried to jerk free, but he wrapped his arm around her upper body, crushing her to his chest with such force it knocked the breath from her. With his hand still over her mouth, she struggled for air.

"Do not do that again. You belong to me. Do not force me to hurt you to prove my love. I prefer you unscarred and willing, but I will cut you if I must." As he continued to propel her toward the door, the pocket of his coat bumped against her hip. The clink of metal-on-metal rattled in its depths. The realization he had brought more than one weapon spurred a spasm of terror causing her legs to buckle.

They made their way to the grand staircase with stumbling, halting steps. He urged her forward with all his strength while she locked her knees in an effort to slow their progress. They made it as far as the head of the stairs before he stopped. Panting from his exertions, he blew moist, warm air onto her neck, making her flesh crawl. The odor of his liquor-laden breath turned her stomach. When his breathing slowed, he pushed her onto the top step and they began their descent. Midway, she lost her footing, causing him to grab the banister to prevent their tumbling the rest of the way down.

With her mouth now uncovered, Sarah Anne screamed. Her cry echoed through the cavernous two-story foyer.

Slowly, the sound of doors opening and feet pounding in the bedroom wing above drifted down the stairs. From the top step, Mr. Littlewood bellowed, "What the hell are you doing? Release that woman at once."

John smirked as he looked up. "Uncle, why should I do that? She is going to be my wife. I have no intention of releasing her until we are well away." He paused then continued with an unnatural calmness, "Perhaps when we are settled, you and Aunt Alva will come for a visit or at least send a wedding gift. Family should stand by one another, don't you think?"

Littlewood took several steps then stopped at the head of the stairs. "By God, I'm finished covering for you, boy. Your other relatives are as well. Since you were a child, you have been torturing and killings helpless creatures and every time there was an incident, we passed you from household to household, but no more. We no longer care if you're hanged. You've done too much." His heavy tread pounded each step as he came toward John and Sarah Anne.

At the bottom of the staircase, John shoved Sarah Anne across the floor toward the service hall and shouted, "Stay behind the stairs, darling, until I have dealt with my uncle."

She stumbled and crashed into strong arms that steadied her then pushed her farther back to safety beneath the stairs. George's gentle voice whispered, "You safe now, Miss Sarah Anne. I seen him sneaking into the house, but he was too quick for me to stop him. I figured what he was after, but he ain't gonna take you. He done had enough of our womenfolk."

Heart in her throat, Sarah Anne grabbed George's arm and whispered, "He has a knife and I think maybe a pistol. We must use the back stairs so we can get to Adelia. This may be our only chance."

Before George could reply, shots rang through the space followed by heavy thuds that could only be a body rolling down the staircase. "Dear God, he done kilt Mr. Littlewood. Get over yonder, Miss. I got work to do."

From the safety of the hall, she watched as George raised his arm and flicked his wrist. The tongue of a bullwhip flew out and wrapped itself around John's neck. He cried out in pain, grabbed the whip's thong to ease its pressure, and turned toward his assailant.

His voice had a strangled quality, but was still clearly audible. "You. I might have known. You've always interfered with my plans. First with Margaret, now with Sarah Anne. I should have killed you long ago." He raised his pistol and took aim.

Sarah Anne could watch in silence no longer. Although filled with terror, she could not stand aside while John took another life. She stepped from her hiding place. "Please, John. If you let George live, if you will harm no one else, I'll go with you wherever you want."

George gasped, but did not turn to look at her. "No, Miss. You cain't go with him. He a monster."

She stepped forward until she stood beside her friend. Placing a hand on his arm, she pressed down so he lowered the whip a fraction. She ran her tongue around her mouth. It had gone as dry as sand. "But I must. It's the only way."

She moved forward toward the man she had once thought she loved. She had daydreamed about a life with him before she learned his true nature. Her dreams had turned to nightmares. How could she have been so blind? What hints had she missed? Yes, he was arrogant, but he was charming, too. He had been kind when she needed a friend. As she drew nearer, her pulse crashed against her eardrums and her heart pounded against her breastbone. Only time would tell whether her sacrifice would be worth its cost.

Without warning, another shot sounded from somewhere above their heads. The bullet came so close, Sarah Anne thought she felt its passing. She screamed at the sound of flesh and bone tearing as a gaping wound opened in John's chest. He looked down at the gushing blood, lifted his hand to cover the hole, and fell to the floor. George kicked John's pistol hard. It crashed against the library door and spun for several seconds before clattering to a halt. By the time Sarah Anne knelt beside John, he was dead.

As George helped her to her feet, they looked up to the only location from which the fatal shot could have been fired. In the confusion, noise, and terror of the scene in the foyer, no one had observed a figure move to the balcony rail. No one had seen him raise his rifle nor had they heard the click of the hammer pulling back. Sarah Anne squinted into the darkness where the lone figure stood.

Jacob met her gaze, his expression solemn in the face of what he had just done.

Her relief was so great it sucked away her remaining energy and buckled her knees. George caught her before she hit the floor and held her upright until Jacob reached them and took her into his arms.

He searched her face with a longing she had not known he felt, but had certainly dreamt of. "I nearly lost you." His finger traced a tear coursing over her cheek. "When you've recovered from this ordeal, I have something I must ask you."

In the next few seconds, the entire household filled the foyer and their private moment vanished. Jacob released her from his embrace, but kept her arm tucked firmly under his. She searched the faces surrounding them, but the face she worried most about failed to appear.

In growing agitation, she screamed, "Where is Adelia? Has anyone seen her?" No one answered her cry.

Law enforcement arrived within the hour. The sheriff took charge of the crime scene and dispatched his deputy to lead the hunt for Adelia. They searched the house and property from attics to stables to boathouse, but the child had simply vanished. By the time the search party returned from the outlying buildings, the sun's rays were painting the Atlantic gold and pink. More men were needed to cover the entire island, so Jacob and the deputy took the motor craft to St. Anne. Oliver was left behind to watch over their mother. Mrs. Littlewood had become so distraught the boys feared she might harm herself. Uncle Zach was summoned to arrive on the morning ferry, his purpose twofold. He would attend Mrs. Littlewood as her doctor and act as county coroner where the dead were concerned.

Too upset to sleep, Sarah Anne sat alone in the library trying to remember her conversations with John. When she caught sight of her uncle coming through the front door, she flew into his arms. "He killed them. John killed them all. And Adelia has disappeared. I won't be able to bear it if he has killed her too. I promised her I would protect her and I've failed."

Uncle Zach patted her back gently. When he spoke, his voice was soft, but firm. "You bear no blame for what a madman has done. You're tired and stressed beyond measure. You aren't thinking straight. Eat something, then we'll talk." Glancing at the sheet-covered bodies lying where they had fallen, he addressed the deputy who sat vigil over John and Mr. Littlewood. "These two aren't going anywhere. I'll see to my living patient first, then attend to the dead."

Alone in the dining room, Sarah Anne stabbed at the scrambled eggs and toast on her plate as she racked her brain for memories of John that might lead them to Adelia. They had talked for hours about so many things. Surely, he had said something useful, but exhaustion slowed her thoughts and sapped her energy. Perhaps if she ate the food instead of punishing it, she might think more clearly. When only crumbs remained, she was still no closer to solving the mystery.

This waiting and inaction were intolerable. She couldn't bear the house another moment. Shoving her chair away from the table, she left the dining room for the service hall at a near run. Once she breathed the clean salty air of the back garden, she knew where she must go.

She found George beside a stall petting Adelia's beloved Merrybelle. He turned a tearstained face toward Sarah Anne when he felt her presence, but did not smile or give his usual polite greeting. Instead, he turned back to the pony and rubbed its poll. The little animal seemed to sense his distress for she leaned against her stall door and laid her head against his chest. He wrapped his arms around her fat neck while his shoulders shook. Presently, the emotional storm passed and he turned back to Sarah Anne.

"Most menfolk would be ashamed to let a girl see them crying, but I ain't. I love that child just as much as you do, maybe more since I've knowed her since the day she was born. So what we gonna do to find her?" Anger tinged his words. Sarah Anne could only hope he did not blame her for failing to protect Adelia.

Dropping down on a hay bale, she pulled at the straw until a clump broke away and fell at her feet. She gave it a vicious kick. "If I knew the answer, I would already have brought her home. I keep trying to remember anything John might have said, but I have no clue. I just don't know what to do. The house and all of the buildings have been searched. Where could she be?"

George was silent for a long time then his eyes narrowed. "You know, they're a few places nobody probably didn't know to look. It's a long shot, but it's worth a try. I'm gonna saddle us some horses."

He led her away from the house to a path so overgrown she hadn't known it existed. As they urged the horses onto the sandy trail, the undergrowth closed in behind them and the house became hidden from sight. Sarah Anne rolled her neck and stretched her back to relieve their stiffness. Her legs might as well have been filled with jelly. She prayed she could maintain her grip on the lower pommel of the sidesaddle. After what seemed an eternity, they pushed through overlapping palmettos into a clearing of sorts. At its center was a mound that once might have been a dwelling.

She pulled back on the reins and surveyed what was left of the structure. Nothing but a rusty tin roof showed above the vines and bushes covering it. It looked like no one had been in it for many years. "Where are we?"

George dismounted, handed his mount's reins to Sarah Anne then headed for the shack as he called over his shoulder, "This here a old slave cabin. Long time ago before the war there was a small planation here. These old cabins is all over this side of the island."

Dispirited, Sarah Anne called after him, "But this place looks completely undisturbed."

George chose not to waste time with further explanations. He took a machete from the sheath attached to his belt and chopped a path to the cabin. After a brief inspection, he sheathed his tool and returned to Sarah Anne.

"Ain't nobody been here in years, but we got more to search."

She silently followed him from cabin to cabin, each one more deserted and dilapidated than the last. Sarah Anne's anxiety grew to the breaking point when George led her into a clearing and turned unhappy eyes her way. "This the last one. You wait here while I check."

Sarah Anne couldn't bear to sit idly by. She jumped from her mount and tied its reins to a nearby sapling. "No, I'm going with you. If she's there, you'll need help."

It became clear as they approached the old shack that someone had disturbed the vegetation. A path had been hacked to the door secured by chain and lock. It took George's strength wielding the machete several times but the lock finally split open.

The shack's interior smelled dank and moldy, but a box of supplies by the door looked new. Sarah Anne ran her hand over the lids of unopened jars and held her fingers to the light. They were clean and free of dust. Her body trembled at the realization of who must have placed the box in the cabin. John had been here all the time. He had never left the island. He could have come for them whenever he chose. She held her hand out for George to see, but nearly impenetrable darkness filled the shack's interior.

He began tapping along the wall. "They got to be a window here somewhere." A few feet beyond the door, the sound of his tapping changed in quality, becoming hollower. "Here it is." Once again he drew his machete and began hacking. A few powerful strokes demolished the window's shutter and filtered sunlight illuminated the space.

Sarah Anne's gaze darted from corner to corner, searching for any sign of Adelia, but found nothing except old boxes and mounds of dirty rags. She was on the verge of running out into the forest so she might scream her heartbreak in agonized solitude when a pile of discarded quilts set in a back corner appeared to move.

Her heart pounding so hard she thought she might faint, she called, "Adelia?"

The pile moved in earnest and a muffled sound like the mewling of a kitten came from beneath them. Sarah Anne and George knelt beside the whimpering mound scraping bits of tattered material aside. Underneath, they found the child bound and gagged, a blindfold covering her eyes. She was terrified and dehydrated, but at least John had not killed her.

Adelia did not utter a word when the gag was removed from her mouth. The only indication she understood she had been released from her prison was her refusal to be set on the ground so that Sarah Anne could mount her horse.

The child buried her head in Sarah Anne's shoulder and clung to her as a young ape clings to its mother. With coaxing, she finally allowed George to hold her while Sarah Anne climbed into the saddle, but before he could lift her up, Adelia grabbed a handful of mane, shimmied up the stirrup leathers, and settled herself against Sarah Anne's chest. With her face once again buried in folds of fabric, Adelia shut out the world.

Despite the joy and relief of finding the child unharmed, another less happy emotion traveled with them as they turned their mounts toward Ripon House. Sometimes trauma marked a child for life.

CHAPTER 48

As they crossed the lawn, the front door flew open. Benson rushed to the end of the walk while Mrs. Bogard assisted Mrs. Littlewood out onto the veranda. Shouts emanating from within the house drifted toward them until the entire household gathered on the front lawn. Sarah Anne searched for the one face she most wanted to see, but Jacob was nowhere in sight. Disappointment dampened the otherwise joyous scene.

Mrs. Littlewood shook off the housekeeper's supportive embrace and strode forward. She stopped beside Sarah Anne's stirrup and lifted her arms toward the child. "Come to your poor Mama. I have been overwrought with worry. I need to hold you."

The only indication Adelia was aware of her surroundings was the fierceness with which she continued to cling to Sarah Anne.

A crimson flush darkened Mrs. Littlewood's face. "How dare you ignore me? I'm your mother. Come down from that horse at once." Her voice pitched higher with each sentence until she screamed at the child. Still Adelia refused to move or look at her mother.

Rage flashed in Mrs. Littlewood's eyes as she transferred her attention to Sarah Anne. "This is your fault. You have stolen my child. Get your things and leave my house today. I never want to see you again."

At this, Adelia finally roused herself and fixed her mother with a glare. "You only care about yourself. Sarah Anne loves me. You don't."

For a woman who claimed ill health and great suffering, Mrs. Littlewood moved with surprising alacrity. She grabbed Adelia's leg and attempted to pull the child from Sarah Anne's arms, unsettling them in the saddle, sending teacher and child crashing to the ground. The woman stood over the fallen pair screaming, but instead of words, her cries were those of an enraged animal. Sarah Anne's rage matched that of the banshee looming over her, but instead of responding in kind, she held her tongue and rose to her knees. Verbally attacking Adelia's mother would not do the child any good nor improve her situation. If she had any hope of remaining at Ripon House to care for Adelia, she mustn't let her usual response to conflict win out.

As Sarah Anne struggled to her feet and lifted Adelia to her hip, Mrs. Littlewood plunged forward. Poised for attack, she suddenly jerked backward. Jacob held his mother in a tight embrace.

"That's enough. Adelia has been through a terrible ordeal and Sarah Anne rescued her. We will let Dr. MacAllister attend to them both." He looked over his mother's shoulder at Sarah Anne. "Go now. Your uncle is waiting for you in Adelia's room."

Sarah Anne sat on the edge of the bed watching as Uncle Zach checked Adelia for psychical injuries. Finding none, he gave her a sleeping draught and her eyes closed almost instantly.

Placing his hand against her forehead one more time, he nodded. "The rest will do her a world of good, but I fear for her mental state. She has experienced significant trauma. "

"But she will ultimately be all right, won't she?"

"I believe in time she'll recover, but you must watch her and alert me immediately of any concerns."

Sarah Anne leaned against the bedpost. The sudden release of tension coupled with lack of sleep left her drained of what little energy remained. She sighed and replied, "I will if I'm allowed to."

"Allowed to what?" Jacob had appeared in the doorway without Sarah Anne noticing.

"Care for Adelia." Her voice was hoarse with anger and despair.

Jacob glanced at Uncle Zach then stammered, "That's . . . that's what I've come to discuss with you. Do you feel up to talking?" As tired and depleted as she felt, Sarah Anne nodded.

"I wish to speak to you in private. Will you walk with me in the garden? The gazebo is pleasant at this time of day."

Every few paces Jacob glanced sidewise at Sarah Anne, but said nothing even after they were seated beneath the gazebo's whitewashed lattice. He seemed inexplicably nervous and Sarah Anne became impatient.

"Jacob, you wanted to speak with me?"

"Yes, but I hardly know how to begin. There is so much I wish to say, but now that I have you alone, I seem to have lost my courage."

"You've no reason to fear me. I would think the opposite is closer in truth."

With his elbows on his knees, he smiled and began. "It's our hope, Oliver's and mine, that you will remain at Ripon House and care for Adelia while we're attending to matters in New York. Once we've buried our father and cousin, Oliver will marry Agatha and they will take up permanent residence in the New York townhouse. Mother will live with them." His explanation ground to an uneasy halt while he appeared to search for words. His discomfort was palpable.

Taking pity on him, Sarah Anne placed her hand on his forearm. "It's all right. You can tell me I will be dismissed after you're settled. In fact, I've known for some time my position ends in June."

"No!" His shout was surely heard in St. Anne. "That's not what I mean."

"Then say what you need to say and end the agony."

"As I said, Mother and Oliver will not be returning to Georgia. Ever. The memories are too difficult. Mother is not well and Oliver has father's businesses to run." He stopped to swipe at the perspiration gathering on his forehead. While the coastal air was as humid as usual, the day was not uncomfortably warm. A cool breeze floated in from the Atlantic, rustling the salt grass at the edge of the garden.

Sarah Anne tilted her head in thought then her pulse quickened. “And where will you live?”

Jacob’s eyes softened and a smile brightened his face. “During the summer, I’ll be in Atlanta studying for the Georgia Bar. Once I’m admitted, I plan to open my practice in St. Anne. Your uncle tells me there is a five county area with no lawyer to serve the people.”

Refusing to give in to false hope, she forced her mind to the practical. “But won’t you miss New York and your family? Life here will be very quiet and there is no way you’ll earn what a big city practice would bring.”

Jacob chuckled. “Oliver despairs of me, but I have always had my heart set on being a country lawyer. Dr. MacAllister and I have discussed the pros and cons of a rural practice. As I see it, the benefits far outweigh the liabilities. In fact there are two benefits that outweigh all others.”

Sarah Anne’s breath quickened. She had no idea when he had spent so much time with her uncle, but she had been so focused on Adelia the world could have stopped turning and she would not have noticed. “And what would those benefits be?”

“Well, I have convinced Mother I can make a better home for Adelia here than she can in New York. Adelia is right. Mother is more concerned with herself than anyone else. It was a hard truth, but Mother has finally accepted that Adelia will be better off with me. Adelia loves St. Anne. More importantly, there is someone here who holds both of our hearts.” He took her hand in both of his, an earnest expression filling his eyes. “I know we have had too little time together, but I’m as certain of this as I am that the sun will rise each morning. In truth, you, Miss Sarah Anne Mercer, are my sun, my moon, and all of the stars in my firmament. Once I’m settled in St. Anne, it is my fervent wish that you become my wife.”

Sarah Anne’s mind whirled. While she wanted to say yes, Jacob was right. They had spent far too little time together. In the depths of her being lay the fear that what he felt was gratitude enhanced by a passing attraction. When the turmoil of the past weeks abated and the heightened feelings began to fade, would this son of wealth and social position regret his proposal? Would he find himself longing for the excitement of New York and its opportunities and society? Worst of all, would he find himself burdened with a wife who could never fit in with the life and people he had always known?

After several seconds of silence, the light faded from his eyes. "I fear I've spoken too soon. Forgive me. You must think me an impetuous fool. If you wish it, you may forget I ever declared myself, but please say we can at least meet as friends."

Sarah Anne's thoughts poured out in rapid succession. "I haven't said no. Please don't take my silence for refusal. It's just so fast, so unexpected. Will you allow me time to consider?"

"This is hardly the answer I hoped for, but I'll give you time if that's what you really need. May I write to you?"

"Of course. How else will we get to know one another better with me here and you in New York and Atlanta?"

"I won't spend all of my time studying. I'll return to the island as often as possible."

Sarah Anne shot him a teasing smile. "That's too bad, because I won't be here."

He stared at her in confusion. "But I thought you said . . ." She stopped the flow of his words with a finger over his lips.

"If I'm going to help Adelia deal with her trauma, it can't be in Ripon House. There are too many terrifying associations. We will await your visits, and I your letters, with Uncle Zach and Aunt Edith. They adore her. She's happy in their house and she fills it with joy. Those three do one another a world of good."

"What you propose makes sense." He looked up at Ripon House's glowering façade. "It is a gloomy, haunted-looking sort of place."

"Yes, I've always thought so."

"You promise you'll give my proposal a chance?"

"I promise." It had been months since Sarah Anne had felt such joy.

He raised her palm to his lips and kissed it softly. "You've given me hope. If you decide in my favor, I promise you will never regret a day of our life together."

As she lay in bed that night, she considered all that had happened since her arrival at Ripon House. The sound of carriage wheels crunching over crushed oyster shells would always remind her of her unexpected beginning. Her plans and dreams had not included being governess to a single student, but coming to Ripon House had changed her life in ways she could never have anticipated. She had found affection and devotion, daresay love, in the unlikeliest of places among people with whom she initially felt nothing in common.

As far as the house was concerned, Jacob was right. It was a gloomy old pile, but maybe it wouldn't feel so depressing if a happy family lived within its walls. She had asked Jacob to wait for her answer, but she already knew what it would be. She just wanted him to be sure she and life in a South Georgia backwater were what he truly wanted.

As she drifted toward sleep, tingling warmth started in her heart and spread throughout bringing peace and contentment. She smiled into the darkness for she was pretty sure she and St. Anne would be enough.

ABOUT THE AUTHOR

Linda Bennett Pennell has been in love with the past for as long as she can remember. Anything with a history, whether shabby or majestic, recent or ancient, instantly draws her in. It probably comes from being part of a large extended family that spanned several generations. Long summer afternoons on her grandmother's wrap around porch or winter evenings gathered by the fireplace were filled with stories both entertaining and poignant. Of course, being set in the American South, those stories were also peopled by some very interesting characters, some of whom have found their way into Linda's work.

As for her venture in writing, it has allowed Linda to reinvent herself. We humans are truly multifaceted creatures, but unfortunately we tend to sort and categorize each other into neat, easily understood packages that rarely reveal the whole person. Perhaps you, too, want to step out of the box in which you find yourself. Linda encourages you to look at the possibilities and imagine. Be filled with childlike wonder in your mental wanderings. Envision what might be, not simply what is. Never forget that all good fiction begins when someone says to her or himself, "Let's pretend."

Linda resides in the Houston, Texas area with one sweet husband and one adorable goldendoodle who is quite certain she's a little girl.

OTHER TITLES BY LINDA BENNETT PENNELL

The Last Dollar Princess

The American Countess

Miami Interlude ... Coming Soon

NOTE FROM LINDA BENNETT PENNELL

Word-of-mouth is crucial for any author to succeed. If you enjoyed *All That Glitters*, please leave a review online—anywhere you are able. Even if it's just a sentence or two. It would make all the difference and would be very much appreciated.

Thanks!
Linda Bennett Pennell

www.ingramcontent.com/pod-product-compliance
Lightning Source LLC
Chambersburg PA
CBHW030818210726
48290CB00002B/641
* 9 7 8 1 6 8 5 1 3 5 7 7 5 *